One-Match Fire

a novel

by

Paul Lamb

Wichita, Kansas

Blue Cedar Press
PO Box 48715
Wichita, KS 67201
Visit Blue Cedar Press website: https://bluecedarpress.com

10 9 8 7 6 5 4 3 2 1
First edition October 2022
ISBN: 978-1-958728-04-8 (paper)
ISBN: 978-1-958728-03-1 (ebook)
Library of Congress Control Number [LCCN]: 2022945368

Cover photo: Anonymous
Cover and interior design by Gina Laiso, Integrita Productions
Editors: Laura Tillem and Gretchen Eick

Printed in the United States of America at IngramSpark

Several chapters first appeared in slightly different form in these journals:

where late the sweet birds sang – *Selected Places Anthology* – Summer 2017
Twice Blest – *The MOON Magazine* – February 2019
When We Were Young and Life Was Full in Us – *The Fictioneer* – Winter 2013
The Lonely Road – *Penduline Press* – March 2013
Men at Work and Play – *Wolf Willow Journal* – April 2014 – and reprinted in
    Defuncted – February 2019
A Tree Falls in the Forest – *Halfway Down the Stairs* – December 2018
Runaway – *Aethlon* – Winter 2016
The Most Natural Thing in the World – *The MOON Magazine* – May 2014
Moving Day – *THEMA Literary Journal* – Summer 2018
Deadfall – *Hedge Apple* – November 2018

I am grateful to the editors of these journals.

For my children and their children

"Only take heed to thyself and keep thy soul diligently,
lest thou forget the things which thine eyes have seen,
and lest they depart from thy heart all the days of thy life;
but teach them to thy sons and thy sons' sons."

Deuteronomy 4:9
Holy Bible: 21st Century King James Version

"We felt that they were not the tyrants to rule our lot
according to their caprice, but the agents and creators
of all the many delights which we enjoyed."

Mary Shelley
Frankenstein

Table of Contents

Prologue

where late the sweet birds sang

His father had once mistakenly claimed the call of a mourning dove was that of an owl. David had been so struck by this error that he doubted his memory. How could his dad be wrong? It had to have been one of the few times he ever was. Yet while he knew his father had considered himself an outdoorsman, he was never much of a naturalist.

His old cabin looked weary now. Not so much run down or neglected as lonely. On the drive David tried to remember the last time they had all been there together. More than a decade gone now. Such a shame. So many of the important moments of his life had been lived at this little Ozark cabin. It had been Curt's eleventh birthday party, marred by biting horseflies that had kept them inside while the cool lake beckoned in the August heat.

He parked on the gravel pad, just as he had countless times, the sides of his car, accustomed to paved streets, splattered with mud. His father had called the place his Cabin at the End of the Road, but it was really just at the end of a gravel track, two miles of washboard after leaving the county blacktop, even less passable now that it got so little use. Jimmy, their neighbor and unofficial caretaker, would see a strange car at the cabin and know it was time to come by.

Stepping out of his car, David was greeted by a familiar smell, one that he forgot every year until it greeted him again. A November forest. The smell of fallen oak leaves and the thin soil still warmed by the sun. A rich smell that convinces him it will last forever, though he's learned that nothing ever does.

A weedy footpath forked from the parking pad. The short, level way went to the cabin; the more steep route followed the old sandstone steps to the lake. As a boy, David would fly down those steps, bursting from the car the same way his dog, Buddy, had when they finally arrived from Kansas City. Now he picked his way carefully down the irregular steps, mindful of a tumble and the remoteness of the cabin.

As he approached the water, two crows rose from the old dock and settled in a nearby tree to watch him. The tilting dock looked unsafe now; even the local kids, Jimmy reported, no longer dive from it. Yet there on the rotting boards he saw a fresh pile of fish guts, what the crows had been after. Someone had been fishing off the tumbledown dock that very morning.

This lake, where he had learned to swim as a boy, was now almost fully ringed by sere cattails. His dad fought them in his time, wanting to keep the shore open for fishing and swimming. But nature always wins, and he had slowly surrendered whole stretches of shoreline as the work grew too much. Since David had last been out, the cattails had nearly completed their conquest. He shook his head, wondering what his dad would say if he could see it, then turned to climb the hill to the cabin.

David was older than the cabin and the lake, though only just, and to him they had always been there. His dad often spoke of golden weekends he and his mother had devoted to building the cabin. David in a basket or toddling about among the hammers and saws and stacks of lumber. He didn't remember any of this. A superhuman effort, building an entire cabin without power tools. His dad had hired a couple of local Amish boys to help since they had the old skills.

For many years David believed that his father had made the lake as well, digging out the entire two acres one shovelful at a time. No one had told him this; it was merely the sensible conclusion of an adoring son standing in the comforting glow of a father who could do anything. By Ozark standards, two acres is just a pond, but his dad had always insisted it was a lake and always corrected anyone who got it wrong. David was supposed to have asked where they had hooked up the hose to fill it.

The lake was silting in now, decades after it was first carved out of the howling wilderness. His dad would likely cry if he could see it, assuming he knew anymore what he was seeing, though he still might. His memory might stir from its stew of fretfulness and confusion. The lake needed to be drained and dug out and tidied for the next owner, but David wasn't going to do that. He'd already decided he would dicker down the price if he must. Just as he had with his father's old house.

The cabin porch was a mess, too. Littered with dried mud and overturned chairs and cigarette butts and faded beer cans. Even discarded clothing that he didn't want to look at too closely. Evidence of trespassing kids from Osceola with nothing to do in town and no one to stop them from partying here. But it had always been a good porch, deep and shady, with a nice view of the lake below; he could understand why a bunch of bored kids would hide out here to skinny-dip and drink away their summer days. Whatever their faults, they'd shown the courtesy to not break into the cabin. Maybe having Jimmy nearby restrained them. He used to call David whenever he spotted a truck bumping through the trees toward the place. But what could David do, two hundred miles away? If he'd had the sheriff run them off, it would only make them spiteful, and they would surely return with hard feelings. He told Jimmy to let them be as long as no one destroyed anything. Jimmy had stopped by once or twice to say howdy; he knew most of the kids, which probably kept them under control.

David supposed that he'd have to put a stop to it so he could keep the place in better order for potential buyers. That was still a bit down the road though. So much clearing out to do first. This place was his dad's hard-won retreat; many times he had told David how he and his mother had scrimped for the money to build the cabin. He would have moved here after he retired if his wife had let him, cooking his meals on the propane stove, staying warm by the potbelly, reading by lantern light, playing out his true identity here.

The place was filled with rusted axes and saws and all sorts of woodland tools he must have thought he needed but many he probably only used once. A mouse-eaten rug Buddy had slept on that his dad had picked up on a trip to Taos before David was born; it still had Buddy's hairs in it. Framed photos. Cast-off furniture. Pots and pans. Stuff and junk. The accumulation of decades that all had to go now. To charity, or to the burn pile.

David thought he could begin by clearing away the cobwebs on the porch. There was a broom in the cabin, and the key he hadn't used in a long time, which he could never remove from his keyring, still fit the lock. The door was snug; he had to put his shoulder to it. A familiar, musty smell greeted his nose, but his dad must have known earlier smells. Of fresh-cut lumber, of sawdust, of wood oil. He must have known every cut and joint, every toenail and dovetail, every fastening nail driven home. The memories he must have had of the place were mostly gone, although he still remembered the cabin. The nurses said he still fretted about it sometimes. But he didn't remember his son.

David's heel crunched something as he stepped in. A piece of glass. A lens from the binoculars there on the floor. His dad had kept them on a nail by the door, ready to snatch whenever he would dart out to look at something, some movement across the lake that had caught his eye. Their leather strap had been chewed away. He could never make the cabin mouse proof as his wife had wanted. When they visited, they kept everything they thought a mouse might get into in ancient popcorn tins. If she hated that, she never told him. He'd assumed she was as in love with the place as he was, overlooking his beloved cabin's flaws just as she overlooked his.

The cabin was disordered within, not from vandals but from time and use, disordered from the snapshots of David's memory that were outdated and inadequate. His father had continued to visit the cabin after David had moved away and his mom had died. Until he became too infirm to be trusted alone there. Before his mind began to slip. Yet he had held on longer than David would have guessed. Perhaps the cabin, filled with memory, baptized by his own blood and sweat, had been the anchor that let his mind hang on even as his memory was ebbing.

In the murk David saw the familiar as unfamiliar. Chairs in wrong places. The unmade bed. Books scattered on the table as though only just set down. The window curtains that were a concession to his mom, who couldn't sleep without them despite the cabin being long miles from anywhere. She'd sewn them herself. They were loaded with dust that rose to David's nose and drifted in the air as he pushed them open. Yet with more light he could see better. Familiar and unfamiliar. His dad's cabin. His sanctuary. His retreat. "I built this for you, you know," he had confessed to David one day as they sat on the porch in the fading light, the setting sun putting the lake into soft focus below. It was David's farewell visit after starting a new job far away. His father was in decline then, though David wouldn't let himself see it, let it interfere with his own long-delayed rise. "It's a legacy, and it will pay off in time." He puffed weakly on his cigar as they sat. "But only after I'm a memory. Curt will come here when he has a boy of his own someday."

Time was running out for the man then, and the crushing cost of his care, which stretched his son thin month to month, would be eased by cashing in his legacy now. It took David a long time to accept that he had to do this. But his father would never be able to return to his cabin now; he wouldn't even know the place had been sold. Did that make his job easier? The tedious job of sifting through the accumulation of a lifetime, of cleaning and clearing and burning and hauling and selling and parting. He knew he had to be merciless, just as he had been when he moved his father out of his house.

The old tractor and brush hog were late additions to his dad's arsenal, kept in repair by Jimmy, who used them to work his own meadows and occasionally to clean up around the cabin. To David these belonged least of all because they arrived after he was gone, after his own memories were fixed. They would be the first to go, and Jimmy would arrive soon to discuss a fair price, which they would both knew wouldn't be fair. Why would Jimmy pay much for things he already had free use of? They both knew that Jimmy would win a lower price, though it wasn't a contest.

The dust from the opened curtains had settled in the quiet cabin; his eyes adjusted to the new light. The cut glass crystal that Curt had given his grandfather one year still hung in the window, casting tiny rainbows. He'd forgotten that detail. Below it on the sill sat the line of fossils David had collected as a boy. "We can only keep the good ones," his father had said because there were so many. Each with a story to tell.

It was not disarray he saw, after all, but use. Untouched for years yet seemingly left only days before. A spiral notebook opened on the table. A mechanical pencil at rest beside it. The chair pushed back as though someone had risen from it moments before. A pair of leather gloves still curled in the shape of the hands that had worn them. A cigar butt in the ashtray. His wife had never let him smoke inside the cabin, but he'd evidently had after she was gone.

A new owner wouldn't feel his dad's presence here, wouldn't see him sitting in that hard wooden chair at that battered oak table.

Doing what, though? He was rarely a man of repose at the cabin. If the night or the cold didn't force him inside, he'd be outside, tending the campfire, sawing logs, or clearing cedars. Swimming in the lake or just rambling in his Ozark hills.

So what, David wondered, was this scattering of books on the table and the open notebook beside them?

He settled himself in the chair and picked up the notebook. His father's handwriting ran down its first page, marked at the top with a date now four years past. He read the inscription:

VISIT JOURNAL #3

Number three? Had his dad filled two prior notebooks with whatever this was? The man who couldn't be bothered to write a grocery list? (And then forgot half of what he needed to buy.) What would his visit journal contain? What would be so important that his father could sit still and fill pages?

David flipped through them. There were dated notes about the temperature, the weather. Chores undertaken or left undone. Animals seen. Had he robbed himself of his precious time outdoors to sit in the hard chair and write such things? It was his handwriting. It had to be so. He stroked his fingers across the writing on the page, as though to confirm that it was real.

• *liberated 27* Juniperus virginiana *today. Not enuf.*

He always cleared cedars when they visited the cabin. "Liberating them from their earthly toil," he boasted. His fear was that with their oily needles they would transfer an otherwise harmless ground fire into the treetops. Clearing cedars was one of his superhuman labors, a never-ending chore. They had the last word now as tiny cedars had reclaimed the space around the cabin.

Yet in all the years his father had brought him here, David had never once heard him use a scientific term to describe anything, and certainly not the cedars he hated. They had bass and bluegill in the lake. Catfish of some kind. They had oaks and hickories and cedars. Just woodpeckers and cardinals and little gray bird as well as a kingfisher that visited the lake below the cabin, but never an *Alcedo alcyon.*

  • Alcedo alcyon *visited again today Entertaining*
  • Picoides pubescens *at the suet feeder*

A *Peterson's Guide* sat on the table before David, its spine broken, its pages dogeared and tattered. Highlighted and underlined. Checkmarks beside many of the birds. His dad's life list? Was that possible? The naughty sounding *Picoides pubescens,* according to one of the books, was a downy woodpecker.

The many pages of his notebook had been filled with entries like these. And two other notebooks were apparently somewhere in the cabin. Was he trying to nail down facts, use these scientific names, David wondered, because he sensed he was losing it all?

  • *KD and I visited today Chest doesn't hurt as much out here*

Who was KD? He'd never spoken to David of bringing anyone to the cabin. Had his dad had a secret girlfriend? The pair of cigar bands taped to that page suggested a man, not a woman, but "KD" alone was surprising enough.

The weak November sun was warming the cabin. The metal roof popped as it expanded. His roof never leaked; he knew how to do it right from a lifetime as a sheet metal worker. It was a job he hated but kept at heroically and one that he claimed to beat in the end by "still having all my fingers!"

  • *forgot wallet again dammit!*
  • *Who cooks for you? Who cooks for you all?*

David couldn't recall the first time he noticed his dad's mind slipping. Or rather, when he first let himself see it. His physical frailty had alarmed David enough. This invincible man was shown to be human like everyone else. That his mind would give way too was more difficult for David to accept.

  • *bring more AA batteries next trip*

But there never was a next trip. His Visit Journal ended there, the remaining pages blank. A bittersweet testament of hope *and* defeat, and David suddenly wanted to see the other two journals he'd filled with his notes, to glimpse at his father's cabin life after

David had left home.

He rose from the chair and began looking in the obvious places. The bookcase with stacks of David's old Superman comics, probably worth more as tinder for a fire than anything else. The table beside the bed. He opened all of the popcorn tins.

He finally found them in the metal cabinet that was a mouse-proof improvement over the old tins, next to a half-empty box of cigars. His dad's beloved Upmanns. Odd that he kept a box of pricey cigars here with no protection from heat and cold or from the drying winter. Why wouldn't he keep his supply at home and just bring a fresh one or two each visit? Surely he didn't still fear his wife's frowning disapproval.

David slid his hand under the notebooks. He would skim them as he waited for Jimmy. Then, on an impulse, he grabbed one of the old Upmanns. Never once had his dad offered him a cigar on their visits. Certainly not while his mother was around, but not even after she was gone. He'd never invited his boy to enjoy them as he did, though David suspected he would have been welcomed to if he'd asked. As a boy, David had watched his father first put on lip balm, then cut the tip and let the match finish flaring before he brought it to the cigar, the flame never quite touching it. He puffed his cheeks to get the cherry going. Whether it was ritual or just technique, it had fascinated the boy.

Fearing his mother's ghostly disapproval, David carried the cigar to the porch; he would smoke outside the cabin. Yet it was breezy there – his dad had claimed that he'd lined up the cabin deliberately to have a gentle breeze cross the porch for summer relief – that breeze made getting the cigar lit challenging. Stepping inside for a moment he had better luck, but before going back out to where the journals waited, he saw one of his dad's old flannel shirts hanging from a nail near the bed. The November morning was cool, and his jacket was in the car, so he lifted the shirt from its nail and slipped into it. It was blue and red plaid, and he recalled Curt picking it out for his grandfather. A small yellow thread ran through it, and Curt had said that made the shirt "pop." It smelled of woodsmoke. A wave of longing swept over David, surprising him.

David settled into one of the righted chairs, snuggling into his father's old shirt, and looked across the lake. He'd forgotten how much he enjoyed this view in November, after most of the leaves had fallen and he could see farther into the forest. He took his first real draw on the cigar. The curling smoke trailed up his nose and he coughed, but the smell of it instantly brought memories of lying on the porch floor with Buddy at the end of the day reading the same comic books over and over while his parents sat in their chairs, relaxing after their chores, or swimming, or dinner. His dad's cigar smoke blending with the murmur of their voices. In David's memory these were perfect moments, and he thought they truly were.

VISIT JOURNAL #1

The information here may be useful. I'll put it down
and see what might be made of it.

- *temp 58 degrees at 10:30 a.m.*
- *birdsong plentyful this morning*

The paper crinkled in his fingers, brittle from having once gotten wet. A cigar band was taped to the page.

The old cigar in David's hand was brittle as well. The wrapper was flaking. The glue on the band had dried long ago; it hung loose and he removed it, slipping it into the pocket of his dad's shirt then buttoning it closed. He spat flecks of tobacco from his lips.

- *splendid solitude!*
- *cut some firewood must stack*
- *sandwich for lunch cookie iced tea (unsweetened, of course)*
- *need more black sunflower seed for feeder*
- *eaves starting to turn – hickries – shagbark?*
- *what is gray bird with crest?*

A snapshot, a moment from years before. His father being reflective. Inquisitive. Passive. A side of him David rarely saw, especially at the cabin.

- *righted Buddy's stone*

David and his father had buried Buddy up the hill behind the cabin. He'd found a spot that had some actual dirt, though they still needed the pickaxe to break up the rubble that comprises most Ozark hillsides. David had told himself he was too big to cry. He was fifteen.

But his dad knew better. He showed David how to swing the pickaxe then put it in his boy's hands to break the ground and make a final resting place for his dog. They took turns digging, working silently. Later his dad found a slab of sandstone and scratched Buddy's name in it with a nail. He must have tired as he worked because the "Y" was not as deeply etched. On some later visit, when David was probably too busy with his friends to come along, his father had tugged the stone up the hill and set it over the grave. Sometimes it was toppled when they'd returned, and they'd set it up again. David thought he should hike up there later.

For a long time, David believed his father could do anything; and then, he couldn't. Maybe his wife's death had robbed the man of some strength or of the need to prove himself. He'd built the cabin with her. He'd built a life with her. With them. Then David moved away. And his mother died. They sold the house and put his dad in an apartment, but he refused to sell the cabin and the lake. Not that David would have let him.

His dad claimed to love his solitary life, but his son was never sure. (Who was "KD"?) They spoke twice a week. His dad sounded delighted to hear from him, and maybe he was. David visited as often as he could. Dragged Curt along sometimes. Bought his father new clothes, new glasses when he needed them. Did little things around his apartment. Met with his doctor, though his dad never liked that. Made a few weekend trips to the cabin where David could feel the gloom lift that had settled on him. Mostly they'd sit on the porch together and his dad would smoke a cigar. Later they would build a fire and sit around it, maybe drink a couple of beers, tell a few familiar stories, but his dad would get cold and they'd retire to the cabin for an early bedtime. Simple oatmeal for breakfast with the iced tea that he'd brought from home. A few chores just for show. Then they'd go back to his apartment in Kansas City. And David would return to his home.

- *funny pain in chest, right side again comes and goes.*
- *hip hurts some but can still get around fine*

This was still his first visit journal, the oldest one. He never willingly shared his ailments with anyone. David felt guilty peeking into his father's secrets like this, into his private memories, even though his dad would never know. He was sure his dad meant to retrieve these notebooks, maybe burn them in some cleansing campfire. He'd surely never meant for anyone to read them. But he'd lost say over that, and now he sat unmasked.

- *gunfire over ridge getting ready for deer season?*
- *mostly blue sky some cottony clouds*
- *crows calling – bring peanuts for them next time*
- Aster anomalus *in bloom*
- *no more swimming this year not warm enuf*

Had he still been swimming in his condition? David wondered. In the lake's condition? On the next page was a photo taped to the paper. His father holding a bass. The familiar lake in the background. Apparently, he had still been fishing, too. David had had no idea. Did "KD" take that photo?

- *Jimmy found old Ford tractor and b'hog that will work for mowing*

As though summoned by his name on the page, Jimmy's old pickup came rattling down the hill at that moment, come to strike the deal. He'd come too soon, David realized, ending his own splendid solitude prematurely.

David closed his father's journal and tapped the ash off his cigar. It was burning much faster than he ever remembered his dad's doing, obviously dried out. He didn't know what one should taste like, but it probably wasn't like this. He stubbed it out and rose to meet Jimmy.

Jimmy stepped on the porch and surveyed the mess David had yet to clean.

"Saw your car." A pause, and then, "Came over quick as I could."

As tight-lipped as David remembered him. "Hello, Jimmy. It's been a long time."

Jimmy evidently agreed, or at least he had nothing to add because he said no more. David offered his hand, which Jimmy crushed in his to establish their roles in the negotiations. Not that they would get to it right away. In this part of the country there were rituals of greeting to perform, seemingly unrelated small talk that must be passed through before the business at hand was reached.

"Nice morning," David said, rolling his head to look at the sky beyond the porch ceiling.

"How's your father?" Jimmy avoided eye contact, looking instead down the hill to the rotting dock and the lake.

"As well as can be expected. Forgetful, mostly. And frail."

"A good man, Mr. Clark."

The crows had returned to the dock and were sparring over the fish guts there. Jimmy eyed them.

"Looks like someone's been fishing this morning," David offered, considering for the first time whether it might have been Jimmy.

"Imagine there's some lunkers in that pond after all these years."

"Lake," David corrected, wondering if Jimmy's words were an admission.

"Your father spoke of getting it dredged. Made nice once again."

David was never allowed to go in the lake by himself until he'd earned his water wings by swimming all the way across and back without resting. A middling swimmer as a child, he was mostly content to fool around in the shallows where he could touch the bottom, afraid of the fish below, always within a quick lurch of the shore. Or he'd hang from the side of the dock, his dad or mom watching him from a folding chair. Their willingness to sit idly in the sun and supervise, of course, rarely coincided with the hottest time of the day when he wanted to splash around. Eventually this motivated him to master the impossible distance across the lake.

It was on their traditional Fourth of July trip to the cabin, in the high heat of the Ozark summer, when David boasted that he was ready to pass his father's test. He was not allowed to dive from the dock, gaining unfair distance and momentum. He had to start from the shore, wading out until the water was deep enough to swim and then taking off from there. His father stood on the dock where he could watch his son the whole way.

The lake was maybe two hundred feet across in those days, but to Little Davey it was oceanic. He had no difficulty reaching the far shore, but as he made the turn he felt fatigue catching him, turning his arms and legs to lead. He began to doubt he was going to make it. He looked across the water, and there was his dad. Standing on the end of the dock, his legs planted firmly apart, his fists on his hips. He had a bright red towel draped over his shoulder, and he'd taken off his glasses, ready to swoop down and rescue his son if he faltered. "Keep your head up," he had urged. That image of him, strong and watchful, stirred in David the strength he needed to finish his return lap. That image had stayed burned into his memory ever since.

Jimmy had droned on about the tractor and brush hog. Not sure the old things were worth much anymore. Needed constant maintenance. Hard to find parts. Wanted to be fair.

David thought then that his father had left his journals so he *would* find them. The mechanical pencil sat on the table inside the cabin. David wanted to begin filling in the blank pages of Journal #3 with notes of his *own* visit that day. Tape his own cigar band to the page. Count the cedars he liberated. Leave his own memories for his own son while he could.

The young cannot understand the old until it's too late. But at least they can come to some understanding of the life lived, if they try.

JOE

Feels like the start of something.

My girlfriend, Peg's, old man, Dave, died, and here we are in Kansas City in the cozy house where she grew up, which is hers now. Sounds like he was a decent guy, but what would I know?

Peg's different lately. I can't figure it out. Maybe because both of her parents are gone now. Or maybe it's this sudden dash here to where she grew up. She's even been talking about how maybe it's time to settle down. Not sure I'm interested in that.

We've been sorting through all the stuff in the house. Her father's lifetime of acquisitions. This is what happens, I've decided, when you stay in one place. There's a seduction to stability, to possessions, and I'm suspicious of it. Fall in love with a person? Fine. You can move through life together. But fall in love with a place and you're stuck.

We cleaned out the back bedroom today. Boxes of who knows what. More flannel shirts than I could count; I'll keep the good ones. A decent twin bed that she wanted me to take apart and haul down to the basement for some reason. Piles for the trash and to give away.

I don't know if we are cleaning up the place so she can sell it or move into it. Either way, she'd promised me a cigar at the end of the day. And a chat.

And so here we are. Sitting in the overgrown grass of her back yard, on a couple of folding chairs I found the basement.

She's plucked a late dandelion from the ground and is brushing her fingers over the soft fuzz.

"If I had a boy," she begins. "I would name him David Joseph."

Chapter One

Twice Blest

A gentle rain was falling, though he hadn't noticed until he rose with the baby. He could hear it dripping over the leaf-clogged gutters outside the window.

Mostly, he saw the black night out there. No light at that unholy hour.

"You're wearing out your mother, kid!" His words just above a whisper. "She can't keep getting up, so you're stuck with me." And I'm stuck with you, he would have added if he dared.

He was in the last place he ever thought he'd be. Or ever wanted to be. Deeply in it. Irrevocably in it. Nearly forty years old, and suddenly with a kid! A sick kid.

But the little house where they had landed was warm enough for the present. He stood in his boxers, an old flannel shirt thrown on, the infant in his arms. The bottle the boy didn't want set aside on the table. He would whimper and then go silent, but never silent long enough to dump him back in his crib so everyone could get some sleep. Joe had carried the boy into the kitchen so the crying wouldn't wake his mother again.

"We all have our pain, kid. You just gotta learn to deal with it." That was the extent of his fatherly advice, the one big lesson he had learned from his own father.

He didn't look down at his son any more than he had to. All the boy did was sleep and cry anyway, and he couldn't do a thing about either of those.

He didn't even know the color of his son's eyes.

"Are you hot? Cold?" He could never tell. Peg could hold her boy against her cheek and know. Another blanket then. Or time for a bath. Quickly, quickly. He needs his diaper changed. He's hungry. Soothe him. Rock him. Talk to him. Touch him.

How did he get himself into this nightmare?

He knew *how*, of course. It has been a delirious summer. But after so long why did this suddenly have to happen? Why did the universe throw this at him? Life was good before. Free. Aimless. Now he had a ring on his finger. (Quickly, quickly.) Had to join the union for health insurance, quit smoking, cut his hair. A tiny house in Kansas City where his wife had grown up, inherited along with a little wad of money and a hundred acres of woods down in the Ozarks. What did they need a bunch of trees for anyway? But the money was being blown on the kid's sickness. If that money ran out, they'd have to sell her piece of property that he hadn't even seen yet. And what if the boy died anyway?

"You're breaking your mother's heart."

In his arms he felt the boy's tiny body shiver as he mewled. He could feel a draft from the window and pulled the thin blanket tighter around the baby – was that what he needed to do? – but one of the boy's arms escaped. "Need to caulk that window," he murmured. Words in the dark, spoken to no one. "And clean those damn gutters. Shit, I'm a homeowner now."

The boy fussed.

"Just stop crying. How about that? I don't know what to do for you, kid. I don't know anything about being a father." True confession, one he could make because no one was listening. "Your damned weakness gives you power over me!" No one but his son heard Joe's words.

As he considered, though, he realized that at least he knew how *not* to be a father. That hard lesson had come easy. Just don't be like his own father. It was an option, fading with every moment, but not altogether run off. "See what you made me do, kid?" he would say if it came to that. "But better for everyone this way," he would say. "You'll thank me eventually. Like I thanked my old man."

Except everyone was praising him. Envious even, which he couldn't understand. "Who'd ever guess you'd be a dad?" The common refrain. Not him, that's for sure. Dad. The name didn't fit. Didn't sound right. Sounded like a word from another language that wouldn't translate well. He smiled and shook hands and accepted all of the good words, the gifts, the advice, the winks and nudges. And all the while no one noticed him looking out the window, down the road, across his remaining years. Not even his wife.

And then, so soon, some of those words he heard hadn't been good.

"Why'd you have to catch this fever, kid? We might have to put you in the hospital again if you keep spitting up your medicine. The doc said you could even get brain damage." He spoke to the black outside the window. And to his reflection. Each man holding a sick, maybe doomed kid in his arms. "Not just stuck with a kid but maybe a retarded kid. Cleaning drool off your face for the rest of my life."

The boy cried. Weakly, with the little force his fevered body could muster.

Joe glanced down. "I didn't make you cry, kid. I did *not* do that. You can't blame me."

He started swaying, unconsciously, as he saw his wife do. The floorboards beneath his bare feet creaked in gentle sympathy.
"It's your fever, kid. That's why you're crying. I didn't make you cry. Quiet now."

The boy in his arms still fussed.

"Stop your damned crying, will you?" he growled. "What do you want? To make me more miserable? I don't have anything you need!"

As though in obedience, the boy went silent, and the man looked down to confirm the child was breathing, alarmed by the unexpected authority of his gruff words. Was this what being a father meant?

"Look, I'm sorry I said that. It's your fever. You're sick and we can't do much about it. Except keep pouring medicine down your throat that you mostly spit up. You have to do it. You have to fight this battle yourself. That's how it works in this world, kid. Sorry about that, too."

What am I doing apologizing to a baby?

A new thought came into his head then, one that left no space for anything else. A cold, dark-of-the-night thought. "What if I catch it from you? What if I catch your fever and you're left without a father? Then what, kid?" What if this squalling thing in his arms, that couldn't do a thing for itself, that couldn't even hold its head up, could kill him? Or worse. "What if you give it to Peg? I would hate you forever."

A bitter-tasting thought he had given himself to chew on in the darkness. What if that happened – if she died and left him with this kid? The *possibility* of these twin horrors twisted his stomach.

Another confession. "I never wanted you. Your mother wanted you. Not me. It was just supposed to be me and her. But you came along. You weren't part of anybody's plan." Another bitter thought. "I knew some people. If it was up to me, you never would've been born!"

The boy cried out. Not a whimper but an actual stab-of-pain cry. The man was alarmed by the authority in his son's voice. The boy grabbed his father's flannel shirt in his free fist and looked at his father's face, his eyes liquid with tears, wide with shock.

Joe stared into his boy's eyes, the beseeching, terrified, blue, blue eyes of his son. The boy's grip on his shirt was unbreakable.

He realized that he was his son's only hold on life at that moment. And then he understood, in a deep way that was beyond words and could only be sounded with feelings. He understood.

"I am so sorry I said that, Davey." Joe whimpered his confession to the one person who could forgive him. "I'm not a monster, Davey. I'm not." He touched David's face. His cheek. His lips. "Forgive me, Son. Let me take it back."

Joe kissed his sick little Davey on the forehead and held him close, understanding for the first time that this was who he was now, who he was supposed to be.

JOE

I said I liked stomping around her Ozark forest and she said I was wrong. It was our Ozark forest. Hers and mine. And little Davey's.

But it's true. For the first time in my forty years, I feel tied to a place. I see what I was missing all those years of wandering. Or maybe what I was searching for. I can sink roots here. Relax here. Maybe heal some old wounds with the gentle medicine that a forest can give.

We'd slashed our way through the scrub and blackberries down in the valley earlier – everyone laughed when we exchanged machetes as anniversary gifts, but I think it was smart – and I dared to tell Peg I could see us building a lake here. Dam the valley and watch it fill with water. Fish and swim in it. And I could teach Davey how to fish and swim.

"Up the hill there is where we'll build our cabin." I was feeling bold because Peg hadn't flinched at the suggestion of a lake. "Where we could look down on the water. Sit on the porch. Smoke a cigar and scratch our bug bites."

When we returned to our tent and put Davey down for his nap, I paced out ghost shapes for a half dozen cabins. Peg followed me every step. We talked and laughed and dreamed like kids.

And then little Davey came toddling up. Somehow he'd slipped out of his diaper and stood there before us, naked but for the dandelion of golden hair on his head. I grabbed him up and held him and began to tell him all about our cabin and lake.

Chapter Two

Comfortable in his Skin

Decades later, after what he considered a lifetime of accumulated loss with only the smallest measure of wisdom to show for it, David must have looked back across his years for the scraps of experience with his family that were swiftly fading, trying to fix them in his memory. Looking for touchstones of his personality, those things that had made him the man he had become.

Memory, David confessed, was unreliable. Sometimes a friend. Oftentimes a foe. Unsparingly truthful. Cunningly deceitful. Which parts were true, and which were merely desired? And after so long, did the difference even matter? As we drove the long, straight highway home one Sunday afternoon, he wasn't sure how reliable his rambling memories were of a certain long-ago trip to the cabin with his dad. If their golden hue was more imagined than real. If this one day in his life, this one experience, was as important as he believed. Or if it had even happened at all. With no way to compare notes any longer, he knew only that these were the memories he had. And so this was the story he contrived about that day.

Their workday had begun with tree climbing, which to a seven-year-old boy sounded great. An old white oak with low, spreading branches stood beside the road up the hill from their little cabin. His dad had boosted him to the lowest branch. "Someday, you're going to be taller than I am." Joe had often said things like that, but the boy was already scampering up the limbs and perhaps didn't hear. "Be careful, Davey," he called.

Davey had learned early that what his dad most feared in his woods was a forest fire that would consume his little wooden cabin.

Before he would ever allow himself to cast a line in the lake or drop a burger on the grill, he always set about clearing the scrubby growth around their cabin to keep an open buffer. The small cedars were the worst culprits. "It's hard work, Davey, but it certainly is the best smelling job in the forest!" The scent of the cut cedar wood reminded Joe of pine forests and Christmas wreaths.

Beneath Davey's favorite climbing tree were a dozen small cedars that needed clearing. Their trunks were too thick to cut with loppers; they needed a saw. His dad claimed that the cedars' low branches, made it hard for him to get in and cut them at the ground. So after Davey came down from the oak, Joe intended to send his lean, little boy crawling beneath these cedars to wield the handsaw.

They had dressed for a cool morning. Joe favored cotton flannel shirts, preferably a little shabby, with a brightly colored tee shirt beneath. He had a pair of thick-soled work boots and always wore tall socks. He'd tuck his jeans into his socks to keep off the ticks. Joe looked comical gotten up in this way, but it worked for the most part. A tick check at the end of the day was always a good idea; he usually found few offenders. A dip in the lake on warm days was a good remedy, too.

Once he was old enough to recognize such things, Davey wanted to wear flannel shirts just like his dad. Joe bought him a pair of boots a couple sizes too big for his growing feet and then, whenever they went to the woods, father and son matched, at least in the boy's adoring eyes.

Davey had come down from the tree much sooner than normal that day. Joe had only just finished setting out their tools when his boy dropped from the lowest branch, then dashed over to give his dad a great hug around the waist. What else could Joe do but return this love, so pure and intense. He was still figuring out what being a father meant, but this part seemed clear enough. His fingers drifted through his boy's golden curls; the world paused for that moment.

"So here's the plan, Davey." Joe unwrapped himself from his boy's embrace. "You crawl under these cedars – you're small enough to get in there – and cut them with this saw. It's new, and it's sharp. And look. I got you some gloves, just like mine."

Davey gaped at this grownup gift, unable to speak, then took the gloves from his father's hand. They were new and stiff. He held them to his nose and smelled the rough leather. Wonderful! He would always remember that smell. "When we're done here, I have a new Superman comic for you at the cabin."

If Davey had the words, then or now, he would have told his father how much he loved their boys-only trips to the cabin. But the feelings were too deep and too complex for the boy to understand. And if he *did* have the right words to say what he felt, those words would fill his father's heart to bursting. Better for them both that they understood it at a level beyond language.

"We gotta get these cedars out from under your climbing tree, Davey. If a fire ever comes along, they'll send their flames into your oak, and then there might not be a tree left for you to climb. Shall we get to it?"

Davey couldn't have known then what he came to understand decades later, that his father didn't expect much from his efforts that day but was just giving his boy a chance to try. To feel he contributed. Davey didn't need to know that. All he wanted was to work with his dad. "Work then play. That's the way," said the boy, echoing his father's motto.

Davey tugged on the stiff gloves. His little hands were lost inside, his fingers not nearly long enough to fill them, but he clutched the new saw then fell to his knees and crawled to the nearest cedar.

Its lower branches met him, scraping against his face as he pushed in. He broke the ones he could and bent aside others until he was at the trunk where he could begin to saw. The angle was wrong though, and with the gloves on he couldn't grip the saw well. His first strokes barely scratched the wispy bark. Already dry needles were falling down the back of his shirt. Grasshoppers clattered in the scrub beyond, and they unnerved him. What else was out there?

Joe had begun on one of the other cedars and cut it down at the ground. He dragged it across the road, far from the oak. Davey watched his father complete the task with speed and ease then turned back to his assignment and tried again.

The low branches were in his way, and Davey saw that if he cut some off, he could attack the trunk more easily. So he turned his handsaw to them and tried that. The first low branch came away quickly enough, though his stiff new gloves made it harder than it had to be. For the next he took the glove off his hand – "my right hand," he whispered – and gripped the saw directly. That worked better, and once he had a few branches cut away, he grabbed them with his bare hand and shoved them aside. His palm was then sticky with sap and when he put his hand on the ground, dirt and twigs stuck to it. Fearing he would transfer this to the handle of the new saw, he reluctantly put the glove back on. But he realized that he was smearing the sap and dirt onto the inside of his new glove, that it would always be there, and that it would make his dad sad if he found out.

The cedar needles itched inside his shirt. The day's growing heat was reaching him. Sweat was stinging his eyes. The work was too hard. He wanted to quit, but he wanted even more to help his dad, so he sniffed back his tears and tried again. Of course, he realized years later that none of this was lost on his father. Joe had taken down two more cedars and dragged them off before he came to Davey's rescue, giving the boy time to feel that he had tried. It was a sort of obligatory thing, he thought, letting his son persist with the work despite frustration. What a father would do to help shape a son, even if it meant the work took far longer than it needed to.

"That new saw must not be as sharp as I thought."

"It's so hard to cut, Dad."

You don't always tell your children what you think, David had later come to understand. Sometimes there are things they need to learn for themselves. More harm than good might result if the right words were spoken at the wrong time.

Joe offered his back-up plan.

"Here's what we'll do, Davey. You cut off enough of those low branches so I can get in there, and I'll cut the trunk. We'll do a bunch, then we'll drag them across the road together. Okay?"

Davey agreed, his faltering confidence restored a little. He turned to the lower branches again and did what he could. His effort made little difference, but Davey didn't need to know that. What he'd needed was to feel he was working side by side with his dad, doing a man's work and believing he was helping. There was a deeper truth than actual truth in this.

Finished with the first tree, Davey crawled over to the next one but backed out suddenly.

"There's a snake under there, Dad!"

"A snake? What kind of snake?"

"I don't know."

"Well, let me see." Joe walked over to the cedar Davey was pointing to with the saw. Pushing aside the branches, he peered below. Then he stepped to the other side of the cedar and looked again.

Davey watched carefully, frightened and fascinated, as his father removed his glove and reached below the tree. A moment later, Joe brought forth the snake that had startled Davey.

"Come here, Son. It's okay. It's only a snakeskin."

Joe held the flimsy, gossamer skin out so Davey could see it. "A snake*skin*?" Davey held back and studied the thing in his father's hand.

"There's no snake inside. He's long gone. Off hunting crickets somewhere. This is how a snake grows up, Davey. When he gets too big, he crawls out of his skin. Then he leaves it behind."

The sun had grown hot that June morning. Davey was sweating. The grasshoppers clattered about the little meadow. The cedar needles inside his shirt itched and poked. But his father told him the snakeskin was safe so it must be safe.

Davey stepped forward and offered an ungloved hand. He touched the skin tentatively. It felt dry and brittle. He could see the shape of the snake's head, even the part that had covered one of its eyes. He could see that there was no snake inside.

"Can I hold it?"

"Of course, Son."

Looking back, David understood how his father wanted him to grow in confidence, each day another bit of preparation for when he became an adult and faced more difficult challenges. He was David Joseph Clark. The finest thing that Joe and Peg had ever done together. The late, and ultimately happy surprise in their lives. But unlike a snake that could shed its skin, Davey would have to grow up inside the skin he had. Joe wanted his son to be comfortable in his skin.

The snakeskin felt weightless on his hand. Made of air, almost not there. He knew then that it was nothing to fear.

"Can I keep this?"

"You can try. They're pretty fragile. Mom won't want it around the house." Over the years, Joe had found numerous snakeskins in the forest. When Peg said she didn't like the things, he had stopped collecting them. "Why don't you put it in the truck. Then we can finish our work here."

"Work then play. That's the way," said Davey as he marched toward the truck with his new prize.

Joe took off his flannel shirt, wiped his sweaty face with it, and threw it over a branch of the oak. When he returned, the boy did the same, struggling a little with the many buttons. The branch was too high for him to reach, and Joe lifted him so he could toss it over a small branch.

Their bright tee shirts were darkened with sweat, but they worked on. Davey continued to reach into his shirt to scratch at the needles. The sun rose higher. The cedars fell. Eventually, Joe called the work done, and they collected their tools and shirts and walked to the back of the truck. Joe dropped the tailgate and took his boy under the arms to seat him on it. Davey's face was red with the heat. His long, golden curls drooped, pasted to his forehead and neck with sweat.

"Put your arms in the air, Davey."

Joe pulled his tee shirt over his head then used it to mop his boy's face and gently brush the cedar needles out of his hair and from his back and chest. A breeze blew obligingly to cool the sweaty boy. Joe pulled his own shirt over his head.

"Any ticks?" he asked, turning his back for Davey to see.

"Nope. Just freckles, Dad."

"Okay. Let me have a look at you now."

Davey stood on the tailgate and held out his arms, turning slowly for his dad. A skinny boy topped by a mop of golden curls. Peg called him her Dandelion. "Not even any freckles. How about your legs?"

Davey sat again and held out a foot.

Joe untied the laces and slipped off the boot. He shook out the pebbles and other debris and set it on the tailgate. He did the same with the boy's other boot. Then he pulled off each sock and stuck it in its boot. Finally, he hiked Davey's pants legs as high as he could and looked.

"Well, here's something that's definitely not a freckle." The tick had not attached itself yet, and Joe was able to pluck it from his boy's hairless leg and flick it into the weeds.

When Davey was younger, his mom or dad would inspect every inch of his body for ticks at the end of each day in the woods. If they found one, they treated it casually, removing it as if it was nothing especially important. Just a minor nuisance. As Davey grew older, he kept his underpants on for these inspections and was trusted to finish the work himself in private. Most days would end with a cleansing dip in the lake. Davey splashing around close to shore as first one parent then the other swam across the lake and returned. Sometimes Joe would swim with Davey clinging to his back.

"Let's say we go for a swim. Mom won't want a couple of sweaty men coming home to stink up the house."

"But we didn't bring our swimsuits!"

"We can swim without them. It's just us men. Tell you what. We can wear our underpants in the lake. They'll be just like swimsuits."

Joe watched as Davey considered this.

"Will Mom be mad about my wet underpants?"

"I promise she won't."

"And you'll stay with me?" the boy asked.

"Always, Davey."

The boy thought of the new Superman comic at the cabin. He could read it on the porch like he always did and dry off while his dad fixed lunch. He was certainly going to remember his swimming suit from now on, but if his dad said it was okay to swim in his underpants, then he would do it this time.

"Okay. I'll go swimming," he said and then added, trying in his best seven-year-old manner to sound sensible, "It will be good to wash off."

It was a short drive down the hill to the cabin. Out of view of the cabin was a small cove where the ground sloped gently under the water. This was where Davey preferred to go because he could get in up to his shoulders and still touch bottom.

The two men had no towels or other gear with them, so all that remained was to wade in.

Before he did, though, Joe Clark ran his thumbs inside the waistband of his boxers a few times. Then, in a swift, fluid movement he had his boxers down and was stepping out of them. Davey tried hard not to look at his father's body, but the challenge was too great. He stared at his father's penis. It hung down and was hairy, but he wasn't frightened by it. One day, his dad had assured him, he would be the same.

Joe waded into the water up to his knees, then turned to face Davey and said, "Coming?"

Davey loved his father. Loved him so much he didn't know how to express it. When he had climbed the oak that morning, he'd gone higher than ever before and could see over the trees of their little forest. The world was much, much bigger than he knew. *That* had frightened him, and he had hurried down to be with his dad, where he knew nothing could harm him.

Davey tugged down his briefs and struggled only a little to get them off. Then he waded in as his father had, only up to his knees. Joe Clark glanced at his son's body. A skinny boy, with his mass of dandelion curls at the top. A tear escaped the corner of Joe's eye. My beautiful, beautiful boy.

Davey splashed water at his dad. Joe returned the splash, and soon they were horsing around in the shallow water. Any lingering self-consciousness was washed away.

Joe turned his back to his son and crouched. "Hop on, Davey!"

Davey threw himself on his father, wrapping his arms around his neck, and Joe swam with his son on his back.

PEG

Joe never had a dog growing up. I think he never wanted to be attached to anything, have anything or anyone depending on him. That part of him is changing now, but still no dog.

Davey, on the other hand, needs to cling. It's not a bad thing. He still needs to find his own footing, and we're here to help. One day we may have to push him out of the nest, but for now we'll nurture him.

He thinks I don't know about the puppy he has hidden in the garage. I'm sure it's some stray he found, and it warms my heart to see him as a nurturer, but I think it's wormy or sick somehow and I worry about if the pup doesn't make it. What would that do to Davey? When you love something with all of your heart, you can't bear the idea of having it taken from you. I go out there when Davey's at school, feed it and change its water. Let it explore the yard a little.

I don't know what he's named it, and I don't know why he thinks he needs to keep it a secret. I guess we've never said anything about having pets before.

I know Davey's already attached. It's his nature to be caring. I need to give the little thing a bath and take it to the vet to find out whether it will live or die. And then prepare Davey for either. Or both.

Chapter Three

Boys are Like Puppies

"Little boys are like puppies," Joe had said. That may have been where the day had started to go wrong, he later considered when he and Davey sat before a dying campfire, Joe pulling on a cheap cigar and gnawing on the bone of the day. More likely, it never could have gone right, he supposed.

It had been one of those warm Saturdays in February that sometimes come along when winter releases its steel grip for a bit so boys can run around in the forest as they should.

"Since Davey got Buddy I've come to see that," he'd continued as he stirred the coals of their lunch fire with a stick. "They need to run and play hard and then fall into a heap and sleep hard. They get dirty. And frightened. They need baths. And treats. They need to be housebroken, and sometimes you have to clean up their messes. But they're also loving and loyal and unpredictable."

Joe and Lee were sitting before the remains of the small fire Davey had made to cook the hot dogs they'd had for lunch. Joe should have understood from Lee's poorly hidden frown that the man didn't see raising boys the same way he did, but it's not the kind of thing you expect, and it was otherwise such a perfect day, so he had missed it at first.

Davey was racing his new friend, Jonathan, and his new puppy, Buddy, around the cabin. They were shouting and cavorting, as little boys and puppies do. Lee looked over at his son, Jonathan, frequently to make sure he was okay.

"What's on the other side of your cabin?"

"Trees. Lots of trees."

"They won't get lost?"

As young as he was, Davey knew their woods. They sometimes let him explore a while on his own, but he never went far unless he was with his father on a ramble to find a new climbing tree or look for fossils. It was clear to Joe at that moment that his son wanted nothing more than to keep circling the cabin, hollering encouragement, with Jon and Buddy in tow.

"Nobody will be his friend, Dad," Davey had said a few weeks before. "Everybody at school is mean to him. They call him 'Ears and Nose.'" Joe could see why. The poor boy hadn't grown into his face yet. "Can we take him to the cabin, Dad? And cook hot dogs?" Of course, Joe had said. He'd talk to Jon's parents and they'd go the next Saturday they could.

Lee had had a lot of questions. Where was the property? How long was the drive? Who would be going? How long would they be gone? What about snakes? Poison ivy? Ticks? Bats? He even wanted to know what kind of hot dogs they would have. In the end he said Jon could go, but he would come along as well, and they would drive separately. Joe should have seen a sign in that, too.

"Well, I still don't understand," Lee was saying, tossing another stick on the coals. He was wearing his winter gloves and a wan smile. "You have all of this land, but you can't farm it. The trees are too small for timber. You don't hunt. Do you have any fish in that pond?"

"Lake. We've stocked it with some bass and bluegill and cats, but they're still mostly too small for good fishing."

Lee didn't seem to hear, or more likely, Joe was beginning to see, didn't think there was a suitable answer to his question. "You're too far from Kansas City to build houses you could ever hope to sell. It all just seems, I don't know. Useless. Indulgent. Know what I mean?"

Joe poked the coals, spread them a little. It was time to let them die down. Lee seemed almost annoyed about what he saw as uselessness, but Joe had heard it before in one variation or another. Some people just didn't understand. "This land is a getaway, Lee. For fun. Boys need places like this where they can run wild and get dirty and just be boys." He included himself in that tribe as he brushed at a smudge of soot on his jeans. "Don't you ever want to just walk in the woods? Strike out without a path and see what you find?"

Lee raised an eyebrow at this. He looked toward the cabin where Davey and Jon were playing with Buddy. They were on the porch now, wrestling like puppies. "I'd be happy if they just stayed on that porch," Lee said, mostly to himself.

"But where's the adventure in that? The excitement? The discovery?"

"Discovery? You mean surprises, don't you? Unexpected. Unplanned."

"I've been rambling these hills for a few years, and even though I'm sure I've set a foot on each of these hundred acres, I'm always on the lookout for what new things they can show me. I really want to find an arrowhead someday. It's possible. The Osage lived here. Haven't found one, but there are a lot of great fossils in the rocks."

"You can't pay your bills with arrowheads and fossils, Thoreau. The taxes alone on your hundred acres of natural history must be pretty high."

Lee, Joe had learned, was an engineer, which he guessed explained the man's analytical view of the woods. In any case, he struck Joe as the kind of person who feels he has a lot of really helpful advice to give but rarely has an audience to hear it.

"Maybe you could rent the place during hunting season. I guess that's what I would do. I'd lease the hunting rights. Make a little money, anyway. You'd have to improve the road first though. Might cost a bit."

"I want to think that bad road keeps out the locals."

"I don't suppose the local riff raff are slowed down by that road's condition, bad as it is. Or by abstract concepts like private property." Lee chuckled ruefully. "Of course, I'd just sell it all if it were mine. Put the money in Jon's college fund."

"Technically, it's my wife's property. She inherited it from her father."

"Oh! I see," Lee said, on the scent now. "That's why you can't sell it. She has a sentimental attachment to it." He seemed satisfied with this, sentiment being, in his experience, an unbreakable, though, he thought, insufficient bond.

The boys had leapt off the porch, leaving their coats behind, and were in front of the cabin, shouting and crashing through the fallen leaves. Poor little Buddy was doing his best to keep up.

Lee rose from his seat on a log to check on the boys, his boy. Downhill from them a short way was the lake, a skim of ice still on it from earlier, colder days, and Lee feared Jon would fall in. But Davey was still wary of the water. Joe's sweet little boy wouldn't go near it unless his dad was with him. Joe was not worried.

"He's taken off his coat," Lee said with a shake of his head. "Why would he do that?"

Because they're running and shouting on a warm February day, Joe thought. Because they're the little furnaces boys are at that age. Joe wanted to be with the boys too, set loose, knocking around and hollering, rather than sitting still before a dying fire with gloomy Lee, bundled up against a cold that wasn't there.

He sat again. "You could probably get decent money for a hundred acres, especially with a cabin and a pond. Get yourself a better truck. Put something away for Davey's college." Lee was kindly working it all out for him. "Or will your boy go to trade school?"

Joe didn't know yet if Davey was college material. Peg was forty-one when he was born, and lots of people had whispered concerns about that. But he was doing well enough in school, smack in the middle of the charts. A solid C student who could even bring home a B now and then. "Don't know yet what Davey will decide about that, when the time comes."

"*Davey* will decide? You're giving him a choice? Jon is going to college! No question about that. And he's going to be an engineer if I have anything to say about it. Graduate degree too. If I had a hundred acres like this, I'd turn it into a college fund right away and have it earning interest. That's what you should do, Joe. I'm sure trade school costs money too."

He'd already worked out Jonathan's future, and he was ready to do the same for Davey. But to Joe's mind, a child wasn't a project or a possession. Or a pet like Buddy. He was a person, a unique human with a life that belonged to him alone, and Joe had the responsibility, for too few years, to raise him and prepare him for his life.

"Maybe the value of the land will grow faster than a savings account. They're not making any more of it, you know. If it turns out Davey needs the money someday, he can sell it then."

Davey and Jon ran up to them, their faces red from their exertions. "I think I have a tick, Dad." Davey tugged down his jeans and underpants and pulled up his flannel shirt, pointing his little round bottom at his dad. Jonathan snickered, but Lee was alarmed. He turned away.

Ticks are a fact of life in the Ozarks. With Davey, Joe tried to treat them casually. Deal with them but not be upset if one happened to find him. He doubted Davey had picked up a tick in February, but he had a look anyway.

"I don't see anything, Davey. Did you feel a bite or something?"

"Yeah. Right here." He reached around and touched his lower back.

There was a tiny stick where Davey pointed, and Joe could see the back of his shirt was littered with bits of leaves. He'd been rolling on the ground with Buddy. Joe brushed the stick away.

Davey turned to him then, his shirt still hiked and his jeans and underpants at his knees. Not at all cold standing half naked before them.

"No tick?"

"Nope."

"Thanks, Dad." He leaned in and gave his father a quick hug.

Only then did he pull up his jeans and let his shirt fall.

Buddy had hurried over after the two boys, panting from his hard play, perhaps looking for more hot dogs. They'd forgotten to bring any food for the newest member of their family, so Davey had sacrificed one of his hot dogs for the pup. He'd been working hard with Buddy in recent days, trying to teach him left from right. Not any progress to show yet, but he had kept at it.

With Davey's pants back on, Lee let his face relax and turned to Buddy.

"Come here, dog," he said, holding his hand close to the ground. Buddy stumbled over expectantly. He was a gangly, cinnamon pup with four white socks and a white tip on his tail, which he was wagging for Lee now.

"Sit!"

Buddy sniffed Lee's hand, and finding it contained nothing, flopped to the ground, exhausted.

"I said sit, not lay down. You're not a very bright dog, are you?" He turned to Joe. "Some kind of mutt, I guess. Dog like this will need constant discipline and training."

"Don't want to train the dog out of the dog though."

"Just like some boys need training. I guess you were right about that."

Joe realized he was saying Davey was a mutt, a not-very-bright boy. Lee really was honest, and not intentionally mean, but a man without much tact. Still, the words stung. His Davey, who had found a starving stray and brought him home, who'd successfully hidden it from his parents for a week. His Davey who had befriended Lee's own stray son when no other boy would. Joe shook off his irritation. They had the day to get through together. But uncomfortable thoughts returned. Joe knew exactly what Lee meant. His boy was going to college. Joe's boy, in Lee's eyes, was fit only for trade school. But what was wrong with that?

"Bye, Dad," Davey shouted as he ran back toward the cabin, Jon in tow, and Buddy pushed himself up from the gravel to stumble after them.

Joe could see in Lee's frown and in the constant movement of his hands, rubbing his knees, turning a stick over and over before tossing it onto the coals, that he was still agitated. He was not comfortable in the forest. Or maybe, Joe thought, not comfortable seeing his son off his leash for once.

"You and Jon should come out in the spring, Lee. It's all grays and browns right now. But it gets beautiful when the trees go green and wildflowers are popping up wherever the sunlight reaches the ground."

"And more ticks."

Joe had hoped Lee would enjoy this rare sunny day they had in the middle of winter, but he was beginning to realize that would not happen.

"In the summer, after a long day, we usually take a dip in the lake to cool off. Wash away the grime. And any ticks."

"You *swim* in that? I'll bet stagnant water like that would be a breeding ground for mosquitoes in the summer. Who knows what other kinds of pestilence! Didn't you take a biology course in college?"

"I didn't go to college."

"Oh," Lee said, drawing out the word as though he now understood everything. Trade school.

The boys continued their untroubled play, shouting, laughing, chasing each other, calling to the pup. This was exactly the kind of day Joe liked to give Davey, and, he thought, what Davey wanted to give to Jon.

"On the weekends, Jon has reading time after lunch." Lee looked at his watch. "Jonathan needs quiet time then. We're training him to focus."

The boys were standing on the edge of the cabin porch, screaming as loudly as they could to hear their voices echo back from the hillside across the lake. Buddy was giving his best puppy bark.

"Jon really needs to settle down."

Joe didn't think Davey's growing collection Superman comics in the cabin were the kind of reading Lee had in mind, but he had nothing else to offer.

"Jon," Lee called, but the boy was still shouting and didn't hear. "JONATHAN!"

The boys stopped and turned to look at Lee. Even Buddy caught the tone in his voice.

"Come here, Jon."

The boy walked carefully down the porch steps and came straight to his father, his head hanging. Davey was behind him. He looked surprised but expectant too, like maybe this signaled a new adventure.

"Yes, sir," Jon said when his slow steps reached his father.

"Sit."

Jonathan dropped to the log beside the fire ring.

"You realize what's happening, don't you?"

Jon nodded his head. "I'm having an episode, sir." Almost in a whisper. He dropped his face to stare at the gravel beneath his feet.

"We've talked about this. Until you can learn to control yourself, we'll have to do what we always do."

Joe feared that Lee was going to spank Jon. What would he do then? What would Davey, who had *never* had a hand raised to him, think of something like that?

Instead, Lee reached into the hip pocket of his coat and brought out a rattling bottle of pills. He removed one of his gloves and shook out a pill that he held before Jon. The boy took the pill in his fingers and then accepted the half-finished can of pop his dad handed to him. He swallowed the pill, and then returned his face to the ground.

Jon was embarrassed that his new friend had witnessed this. Joe could see that. No wonder the boy didn't have any friends and was an easy target for ridicule. Davey had taken a half step toward his dad. They would have something to talk about later, if Davey wanted to. Joe wished his boy didn't have to learn such ugly things about the world so soon.

"It's time to settle down now. Your medicine will help you get in control. You understand, right?"

Jon nodded again.

"Say 'Yes, sir.'"

"Yes, sir."

Only then did Lee look at Joe. "It's a little condition he has that he's supposed to grow out of it. We have to manage it for him."

"Sure," Joe said, not knowing what else to say.

"You drank a lot of pop today, Jon. That's why you're so hyperactive now. Do you need to use the toilet?"

"No. Davey and I did that before."

"Together?"

Jon's head rose and fell twice.

"You went to the bathroom together?"

Joe wondered how it could be so surprising.

"No," Jon said. "We went on a tree behind the cabin."

That was what Joe had feared Jon would say. Lee didn't speak for several moments. He dropped the pill bottle back in his pocket and rubbed his hands on his thighs.

"Jon," he said carefully. "I want you to *walk* over to the porch and get your coat. Put it on, and then come back here."

The boy rose from the log and headed toward the cabin. Davey tagged along, silent but close. Joe did not say anything. Lee did.

"Your boy has taught my son how to take down his pants and urinate on a tree. Like a dog." He pulled on his glove again. "And casual nudity. Maybe in your family, but not in mine. And not something I wanted Jonathan to have even the *idea* of."

He was whispering so the boys couldn't hear, but he spat the next words at Joe.

"I don't want my son playing with your son again. I'm sorry I have to say this, but your boy is a bad influence. A bad influence and a vulgar one. I try to raise my boy properly, and he certainly doesn't need exposure to this kind of lifestyle."

With his judgment delivered, Lee stood and zipped his jacket. The boys were back by then, and Lee painted a smile on his face.

"Jon, I'm sorry, but we have to be going home now." He zipped Jon's jacket up all the way to the collar. "I know you had a lot of fun today, but it's over now. You can settle during the ride home. Okay?"

Jonathan nodded mutely. Davey's shock and disappointment were obvious.

"Bye, Davey," Jon said without making eye contact. "Thanks for inviting me." He waved his hand, but he didn't raise it higher than his stomach.

Davey understood some of what was happening, but he said no more than "Bye, Jon. See you at school Monday."

Lee laid his hand on his boy's shoulder and steered him to their car. They got in and, with a spray of gravel, passed up the rutted road. Through the winter-bare trees Joe and Davey could see the dusty cloud of their wake long after they could no longer hear the crunch of the tires on the dry gravel. Jon and his father had spent less time at the cabin than they would spend driving to and from it.

Davey stood in silence next to his father as he watched his new friend disappear. He sniffled.

What could Joe say to his boy? How could he explain what had just happened when he barely understood it himself. It looked as though Lee wanted to *humiliate* his son. In front of his only friend.

There are many ways you can help a boy, Joe thought. But sometimes what looks like help is just a form of abuse. He laid his hand on Davey's shoulder and pulled him close into his arms. Davey hugged him back and buried his face in Joe's shirt. He was crying.

They stood that way for a few silent moments until Buddy began tugging at Davey's shoelace. Davey looked down at his puppy and bent to pick him up.

Joe took a few deep breaths. He leaned down to kiss his son's forehead before he spoke.

"Davey, why don't we stay here tonight. Here at the cabin."

Davey looked up at him. "But we ate all the hot dogs!"

Joe withheld a chuckle at this reasonable concern.

"We can drive into Osceola and get some supplies. Anything you want."

"And dog food for Buddy?"

"Yes, dog food for Buddy." And maybe a cigar or two as well, though the stogies they had at the gas station were pretty harsh.

"And I can call Mom from the payphone there. Tell her we're staying the night. Just us men."

"I think Buddy's bright, Dad."

"Bright enough to learn left from right, if you keep at it, Davey."

"Will we hear whippoorwills tonight, Dad?"

"Sorry, Davey. Not this time of year. It's too early."

"Have you ever seen a whippoorwill, Dad?"

"No, but I've heard them, so I know when they are there."

Davey considered this.

"Davey, if we stay the night, it might get cold. I'll show you how to build a fire in the new wood stove. That's an important skill for a young man to have."

Davey said something then, but his face was buried in Joe's shirt again. Joe thought it sounded like "I love you!"

Peg

My baby boy is growing up. Becoming more himself every day. Perplexed by a world that keeps getting bigger all around him. Bigger, and not always fun. Or fair. I wish I could protect him from some of it, but I can't. He comes home from school now bearing whatever insult or harsh realization he's had about life. And sometimes he still talks to me about his troubles, but more often he goes to Joe now. And I guess that's fine. He loves me, but he adores Joe.

I can feel him pulling away. Do all sons drift from their mothers? Is it part of what they need to do to become men? This boy who would run around the house all day without a stitch on, run down to the basement naked to find a particular shirt in the dryer, as though it were the most natural thing in the world. And I guess it is really. But now that he's started puberty, he's more cautious around me. Careful to be wearing something all of the time, and apologetic if I catch him naked for a moment between the bathroom and his bedroom.

He's keeping his life more shrouded from me too. I learn from Joe, more often than not, of Davey's latest mishaps or adventures. Apparently, they have goings-on at the cabin that I know nothing about and likely never will. Guy stuff, I suppose. Harmless and healthy. It's not that I need to know, but he's my boy, and I want to know. I want to share in his life, at least as much as he will let me, because in many ways, he is my life.

Chapter Four

Rite of Passage

"You and Davey need to have a man-to-man talk, Joe."

"About what?"

"About something I think a growing boy would rather discuss with his father than his mother."

"Oh!"

That was on Wednesday. By Saturday, Joe and Davey, and Buddy, were breezing down the highway, windows open, the July wind buffeting their hair since the air conditioner in the old truck hadn't worked for years, on their way to the cabin with a list of chores to maybe complete, or maybe ignore. It was the middle of Davey's aimless summer, between finishing eighth grade and starting high school, and Joe could see that his boy *was* on edge, once he looked. And so, cabin time, a relaxed time when the boy might talk about what troubled him.

Buddy sat on Davey's lap the drive down, or beside him on the bench seat. When they finally got to the edge of their hundred acres of forest, Joe stopped the truck. Here, at the top of their land, the beginnings of a wet-weather creek cut through the exposed sandstone that capped whatever else lay beneath the thin Ozark soil of their forest.

Joe and Davey had been harvesting large, mostly flat chunks of this sandstone – much easier to shape than the limestone farther downhill. They were using it to make steps leading from the cabin to the lake below. The process was slow, dirty, and better suited to their winter visits. Under each new step they placed a quarter showing the year it was laid, a ritual that had captivated Davey, both as a hidden treasure and as a permanent sign of their presence on the land.

Joe had thought they could add another step during this visit. It would be a tangible achievement Davey could point to, and they could work side by side as two men. When his son was tired, maybe he'd be more relaxed and around the campfire that evening they might talk. He'd brought a quarter – minted that year – from the bowl of change by their front door to plant with this step.

As they climbed out of the truck, Buddy began sniffing everything. Joe tossed a pair of curled leather work gloves to Davey.

"Let's grab a chunk while we're here."

The sandstone was fractured where it was exposed, and some pieces were larger than man and boy could lift. Others were more suited to making steps. It was just a matter of finding the right one and prying it loose from its neighbors. Joe supposed that Davey thought his father knew what he was doing, but he was mostly winging it, never knowing if the next slab would be big enough or too big, whether it would snap in half as they worked it free, or if the two of them could even carry it back to the truck and heft it onto the tailgate. But he figured that as long as he pretended confidence, Davey would think that's what it was. And confidence, Joe suspected, came as much from belief as ability.

"What do you think, Davey?"

The boy was pawing at the exposed ledge, working out smaller pieces and tossing them into the leaf litter, focused on a slab that would take some work to free. From what Joe could see, the piece looked suitably thick and wouldn't crack once it was in place, but getting it in place would be hard work.

"How about this one, Dad?" Davey grabbed the corner of the slab he had chosen and began a back-and-forth tugging that slowly edged it free. The stone ground against its neighbors, and bits of gravel and dirt rained down to clatter on the dry leaves as Davey teased it farther from the ledge that held it.

The more Joe saw of it, the better he liked it. And hated it. Davey had found a fine piece, with good dimensions, but it would take the two of them, and possibly some cursing, to get it to the truck, and when they got it to the cabin and down the hill toward the lake, they would have to dig a large hole in the hardpan to receive it. In all, more work than he'd intended, but the boy was already deep into that hard work, and Joe didn't want to interrupt his focus.

When Davey tugged the rock free, it thudded to the ground at their feet, and he began brushing off the dirt that clung to it.

"Good choice, Davey."

With lifting and dragging – and no cursing at all – they managed to get the piece of sandstone to the truck. Davey did most of the work, surprising Joe with a strength he didn't think his skinny boy had. Once they had the chunk onto the tailgate, and both had pulled off their gloves, Joe fished in his pocket for his keys and tossed them to Davey.

"We won't tell Mom about this," he said with a wink.

"About what?"

"That I let you drive the truck."

"But I'm not old enough to drive!"

Was there fear in his son's voice? Did he think he was going to get caught breaking the law? Doing something wrong? Something that couldn't be right if he wasn't going to tell his mom about it?

"You only need a license to drive on public roads, Davey. Out here we're on private property, and a boy can drive up and down our gravel road as much as he likes. Time this boy started doing it, I think."

The idea was spontaneous. Joe hadn't planned to give Davey his first time behind the wheel that visit, but when he watched his boy wresting the rock from the ground, not needing any direction or even much help, he realized Davey was ready for other chances to build his confidence and see that he was more mature than he realized.

"I don't know about this, Dad."

"You'll do fine, Davey. I'll be right beside you. And the brakes still work pretty good on this old truck. We'll take it slow. Take all the time you need to get to the cabin. What can go wrong?"

"I could hit a tree."

"I won't let that happen, Davey."

And because his father said that, and because his father was never wrong, Davey thought maybe he could do this thing. The road to the cabin was bumpy, but it was mostly straight, and he'd walked on it hundreds of times, so maybe he could drive on it this time.

When Davey climbed behind the wheel, Joe watched with a bemused smile as the boy first carefully buckled the seatbelt then reached up to adjust the mirror, though only a little because he was nearly as tall as his dad.

"Now, you see the gas pedal and the brake pedal. Touch each of them with your boot so you know where they are. You need to be able to use them without looking down."

Davey did this, having no trouble reaching them with his lanky legs.

"When you use the brake, use your right foot. That way you take it off the gas and the engine slows." The boy looked at his feet and then at his father, something like terror in his wide eyes.
"Okay, so put the key in and turn it. You don't have to give it any gas to get it started since it's already warmed up."

Davey did this.

"Now press on the brake to hold us in place, then shift into drive . . . that's right . . . now ease off the brake and we'll start moving forward slowly."

Davey gripped the steering wheel as though he thought it would try to escape. He dared not look at his father beside him but instead peered straight ahead at all of the looming trees as the old brown truck crept forward. And if that weren't hard enough, he had to make a turn up ahead. He had to turn the truck, while it was moving, in a forest, with his father watching. Even Buddy sensed the tension, for he sat still on Joe's lap and didn't try to stick his nose out the window.

Davey flicked on the turn signal and Joe had to swallow a chuckle.

"Now, depress the brake, Davey, and we'll just take this turn slowly."

Davey stomped on the brake and Joe lurched forward while Buddy pitched to the floor, where he chose to remain. The truck was stopped before the turn, the brake pedal pushed as far as it would go, and once Joe composed himself, he began talking Davey through the turn.

This worked well enough, though Joe had to tell Davey not to over steer when he tugged the wheel too sharply, and then to straighten the wheel once they were around the corner, and once or twice Davey touched the brake when things were happening too fast at their tortoise pace, but eventually they were on the straight, mostly flat stretch of gravel that led deep into their forest where the cabin waited.

"You can give it a little gas here, Davey. If you want."

Davey's foot felt full of lead as he shifted from hovering over the brake pedal to hovering over the gas pedal. And when he let his foot down, he gave it more than a little gas, and the truck leapt forward with a spray of gravel. It startled Davey and he pulled his foot back. Buddy, still safely on the floor, didn't share his thoughts about any of this.

And so it continued for the long quarter mile journey to the cabin. The truck retained both of its side mirrors and its bumpers, and if any tree branches had scraped it, well, Joe told himself, that was just a sign that they needed to cut them back from the edge of the road and not a sign of a beginning driver having trouble staying centered. No, he thought, they would not tell Peg about this adventure.

Davey stopped the truck a few feet short of where Joe normally parked behind the cabin, and that was where it remained until they drove home the next day. As they each stepped out of the truck, and Buddy eagerly exited too, Davey slipped the keys into his pocket. Was this, Joe wondered, a sign of the boy's growing confidence? It couldn't have been automatic; he didn't carry keys. Was he asserting that any further driving that weekend would be his responsibility? Did it just feel good, feel grown up, to carry his dad's keys for a while? And did he forget that Joe needed them to open the cabin?

Joe grabbed some of their gear from the truck bed and carried it to the porch. He expected Davey to do the same, and then Davey would be the one to unlock the cabin. Yet as Joe waited, Davey did not appear, and when he returned to the truck, he found that Davey had thudded the chunk of sandstone from the tailgate and was turning it end over end down the hill. The stone would need to be dug in, and they would need tools to do this. Thus Joe knew Davey would come to the cabin eventually to collect them, so he just continued to unload the truck and set their gear on the porch.

When Davey finally climbed the hill to the cabin, he found his dad sitting in one of the porch chairs, back in the shade, and all of their weekend gear sitting beside him. Joe had wanted to light a cigar, but the matches and cutter were locked inside the cabin.

"Oh," the boy said as he realized what had happened. He fished the keys from his pocket then held them out to his father.

"Go ahead and open the door, Davey. And hang on to the keys if you want." Maybe that would give the boy a little swagger for the weekend, but it was probably a good idea, he thought, to hide a key somewhere around the cabin from now on.

Davey unlocked the door, and together they moved their gear inside. Joe then began opening the windows to let fresh air into the stuffy cabin, and Davey stuck his hand into the cooler to get himself a can of pop and whatever else he could devour before they had lunch. Davey, Joe saw once again, was a different boy at the cabin, more at ease and less timid than at home. Davey held a piece of beef jerky before his dog, which Buddy accepted, jumping on the bed to eat it.

"So do you want to work on that step now? Or go for a hike? Liberate some cedars? Or whatever?"

Davey thought for a moment and then said, "We should get that rock in the ground first so we can swim afterward and get cleaned up."

"And lunch sometime in there?"

"Absolutely, Dad!"

Because they had both already set a half-dozen stones in place, they knew what tools they needed: the pickaxe, a spade, a hand shovel. And maybe some expressive vocabulary. They collected the three tools, and Davey finished his can of pop. Then they walked down the hill toward the lake where Davey had left the stone. It was late enough in the morning that they would have to work in the sun, and they sweated copiously as Joe swung the heavy pickaxe and they took turns shoveling out the resulting dirt and gravel. Neither complained, and Davey soon shed his tee shirt, wiping his face with it then tossing it over a sumac branch.

"There's some suntan lotion in the cabin."

"Yeah, if I go back up there for anything, I'll get it, but I really want to get this job done."

Joe was pleased with the boy's clear-eyed devotion to the task, and it seemed on the surface that what was bothering Davey, that *other* chore they had for the weekend, was gone. Joe guessed, though, that it was really just pushed aside for now and that it would return once Davey's focus relaxed.

The hardpan did not yield any more easily for this new step than it had for the others below. It exacted its price in labor and sweat, but the two of them created a space that could accept the stone they would wrestle into it. First, though, Joe dug in his pocket for the quarter. He gave it to Davey, who examined it then centered it carefully in the hole. Next, they tugged and shifted the slab of sandstone into place, putting some wedge rocks under the front of it and backfilling around it with the dirt and gravel they'd created. Then they took turns jumping on it to help set it.

"A couple of good rains," Joe said, pulling his shirt up to wipe his face, "and that ought to be solid. Agreed?"

"We do good work together, Dad."

They'd worked through lunch, which Joe had not expected Davey to ignore, but he hadn't wanted to interrupt him either. Now, he thought, they would retreat to the shady porch and too many cans of pop and bottles of water and sandwiches and chips as they assessed the remainder of the day before them.

Yet once again, Davey surprised him. The boy sat on their new step and began unlacing his boots. Off they came, and then his socks, and soon his jeans were in a heap on the ground and he stood before Joe is his briefs. If ever there were a time for suntan lotion, Joe thought, this was it as Davey slipped out of his briefs and walked nimbly down the steps to the lake.

By the time Joe got undressed and to the water's edge, Davey had waded in up to his knees. His mop of golden curls dripped sunlight. He was smiling, showing plenty of white teeth. My perfect boy, Joe thought. Free of his troubles for the moment.

He stepped into the water and stood before his son.

Davey bent low with cupped his hands and brought water to his face to wash away the sweat and salt of his labor. Then he cupped them again and collected more water, which he threw at his father, laughing. Splashing ensued, and their feet shifted on the uneven, muddy bottom. Soon they were up to their waists and pitched themselves forward, swimming, side by side, across the lake. Joe was the stronger swimmer, and he checked his pace so Davey could stay with him.

They paddled around the lake in the sun, checking for any sign of muskrats and their problematic dens, but finding only dozens of frogs that leapt into the water when they were startled. They swam to the middle of the lake and floated on their backs, feeling the sun touch their skin. Curious dragonflies patrolled the air just above them. A plane droned across the blue vault of sky. They dove under the water and came up far away. They secretly scratched a few itchy places. They washed away the grit of their morning work and then lurched from the water, carrying their clothes to the cabin. Instead of dressing, they flopped into the chairs on the porch and let themselves dry in the air. Buddy heard them and began scratching at the cabin door to be let out and, released from his confinement, settled on Davey's pile of clothes for an afternoon nap.

As he began to drift into sleep, Joe felt content. This was the kind of day he had wanted to give his son. Whatever the boy faced, he always had this.

Neither knew how long they had slept in those chairs on that porch. When they woke, Davey rubbed his hands on his legs to brush out the lake silt that had dried on his hair. Then they pulled on their clothes and decided what they should do next.

Davey's stomach suggested that lunch would be a good idea, and so they went into the cabin where the coolers waited and made themselves semblances of sandwiches, which soon disappeared. Buddy disdained his kibble and begged meat from Davey, which worked well for him.

Muscle tired and lethargic in the July heat, they didn't undertake any new projects that late afternoon. Joe poked around the cabin, pulling weeds from the gravel, gathering fallen branches, and thinking in the abstract about maybe splitting some logs into firewood and stove wood. And all the while, he watched his son, watched as the boy copied his actions, enjoying the uncomplicated pleasure these familiar chores gave in this holy place.

They retreated to the cabin often for water or pop. Davey threw a stick for Buddy to chase. He visited the new step to examine his work. Turkey vultures circled over the south ridge beyond the lake. The afternoon buzzed with forest sounds.

Joe could see that his boy was immersed in the safe comfort of a cabin weekend, and he hoped that would allow him to share his worry so they could talk it through. But Davey wasn't speaking up. Not yet.

His attempt to build a one-match fire had been unsuccessful. He could still only do it about half the time, and Joe knew his boy was too impatient to build it carefully so it was a success. He was too eager to strike the match when he didn't have all of the preparation done first. A few gentle suggestions as the boy worked sometimes helped, but Joe knew there was a line between helping and annoying, so Davey would need to figure it out on his own, which was how some people learned after all.

"I don't always get it right either," Joe confessed as Davey watched the flames ignite the kindling too high and then fizzle out. So he had to start again, laying down more tinder and resetting the kindling over it. Then he drew another match from the box. "Takes practice."

Davey managed with the second match and soon the flames reached into the air as the kindling caught. He'd readied the bigger sticks earlier and now added them carefully to his fire. Once its enthusiasm waned and the fire settled into a more mature crackling of logs, they would toss their burgers on the grill and burn them enough to be called cooked. More pop. More tending the fire that didn't need much tending. Night would finally fall. The owls would hoot. Maybe a whippoorwill. Joe would light a cigar and muse. And somewhere, during all of that, he hoped Davey would feel safe to tell his dad what was worrying him, what his mom had overheard him discussing with his friend, Jon.

But that hadn't happened. They'd eaten. They'd added more

wood to the fire. The forest gave its sounds. Buddy lay curled in the gravel close to Davey's feet. The stars began to emerge. They talked about the new step, about maybe placing another one in the morning, but Davey hadn't spoken about what was really on his mind.

Joe grabbed a stick from the woodpile and then opened his pocketknife and began whittling it. When Davey saw this, he did the same, having remembered to retrieve his knife from the old cigar box of treasures he kept so cleverly hidden under his bed at home.

"So," Joe said, deciding finally to try to tease the needed conversation from his boy. "High school in a few weeks."

Davey grunted an assent but gave nothing more.

"You and Jon excited about going?"

Davey didn't have a large group of friends – he was shy in that way – and Jon was about the best one he did have. They hung out a lot, mostly in Davey's room or on their bikes to McDonald's. They were a mismatched pair. Jon was still a squirt compared to Davey, who was sprouting so much now that he'd need new clothes before school started.

"I guess."

"Big adventure."

"I guess."

This wasn't working as Joe hoped. He whittled his stick a little more then collected the shavings and threw them on the coals. After a moment, they flared up briefly. Davey did the same.

Davey was a conscientious student, Joe knew, and he worked hard to bring home the best grade card he could, but Joe also knew that high school was going to be tougher for him. They'd already begun discussing what they could do about it. Peg would give more time to helping him with his homework, with choosing suitable classes. They wouldn't hesitate to hire a tutor if that was needed. They'd encourage him to take whatever extra credit work he could. They'd keep an eye on all of it with the sole purpose of maintaining the boy's self-esteem in the onslaught.

But none of that was what was troubling Davey.

Joe examined his stick in the orange firelight. "A little more work and I should have a perfect toothpick."

Davey laughed at this but didn't look up from his own busy hands.

"Jon said something, Dad."

"Oh, what did he say?" Joe responded as casually as he could. In the firelight they could not make good eye contact, and that, Joe knew, would help.

"About . . . gym class."

"You're a fit boy, Davey. You muscled that rock around like a champ today. Gym won't be a problem for you." And Joe knew this was not the point anyway.

"Yeah," Davey said barely above a whisper. "It's not that."

Joe waited, fearful that if he said another word, even one intended to be encouraging, he might stifle the boy's willingness to share his confidence.

"He said they have . . . gang showers in high school. I have to shower with other boys."

There *was* fear in his son's voice this time. Joe could hear it. The boy was facing a rite of passage that all boys his age did. And while Joe knew that after a month or so, showering with other boys would no longer be traumatic for him, he also knew that Davey was not at that point yet. Davey knew only shyness and fear then, born of his general lack of self-confidence.

What Davey didn't know, what he couldn't know yet, was that he had nothing to be ashamed of being undressed before the other boys. Joe wasn't quite sure how to tell him this, and Davey would quickly discover it on his own anyway, so Joe tried a different approach.

"You and I swam naked in the lake today. No big deal."

"That's not the same. You're my dad."

"Davey, you're going to see a lot of difference among the boys when you get to that locker room, and the important thing to know is, it's not important. Every boy grows up at his own pace. Some are farther along than others, and that's normal. And trust me, Davey. You have nothing to be worried about in that."

Davey kept his eyes on his whittling, but Joe wondered if maybe he saw the smallest smile curling at the end of his boy's lips.

"You're getting to the age where you need to shower more often. You're not a little boy any longer. Shoot, you're nearly as tall as I am. First couple of times after gym class when you go in there and wash off, it's going to feel awkward, but trust me, that will pass. And I guarantee, every other boy is going to feel the same way. Pretty soon it won't be a big deal. And that's the key, Davey. Don't let it be a big deal. Just go about your business and let the other boys go about theirs. Just focus on what *you* need to do in there. Get undressed. Get washed off. Get dressed. Either don't say a thing, or just talk about anything in the world. Stride in there as though everything was normal, even if you have to pretend for a while. It *will* get easier."

Whether Davey understood any of this, even less whether he agreed, Joe didn't know. The matter would resolve itself. That he did know. And then perhaps Davey would look back on this conversation and see the truth in it. But for now, Joe hoped something sunk in and that he hadn't spoken too much about his boy's worry, hadn't been too ready to dismiss it.

And then Davey spoke. "You're my best friend, Dad."

DAVID

I knew it. Dad knew it. And Mom didn't need to know it, until it was done.

I said I wanted to go to the cabin by myself. Drive here and do whatever and drive back. Alone. I knew I could. I know the way. I can drive the truck as good as Dad. Then he said, "Let's find out." And here I am. First time I've ever been here on my own.

"Don't touch the chainsaw," Dad said, and I won't. That would be stupid. But I can still wander the woods, climb a tree maybe, cut some cedars or buckbrush with the loppers, make a fire or not, jump in the lake before I go home. Anything.

Or just sit here on the porch like Dad. He'd smoke a cigar, but I won't, even though it smells good. It's funny. I could be anywhere in the forest, doing anything I want, but I'm sitting on the porch.

It's different, without Dad. The birds are all singing. I can hear the bullfrogs down at the lake. But something's off. I don't feel unsafe – I won't do stupid stuff that could get me hurt – but everything here seems, I don't know, bigger. What if I get a cramp when I'm swimming or fall out of a tree? Or a snake bites me? If I shouted for help, no one would hear me. I never thought like this before, I guess because Dad was always around.

Maybe just getting here on my own is what I really wanted. Show myself I could. Maybe just leave it at that. Except he'll ask what I did, so I have to tell him something. Split some firewood maybe? Clear some scrub?

I don't think I'd like spending the night here alone. But Dad doesn't need to know.

Chapter Five

When We Were Young and Life was Full in Us

David Clark was naked. He was seventeen. He was in love. And he was as naked as the day he was born. He had paused, despite the chill, to stand before the cabin window and watch the snow falling outside. When they'd arrived that morning, he had stoked the potbelly, but he was in a great, heart-pounding hurry then and hadn't been careful. Because of his fumbling first effort, the fire he laid didn't catch, so the cabin was still cold.

The snow wouldn't last. It had been a warm December so far, and the little that was falling would soon melt. No one would happen upon their two sets of tracks. There would be no sign that they had ever been there at all. And for now, the snow was wrapping the little cabin in a conspiracy of quiet for them, sending in a soft, white light.

David felt the energy of his seventeen years in every muscle of his body. It trembled within him as a dawning sensation. It tingled in the downy hairs of his skin. It radiated from his gut. A force too strong to resist, too elemental to understand. He was awakening finally from a long, dreamless sleep. It was a realization, a newfound essence swirling inside him. His life before was already a pale memory, or maybe he had just never opened his eyes. The world had changed for David that day. This, he now understood, was what life was about.

"You're the best thing that's ever happened to me, Kathy," he sang out with all of the purity and ardor of his seventeen glorious years.

David had just risen from the bed where, only a half hour before, he and Kathy had lost their virginity. They had tumbled into that bed like a pair of wrestling puppies. There was a great deal of giggling, and a little bit of fumbling, but they eventually found a happy rhythm, and it soon satisfied them both. Once they were able to give their attention to something beyond each other, they realized that the cabin was still cold. So David had risen to stoke the potbelly properly and make the place toasty. But he hadn't gotten there yet.

He was restless. Something in him felt uncontainable, some energy that had him burning hotter than any fire in the belly of any wood stove. His body was talking to him in a language that he was only beginning to understand. He couldn't have explained what was rushing into his head. All that he was feeling. He didn't know it was simply being alive that he had suddenly awoken to. He only knew that he had to get up and move, use his muscles, feel this new knowledge burning in his flesh where every sensation was suddenly more intense.

In this way, the cold felt good against his bare body. It convinced him that he was alive, alive in a way he hadn't recognized before. His nipples grew erect in the cold. He touched them briefly then ran his fingers across his chin, seeking a bit of acne he remembered there but finding soft beard stubble instead. I should shave more often now, he thought.

Kathy had remained under the blankets where the shared warmth of their two bodies lingered. She stretched with a luxurious sigh, then rested her hands on her stomach.

"I love this cabin. I love coming here. My dad built it." David was chattering now because something within him was brimming, and he used words since he didn't know how else to release it. "Someday, when I have a boy, I'm going to bring him here too. Next summer, you and I can go skinny-dipping in the lake. I'm glad you're not going to Notre Dame like your dad wanted. I'm glad you're staying in Kansas City. We can keep coming here. I can show you the forest in the spring. We can have campfires. Look at the stars at night. Go on hikes in the fall. Look for wildlife."

David snatched the binoculars from their nail by the door and trained them on the opposite shore of the lake. Sometimes he saw deer there. Once, a fox. He wished he could see a bobcat so he could tell his father *something* truthful about his visit to the cabin. Be able to share at least one part of this big, big day with his dad.

"Do you think they know about us?" Kathy said. "Your parents?"

"What do you mean?" he said, still scanning the far shore. "They know you. They like you."

"No, I mean, about us. Being together. Like this."

"Are you kidding? No way!"

David turned the binoculars down to examine himself, but he couldn't focus that close. He knew what he would see though. Pendulous. Well used and sated, for the moment. He felt great strutting about the cabin naked. Davey was once a tree-climbing, dog-loving, ball-throwing sweet little boy, and now, with his toothy, confident smile and mop of golden curls, David was on the threshold of becoming a man. Soon to graduate, to go to college, to become an adult finally. Invincible. He turned his body slowly before Kathy's eyes, his arms held out from his shoulders, every muscle sharply defined beneath his skin. "Look. No ticks this time of year!"

"You are beautiful, Davey." A statement so true that it seemed untrue, as though such perfection couldn't possibly be.

"So are you, Kathy. I'm the luckiest boy in the world!" And he meant it. He put his dad's binoculars back on their nail. The clinging warmth of their little nest had finally left him, so he crossed the room and squatted before the stove, giving attention to laying the fire more expertly this second time, the way his father had taught him.

"Hurry, Davey." Kathy's words came from somewhere deep in her throat. She rustled the blankets. "I want you back here!"
He finished, and then, with the loose-limbed grace of youth, scampered over to their bed. Kathy lifted the blankets to welcome him. The snow light caressed her milky skin. So did his eyes. Her coppery red hair was spread on the pillow like a fire of its own, and he curled in beside her with a moan. Wrapped again in her nurturing, life-giving warmth.

She rested her head on his hairless chest. One hand low on his stomach. He snaked his arm under her neck and wrapped it around her shoulder. Then he began twirling a finger in her hair.

Their bare legs twined. They warmed each other. Cocooned in the quiet and the solitude, they snuggled deeper into the blankets with soft murmurs and began to drift. As morning drowsily slipped into afternoon, they slept, and every time they woke, they celebrated their love anew, floating into another blissful slumber soon after. And so the heedless hours passed. The cabin was warm. The bed was soft. Their bodies were one. And the world, it was far away. Couldn't it stay like this forever? he dreamed.

Like a shed skin, David's clothes lay in a heap on the floor by the stove. Kathy's were on a chair, folded hurriedly and cast aside. He and Kathy had been growing closer over the last year, their discoveries of each other becoming more intimate, both feeling that their love was the real thing. As what seemed inevitable raced toward them, David said that he knew the perfect place. Kathy quickly approved. They had carefully planned their trip to the cabin for weeks, picking a Saturday when he knew his dad couldn't show up unexpectedly. David didn't think he was being devious, lying to his father as he had, but resourceful, compelled by a very human need. And he thought his dad would even understand, if it ever came to that.

Kathy had risen early that morning, but not so early as to be suspicious. She spent more time than she usually did in the bathtub, shaving her legs and painting her toenails. She brushed and flossed. Braided her hair, then dabbed the slightest perfume on her neck. Dressing warmly but comfortably, she threw a few extra things in her purse.

David had awoken early because he was too excited to sleep. He showered, taking less time than he usually did. He checked the condom in his wallet again, then screwed up the courage to lie to his dad, saying he was going to the cabin to look for bobcat tracks in the snow. The snow had been a bonus, giving David a plausible reason to go, and he thought it a sign affirming the rightness of what ached inside him. His dad was doubtful that he would find anything more than rabbit tracks but said he hoped Davey would get lucky, then tossed him the keys to his truck. "Be careful."

When David came by to pick up Kathy, she told her mom they were going Christmas shopping all day at the mall.

Some years before, Kathleen O'Donnell's mother had sat her down to explain the distressing facts about becoming a woman and a wife. Distressing only to her mother though, and only because she had to speak of such things out loud. Kathy had already learned most of it in school. Hesitant and halting, their talk included several church pamphlets but little eye contact. There were some words about virtue, a little discussion of biology, and even a quick mention of sin. Kathleen was encouraged to come to her with any questions, but her mother had been so stressed by the effort that Kathy knew there wouldn't be any further talks. Still, she understood the mechanics of being a woman, as well as what was expected of her.

David's training had been more scattered and sporadic. His dad found seemingly random occasions, beginning when Davey was about ten, to bring up this or that fact of life, blunting its impact by tossing it toward his son as merely a casual thing he ought to know. It was when they were fishing off the dock together one boys-only weekend at the cabin that his dad gave him the most complete explanation of sex. They were able to stay occupied with casting and giving minute attention to their lures as his father spoke. Had either of them gotten a strike in the middle of it, both would have welcomed the interruption. On the whole, though, it was a comprehensive body of knowledge that David had received over the years, in doses he could absorb, and it was all certainly less stressful than Kathy's had been. Sex was simply a natural fact of everyone's life, his dad had assured him. One Davey shouldn't be ashamed of or embarrassed by. And David *did* believe he could talk to his dad about it if he ever felt the need, which he sometimes had.

There had been no moralistic tone to it. About as close as it came to that was when his father had said, only a bit more sternly than in his usual calm voice, "Just don't get some girl pregnant!"

David and Kathy were never again as young as they were that day at the cabin. Although they continued to share many perfect moments, they could not hold onto the dreamlike, playful innocence of their youth for long. Adulthood rushed toward them, with its own implacable inevitability, and they faced new responsibilities far sooner than they had ever dreamed.

JOE

Davey has gone somewhere, somewhere that he won't let me follow. Something is bugging him. Once we'd gotten him into high school, he found some self-regard – we're going through toothpaste and shampoo like crazy – and I thought we'd turned a corner. But now this. I don't think it's his schoolwork. I really think he's doing as well as he can. Peg helps him. He and Jon do homework together sometimes. And this girl, Kathy. She's been coming by the house all year. They sit at the kitchen table, talking and laughing and even sometimes giving a little attention to his homework. He said she's not even in some of the classes she helps him study for. It's showing in his grades.

It's obvious she's more than a friend. Once their studying is done, they sit close on the couch in front of the television, and he puts his arm around her or they hold hands and laugh at the shows. Or maybe they retreat to his room, though Peg has told him he has to leave his door ajar. "What for?" he jokes, and she quips, "Well, if you don't know, I'm certainly not going to tell you."

No, it's something else. The last few weeks it's like he's in a daze. Peg's noticed it too. We need to get out to the cabin. Just the two of us, father and son. He's a different boy when we're out there. He talks to me more readily. I've suggested a visit a couple of times, but he says it's too cold. A February overnight at the cabin never daunted him before so I say we can just lay a fire in the woodstove to keep warm, and he acts like this is the worst thing I've ever said.

Chapter Six

The Lonely Road

David knew the words. Every one of them. But he'd never known people who actually used them so much. So casually. Especially girls.

"All men are after only one damn thing," Marti had shouted across David's line. "Pussy."

"And if they're not," hollered Suzette back, "they're no damn good!"

The two of them taunted him ceaselessly. Mostly about sex. He couldn't tell if they hated all men or if they were just having a jolly time with him. Embarrassing him and laughing when he blushed, which he did so easily. Each shift something more personal, more humiliating. He was only nineteen, just a boy in that warehouse. Fresh-faced fresh meat. Up past his bedtime, the women teased. And the stuff they talked about! They quizzed him, guessing how experienced he was with girls, what he knew, what he had tried. How was he hung? He wasn't still a virgin, was he? Not that! How many girls had he nailed? How many at once? Or was it guys he went after, pretty as he was? And when he wouldn't answer, they'd come up with answers for him. Outrageous stuff. Terrible stuff.

"That looks like peach fuzz on your lip. You ain't even shavin' yet. Got any hair on your balls, little boy?"

"Maybe he's curly blond downstairs just like he is upstairs. Let's see your junk, Davey! And that tight little ass you got. I want to bite it!" They laughed, eyeing him up and down. Whistling. Grunting. Rubbing against him when they passed.

And then they'd tell him about themselves. Marti, with three kids by three men. Suzette made him regular offers – anything he wanted. "I come cheap. Someday I'll show you my tattoos, little boy. Every last one of them." The other guys in the warehouse just chuckled as David tried to cope. His parents had given him a sheltered life; his imagination had never prepared him for this. He had no idea these kinds of people really existed. His heart grew heavy learning he lived in such an ugly world.

One morning a few weeks before, when they were all stumbling out after their shift, Marti and Suzette ragging him as usual, they saw the child seat in the back of his car and quizzed him eagerly. But he was tired from the work, from fighting so hard to ignore them, to keep his life out of his job, and he broke down. He wearily told them that he was married and had a boy.

"Married? You're just a kid! What do you want to be stuck married to some bitch for at your age?"

He shouted. "Don't call her that!" Then the bitterness replaced the anger. "We *had* to get married, okay? I got her pregnant. That's why I work all night loading stupid trucks. To make some money so we can move out of my parents' house." He sounded pathetic, even to himself. And he knew instantly that he'd said too much. Now they would have fresh material to torment him with.

But Marti and Suzette eased up after that. He didn't know if they'd suddenly found a little respect for him or if they now considered him to be one of them. A screw up. A loser who couldn't keep it in his pants.

And that was what he feared the most. That in the end he *was* one of them. That he'd cashed in his future like a stupid, horny kid. Robbed Kathy of hers too. Most of their friends were at college now, off having adventures; he was stuck in a job that was like a nightmare he couldn't wake from. He'd doomed his little family to a dead-end life that made him cry when no one was looking. It was all he could think about anymore. What he had done to himself. To Kathy. To little Curt.

Ice had come down in the night. The parking lot was slick, and he could feel the cold through the soles of his sneakers. The defroster in his car was broken, and there wasn't any money to fix it. The road home was going to be difficult. He sneezed more cardboard dust out of his nose, pulled on his knit cap, and found the ice scraper under the front seat.

"It's too early to go home, Davey," one the guys said, sauntering over. "Join us for a couple beers? C'mon." They kept coolers in their cars and sat in them during the early morning with their engines running, getting wasted before driving home. But David had heard about the busts out there. Stuff a lot worse than beer. And anyway, he wasn't old enough to drink. They seemed like good guys, but they had hard lives with hard edges. He didn't fit in. Worse, he didn't want to find out that he *did* fit in.

He'd had another bad shift. His belt backed up again. Packages coming faster than he could load them. The other guys could handle it. Even Marti and Suzette could keep up despite their chatter and complaining. "Hey, Davey, let me know if you want me to handle your big package," Suzette had cackled. He didn't even get it at first. His supervisor finally came over to help, like so many nights. Seven months now and still getting behind. "You'll get better," she told him. "You're doing fine, David." He didn't think so. How much longer were they really going to put up with him? Pretty soon, if he didn't improve, he was sure they'd fire him. Another disappointment. To his parents. To Kathy. To Curt. What kind of husband am I? What kind of father?

As soon as they learned she was pregnant, Kathy's parents had cancelled her spring break trip to Italy. He and Kathy had skipped prom; she was showing by then and the dress she had picked out no longer fit. They talked about skipping graduation too, but his parents objected. Their friends all had a wild summer and left for college in the fall. The best he could give Kathy was his boyhood bedroom in his parents' little house and a nervous promise that someday they'd be able to move out. But any apartments they thought they could afford, ones that were decent enough to bring a baby into, wouldn't take them because he didn't make enough money or have any credit. So there they were, living in his folks' two-bedroom house with a crying baby. His parents insisted they didn't mind, but David did.

He'd first noticed Kathy when they were sophomores. She

had freckles and long red hair. Sometimes she wore it in braids. Sometimes in a ponytail that she flipped about. He'd noticed. When he finally screwed up the courage simply to say "Hi," his buddy Jon pushed him in her direction. Kathy turned and looked at David with her green, green eyes. He hadn't known she had green eyes. Two of them. They looked right through him. He immediately forgot what he was going to say, which she thought was endearing, so she did the talking that first time. It got easier after that. All of their friends agreed they were perfect together. By junior year, they were a couple. By senior year, they were pregnant. After all of the trouble over the last year and a half, Kathy still claimed she was happy. Happy to be Davey's wife and Curt's mom. And he was happy with her too, but he didn't see how long he could keep her happy. Or keep her at all. Not the way it was all was turning out. How could she love a failure like him? Nothing would delight her parents more, he knew, than for her to move back home with them, to admit marrying him was a big mistake. And to his eyes, that looked more true every day.

His first semester at college had been a disaster. He tried going to class in the morning after his shift, covered with cardboard dust and stinking of sweat. Bleary and wanting to sleep. Trying to pay attention and take notes. No one would sit by him. He'd been a C student in high school, even when he tried. And there he was in college, thinking it might be different, that *he* might be different. He dropped most of his classes. A full load was unworkable. With the spring semester he shifted to night school, but he didn't have as many choices there. It was going to be a long road, piecing together a degree that way. And his father, who had never gone to college, told David that he had to get a degree. There was nothing wrong with honest, manual labor, Joe had told his son. It was how he had put bread on the table for his family. But the world was different now he said. And so David saw himself on course to disappoint his dad in yet another way.

It was Kathy who should be in college, David knew. She had the brains. Kathy had aced her way through high school, even her last semester when she was pregnant and fighting with her parents all the time. She'd spoken often of getting a degree in graphic design, of being creative and making things. She even got some scholarships. Not that she needed them, as rich as her parents were. But now she was stuck changing diapers and trying to keep their boy quiet during the day in that little house because his daddy needed to sleep. What did she do all day, he wondered, while her husband was sleeping? And what did she feel at night, when she was alone in their bed?

He *was* stupid. He was a stupid kid who had done a stupid thing. And look where it left him. Now he had a son that depended on him. David loved his boy, but he knew Curt needed a better life than he could ever give. The nurse at the clinic said that Curt was already way ahead of the development curve. He was going to be talking soon. And then how long until Curt, too, recognized his dad was a screw up?

Finally home, David parked in front of the house and turned off the engine. He had made this life he must live. So he cried until some of the anguish was out of him and he could go inside where his parents, his wife, and his child waited. Already the neighborhood was waking. He wanted to get in before anyone saw him.

He entered by the kitchen door and welcomed the warmth inside. He shook off his coat and kicked his shoes into the corner as he always did. Then he slapped his wallet and keys on the counter, peeled off his gritty shirt and jeans, and threw them down the basement steps to the laundry. His mom was in the kitchen, making coffee.

"Good morning, Davey." She kissed him on the cheek, ignoring that her grown son was before her in nothing more than his white cotton briefs. Loading trucks had filled out his lean body. He was fit, and a hard body was about the only good thing to come from all of this, he decided. He could give Kathy that much anyway, but he didn't see what good it was. Not in the long run.

"Hi, Mom."

"How was work?"

"Great. Fine."

"Want some breakfast?"

He sighed. "I'll get some cereal later. I'm beat." He felt unclean. Unworthy. His parents wouldn't let him buy even the groceries for his own little family, much less pay any rent. When he'd come home with his first pay stub, he was alarmed that so much of his money was already gone. His mother had sat with him and Kathy at the table that early morning and explained taxes and healthcare deductions and life insurance premiums. It was horrible. "We'll never be able to move out!" he had moaned. She assured him they would.

The house had always seemed big enough when he was growing up. But with Kathy living there now, the three steps between their bedroom door and his parents' seemed to leave her no privacy at all. At *her* parents' house, she'd had the whole upstairs to herself. Her own bathroom, and a bedroom twice the size of what the three of them were crammed into now.

He padded to their room in his socks and quietly opened the door. Kathy was asleep. Beside her on the bed was little Curt. The two things that were most important to him. Peaceful and innocent. They didn't know what the real world was like, a world he wanted more than anything to protect them from. How impossible that was proving to be.

From the state of things, David could see that Kathy had been nursing Curt. His boy was asleep. His wife, uncovered as she was, was beautiful. David held his breath as time stopped, giving him this perfect moment. But only a moment.

David scooped Curt from the bed and held him. It almost looked as though his son smiled for him then.

"Hello, little man," he whispered. "Smells like someone needs his diaper changed." David laid Curt in his crib and cleaned him, putting on a fresh diaper, then he carried him to the rocking chair they had squeezed into their room.

"Here we are," he whispered, rocking his sleeping son. "The two Clark boys in their underwear."

He ran his fingers through Curt's wispy hair. It was coming out red, just like his mom's. David looked at his little boy. Sweet. Trusting. He held Curt tight and dropped his face to his son's shoulder.

"Please, please, please be like your mother," he sobbed. "Don't be like your dad. Please, Curt!"

Kathy stirred then and saw them.

"There are the two men I love," she murmured.

David couldn't look up, didn't dare meet his wife's eyes that saw through him.

"The two best things that have ever happened to me." How he wished that were true. Wished he could make it true. But he didn't know how. Didn't see how she could even *pretend* to believe that.

"Is Curt asleep?"

"Yeah."

She rose onto one elbow. "Well, why don't you put him in his crib and come be with me?"

"I'm a . . . I'm a mess, Kathy."

"You're fine, Davey. C'mon."

David eased Curt into his crib, careful not to wake the sleeping boy, and pulled a blanket over him. Then he turned to Kathy. She reached up and hooked a finger into the waistband of his briefs, pulling him closer.

They loved each other then, patiently, quietly. And for a while, David felt his cares fall away. Maybe it was true, he thought. Maybe she really did love him. And maybe her love would be enough to save him.

KATHY

Dad is still in denial. Or something. He won't hold Curt. He would leave the house those first few times Davey came with me. Mom says I just need to give him time, but she's hardly better. She keeps referring to Davey as "your husband" and never uses his name. It's like Curt was another virgin birth to her. Davey can tell. He always has some errand to do when it's time to visit my parents. And the truth is, I don't blame him.

But when it's just the three of us together, like when we're all in bed after I've fed Curt and we're right on the edge of sleep, I don't think there's anything better, anything more perfect in all the world. Sometimes I wish I could just live in that moment forever.

I was never ashamed of my choice. I've never regretted it. And as each day passes, I see more clearly how right it was. Davey loves me, in his inarticulate way. He talks incessantly about the health insurance we have from his job. About getting a raise. Getting more overtime. I'm pretty sure when he splurges on flowers, it's because his mom has told him to.

And with Curt, Davey is a different man. The defeat that weighs on him disappears. He's happy; I can see hope in his eyes. He speaks about the future. About ideas and dreams. He can barely wait for the weather to get warm again so we can take Curt out to his dad's cabin. Or I guess, return with Curt to the cabin.

Yes, he needs some work, some propping up. But I've bound myself to a good man, and if I'm the only one to see that, it's enough.

Chapter Seven

Name of the Father

David trailed Kathy and her mother, navigating the racks of clothing with Curt in the new, bigger stroller. The one that Kathy's mother bought to replace the tattered umbrella stroller they'd found at a garage sale. They were headed for the juniors department, to buy Kathy a new outfit. For her mother to buy, that is. She'd just bought a closetful of clothes for little Curt.

They'd met in the children's section of the department store at the mall out in the suburbs. Kathy's mom said she wanted to get Curt some new clothes so he wasn't always in thrift store things or even in David's own baby clothes. "My little Curtis is such a pretty boy," she said. "I'm glad he got our family's red hair." Then she added, barely under her breath, that her grandson deserved *some* nice things.

She had breezily picked out a dozen shirts and pants for Curt, giving them to the clerk to hold at the counter. Kathy finally told her to stop, that they had enough.

"He's ten months old, Mom. He'll grow out of these before he has a chance to wear them more than once."

Her mother frowned but deferred. David stayed out of it and kept Curt entertained, playing peek-a-boo and tickling his nose with his stuffed tiger until his boy laughed. Such a beautiful sound.

When they had finished, when Kathy's mother was paying for all of it, she decided, perhaps not so spontaneously, to dress Curt in one of the new outfits. "Why don't we see how handsome Curtis Daniel can be?"

"Curtis *David*, Mother."

Her mother didn't hear, or pretended so.

Kathy lifted her boy onto the counter and her mother took over, tugging Curt's pants past his bulky diaper and pulling his little Superman tee shirt over his head. She handed these to the clerk and said, "You can just throw these away. Thanks."

Afterward, when Kathy's mother was marching them out, David held back and retrieved the Superman shirt from the trash. He folded it carefully and slipped it into one of the bags with the new clothes.

"It's just that I don't get to see you as much as I'd like, Kathy," her mother was saying as David caught up. "I wish you'd let me take you to Italy. You should see the world."

"I can't leave Davey and Curt, Mom. Besides, they *are* my world."

"Well, I'd pay for a nanny to take care of little Curtis so you wouldn't have to worry. And your husband could go to his job just like he does now."

She rarely spoke directly to David and almost never used his name. For a while he wasn't sure she even knew his name. Kathy's father was far worse, storming out of the house whenever David was over. David knew he wasn't the husband they'd wanted for their daughter – not even close – and certainly not the father they had in mind for their grandson. He and Kathy had been married for just over a year, and once he realized that he would never be welcomed by her family, he resigned himself to it as much as he could. It hurt, but he didn't want to make things difficult between Kathy and her mom, so he just shut up and lied to himself that it didn't bother him. Not that her mother ever made it easy. She spoke now as though he wasn't just a few feet behind her, hearing all that she said. And, he realized, maybe that was what she intended.

"You're looking a little peaked. Are you getting enough to eat?"

"Kathy," David interjected. "I think Curt and I will just wander in the mall while you two shop."

Kathy darted back to him. She knew what was going on as well as he did. Balancing her loyalties was just as unsettling to her.

"You know I'm still trying to lose my baby weight, Davey," she whispered.

"Yes, I know. Just go on and have some time with your mom. We'll be fine. Go."

She placed a soft hand on his cheek and kissed him, then bent to kiss her smartly dressed son.

"Be good for Daddy. I'll see you in the food court at noon."

"At noon," David said. "Remember that, Curt."

Mother and daughter wandered off while father and son steered themselves to the mall.

The mall was busy that morning, but there was nothing he needed to buy. Nor did he have the money to buy it with. They were saving every penny he made so they could move out of his parents' house, a house too small for four adults and one baby.

The mall was oppressive to David. The loud, colorful advertising. Urging him to buy things he couldn't afford, hinting that he was only marginally good as a provider for his family. Sometimes he wasn't sure just what his role was, living in his parents' house, sleeping when everyone was awake, relying on his mother-in-law to clothe his son, his own parents to pay most of his bills. Half the time he felt more like a babysitter than a father.

So he wasn't shopping; he was just wandering. Wheeling the big stroller between knots of shoppers. Past the splashing fountain, the noisy carousel, the flashing marquees, the conversations. Curt was babbling, chewing on his stuffed tiger. Happy for the moment.

David paused before a shoe store. A pair of Nikes in the window had caught his eye. He looked down at his own sneakers. They were ratty, but he told himself they were sufficient. Standing all night at work. Knocking about on his free time. He wasn't a runner. He didn't need fancy Nikes. If anyone needed good shoes, it was Kathy, who had started running to lose weight and, he reluctantly admitted, to escape for a little while from that tiny house they were all crammed into. David wouldn't be surprised if her mother bought Kathy the Nikes before the morning was over. He was pretty sure she was slipping Kathy money to supplement his salary; she always seemed to have cash when they needed it.

At the far end of the mall was a toy store, and David thought he would take Curt there to poke about and see what interested him. His first birthday was still months away, but David's dad kept asking what kind of gift he could give him. "Another box of diapers just isn't a birthday present, Davey." But what did a little boy really need besides love? And David thought that Curt got lots of that in his parents' house. Still, maybe he could find a gift to suggest to his dad.

David wheeled the big stroller into the toy store, which was lively and noisy, full of children, and the displays quickly caught Curt's attention. There were plenty of toys and gadgets for older children, but the things suited to babies were at the back of the store, so he headed there. A salesclerk hurried over.

"Can I help you find anything?" she said. She eyed the bags that hung from the back of the stroller and then gave David a once over. He was dressed comfortably, which for him meant a torn but more or less clean pair of jeans and a comfy flannel shirt that he'd liberated from his dad's closet.

"No thanks. Just killing some time."

"Okay. I'll be just over there if you need anything," she said with a crispness that betrayed her missing sincerity. She walked away but turned and looked at him again, pasting a smile on her face.

David nodded and then pushed Curt to a cage of brightly colored balls. Their house was full of balls. David's dad could never see one that he didn't think his grandson ought to have. And for the moment, a bright blue ball would keep Curt happy and occupied. David slipped it from the cage and held it before his son. Curt dropped his tiger and reached for the ball.

"Ball," said David. "This is a ball." Kathy thought that Curt was ready to start saying words. Deliberate words. They both worked with him, showing him objects, and using their proper names. Reading to him. It wouldn't be long.

Curt took the ball eagerly in his hands and pressed it to his mouth to taste it. His teeth were coming in, and a bit of drool escaped and fell on the front of his new shirt. David grabbed the diaper off the back of the stroller and wiped Curt's face and shirt.

"Gotta keep you clean, little man, in your new outfit."

Curt twisted away from the diaper and then pressed the ball to his mouth when he was free.

"Ball, Curt. Can you say ball?"

Curt was excited. He pumped his legs and waved his arms, and the wet ball flew from his little hands and rolled down the aisle. The clerk hurried over and picked it up, then realized it was covered with baby slobber.

"Sorry," David said. He took the ball and dried it with the diaper then put it back in the cage. Curt wailed and stretched his hands toward the balls.

"Here's your tiger, Curt. He wants to play with you."

But Curt didn't want his tiger. He wanted a ball, and he began to scream for one. He wasn't the only screaming child in the store, but he was David's screaming child. So he quickly wheeled the stroller away from the balls and down another narrow aisle to a low shelf full of stuffed animals.

"Look at all of the animals, Curt. Animals."

Curt was barely diverted. He remembered the ball and was wailing for it.

David grabbed a toy horse and walked it through the air to Curt, nuzzling his nose with it. This got Curt's attention, and he forgot the ball, wanting to put the plush horse in his mouth now. David knew this would be a mistake, so he pulled the horse back, then galloped it toward Curt again. The boy laughed, and David sat himself on the floor to play with his son.

"Can you say horse?"

Back and forth the horse galloped, and Curt giggled each time it touched his nose. He reached for it, but he never seemed frustrated that he didn't get it because it kept coming back to him.

"Here comes the horsey."

Soon David had the tiger riding on the back of the horse, which Curt liked even more. He squealed with delight. And the two of them might have stayed lost in this play for a long time had the store manager not come over.

"Sir, do you intend to purchase that?"

"Uh, no. We're just playing."

She sighed. "Well, this is a store. Not a playground. So if you're not here to buy something, I really need you to move along. People have to get through this aisle. You're in the way. I'm sure you understand."

He understood. There were plenty of other children in the store, running around, playing with toys. Plenty of strollers blocking aisles. The clerks were ignoring them, but they didn't like the look of him. Old shirt, worn through at the elbows. Torn jeans. Ratty sneakers. Long hair. They assumed he was going to slip something into one of the bags hanging off the stroller. That's what he understood.

"Sure, I understand," he said mildly as he pushed himself up from the floor. "Here's your tiger, Curt. But the horsey has to go back to the barn now. Say bye-bye to the horsey."

Curt was wary of the store manager standing over him and clutched his tiger. David pushed the stroller toward the front of the store. The manager walked behind him until he left. He could feel her eyes on his back as he slunk down the mall, adrift once again.

He had nowhere to go and time to fill before he met Kathy at the food court. He wheeled Curt ahead of him aimlessly, joining the flow of people. Then David thought that maybe he and Curt could share an ice cream. Kathy didn't need to know. It wasn't so bad to give a nine-month-old a few spoonfuls of ice cream, was it? Yet when he reached for his wallet, he discovered he didn't have it. He had left it atop his dresser at home. He did have a few dollars in his pocket, though, and hoped that would be enough.

David pushed the stroller to the ice cream store and got a small cup of mint chip. His favorite. Then he wheeled Curt to the splashing fountain and sat on the edge of it before his son.

David tasted the ice cream first, then he put a little on the tip of the spoon and held it before Curt, who opened his mouth eagerly. The two little teeth in his bottom gum made David smile. He dabbed the ice cream on Curt's tongue and watched his boy's face light up. Curt worked his mouth for a moment and then opened it again, ready for more.

"One for me and one for Curt." David took a tiny bit for himself then spooned more into Curt's waiting mouth. Curt grew excited again, pumping his arms and legs, knocking his tiger to the floor. David bent to pick it up.

"I think that's just wonderful," a woman said, stopping before them. She smiled down, and David returned her smile.

"You don't see a lot of boys your age willing to look after their little brothers. I'll bet your mother is very proud of you."

"Actually, he's not my brother. He's my son."

The woman's approving smile melted into a disapproving frown. David understood this too. He knew he didn't look old enough to be a father. Or maybe to be a *responsible* father. With his smooth, ruddy cheek and mop of golden curls, he barely looked sixteen, much less the nineteen he was. And without a ring on his finger, he knew what she was thinking. It wasn't the first time.

The woman stalked off, shaking her head.

That was her problem, David told himself. And he almost believed it. Believed it, at least, when he didn't doubt his sufficiency to be Curt's father. Questioned every day and at every turn.

Curt was begging for more ice cream, and David turned back to his son.

"Here you go, little man." He spooned ice cream into his boy's mouth. Curt worked it with his tongue and squealed with joy. A string of green drool rolled from his lip and onto the front of his new shirt.

"Uh-oh. Mommy's not going to like that."

David grabbed the diaper again and tried wiping the drool from the shirt, but it left a green smear. Curt turned away as David tried to wipe his face. He should have thought to put a bib on him, but it was too late now.

The cup of ice cream was only half finished, and rather than fight the inevitable, David decided to simply enjoy the time with his boy. He'd change Curt's shirt after they were finished; it would wash clean later.

Curt's mouth was soon ringed by a pale green halo of melted ice cream. His fingers were sticky. Plenty had dripped onto his new shirt, and the tray of his stroller was smeared with it. David and Curt shared spoonfuls, the boy delighted with every taste and the father delighted with his boy. The world of the mall went on around them, but David settled into in the small world before him. He could do this much, he thought.

When the ice cream was finished, when David had dripped the last of it into Curt's eager mouth, he set the empty cup and spoon on the edge of the fountain and reached for the diaper bag that held all of the things a toddler's parent needed. From it he pulled a wet wipe that he used on Curt's resisting face. Then he cleaned his boy's fingers and the tray as well as he could, but he needed a second wipe to finish it. Once he had this done, he gave Curt his tiger again. The boy babbled and put the tiger in his mouth. David hoped Curt was a little sleepy now.

"I should put a clean shirt on you before we see Mommy." There were a dozen in the bags on the back of the stroller. As he reached in, his fingers touched the soft fabric of the Superman tee shirt. David pulled it out and flapped it open. The shirt was faded and stained. The emblem on the front was flaking. His mother had repaired one of the seams so it didn't look too bad when Curt wore it. David studied the little shirt and smiled.

"I looked a long time for this, Curt," he said as he unbuttoned his son's ice cream-covered shirt. "Because you are my super boy."

Curt watched his father talking to him. David slipped off the stained shirt and turned it inside out before folding it carefully.

"And I finally found one at a garage sale that was just your size. See," he said, holding the shirt before Curt. "Superman. That's you!"

David slipped the shirt over Curt's head, and this time the boy did not resist. Then he worked each arm into its sleeve and pulled the shirt down over Curt's round little belly.

"There we are. My boy again. Who loves his little Curt?"

The buttery smell of the nearby pretzel kiosk filled the air. David half heard snippets of conversations from passing shoppers. The squeak of their shoes on the polished floor. Background music overhead.

"Dada," answered Curt.

JOE

He's working hard at it, and it's coming together, but he's impatient.

You look at your child and it's hard to admit he's more than that. More than a child anymore. He's not just playing at adulthood. He is an adult. A man. A husband. A father. And somewhere in there, some of the time, still a son, too.

He's squirreling away every nickel he makes, saving up to move out. He wants his family to have their own place. I understand. It's a tight fit here, sure, but we make it work. Still, it's not the same as having a place of your own. I'm sure it's even harder for Kathy, but she's too polite to complain. At least to us. I don't know what she might be saying to Davey. If she's pushing him, or if he's doing it all on his own.

They go out on the weekends to look at apartments while we watch Curt. And when they come back it's always the same glum look on his face. Life is hard. And expensive, and he insists on something decent for the three of them. But that means waiting longer, waiting for more money in the bank or another raise at work.

And so he does without. Stays in. Takes all of the overtime he can get. Won't spend a cent on himself ever. In some ways I think he's still punishing himself for what he thinks is the mistake he made. I could try to tell him he's wrong, I have told him he's wrong, but he's keeping his own counsel. This is what it means to him to take responsibility. Maybe I taught him that lesson, though if I did, I don't know how or when. I've always winged it.

Chapter Eight

Sins of the Father

It was hard for Joe to listen to David's stories. The ones he'd already heard and these new ones he hadn't.

Kathy's father sounded like a terrible man. What kind of father calls his own daughter a "rutting, backseat bimbo"?

"And it wasn't like that, Dad. We . . ." David paused and looked away. He had grossly disappointed his father over the last year. He knew it. There had been no harsh words, no doleful looks, but how could he have not been a disappointment? He'd been stupid. He'd really, really screwed up his life.

David turned back and looked his father directly in the eye, the way a man should. "We came out here to the cabin. Me and Kathy. That's when it happened, we think." It was *not* the particular moment of their lives that most sons talked to their fathers about. Even a father you shared nearly everything with. But he deserved to know the truth. "And we were in love, Dad. We *are* in love."

David's little boy, Curt, sat on the table between them. Curt was eleven months old. He was lean, like his father, but had the red hair and fair skin of his mother. David was slowly undressing him, taking off his little shoes and socks. Curt gnawed on a ring of plastic keys.

Not long after they had snuck off to the cabin for that too brief, endless afternoon, Kathy had read the signs and realized she was pregnant.

What they had done terrified them. Kathy already knew what her parents would say. A good Catholic girl. Pregnant at seventeen. But she hadn't anticipated the ferocity of her father's reaction.

"There will be no bastard in my family," he shouted. "The thing will be put up for adoption the moment it's born. You aren't to hold it one time, Kathleen. Or give it a name. Or even know if it's a boy or girl. It will be taken away immediately, and that will be the end of it, and we'll all try to live as though this horrible sin had never happened."

Her father would arrange the adoption himself. One of the other lawyers at the firm would take care of the details. "There are plenty of properly married couples who will line up for the chance to take it."

Kathy was so shattered that she didn't question her father's will. He was not a man who allowed questions. And what else was there to do? She knew what she had done. How young she was. How she had failed her parents.

She was forbidden from seeing David, of course. "Did he force himself on you?" her father roared, as though there could be no other possible explanation. "Get you drunk at some party?"

David didn't know what he would say to his parents. Or what they would say to him. At first Kathy suggested he didn't need to tell them anything since the baby was going to be given up. His parents never needed to know. But that felt cowardly to him. He always took his problems to his father, and this was certainly one that needed confessing. He knew how disappointed his dad would be. Regardless, things were going to be obvious soon. His parents knew they were a couple. And what if her parents wanted to talk to his? It wouldn't be long before the whole thing found its way to them. Sooner or later, David had to speak up. But how to do it? He had no idea what he would say.

Slowly, Kathy realized that despite what her father said, they would not go on as though this horrible sin had never happened. It might be hushed, but it would never be forgotten. She would never be *allowed* to forget it. Her mother found occasions to speak glowingly of Kathy's older sister, and what a fine woman and wife she had become. Her father barely spoke to her at all. Their rebuke was loudest in its silence. Kathy grew larger by the day, yet her mother pointedly ignored this fact of her daughter's life. No bits of motherly advice were offered. No ways of coping. No anecdotes of experience. Her mother talked about it incessantly by not talking about it. Kathy understood then that this shame would be pressed upon her in subtle ways for the rest of her life.

Each morning she looked at her body in the mirror. Her flat stomach, her pale skin at first betrayed no sign of what was happening inside her. Couldn't it all just be a mistake? But it wasn't, and as the weeks passed, she watched her stomach swell. Her hands encompassed it. Embraced it. *Understood* it. She and David had put a life in there. Her job was to nurture it. To love it. And she found that she did. She loved their baby. But there was nothing she could do about it.

Then one evening, the very worst happened. Her father brought home a young couple. They weren't Catholic, but they were good people. Good jobs. A nice house, right there in Brookside. But they couldn't have children. Wouldn't it be sensible to admit how much better a life they could give it than Kathy ever could?

She refused to see them. She spent the evening crying in her room. It was horrible. How it was already arranged. Her body was a factory; her baby was a product. Her baby. She wanted Davey. She wanted to be with him, to hear him tell her there would be an answer.

"What about David?" she had screamed through the door as her mother fretted and her father fumed in the hallway. "What about what he wants?"

"Is that his name?" her father stormed back at her. "He has no standing. He doesn't matter in the slightest. He was just the randy goat that took his pleasure and left you pregnant!" And in his mind this was the only imaginable explanation for what had happened. Come August, her father had made clear; that bastard would be gone forever. It was already settled. Her father's will would be done, and Kathy knew it.

The weeks passed. David and Kathy met whenever they could at school and tried to see their way to some solution. And the answer came.

David rose early one Friday in March and confronted his parents as they ate their breakfast. He'd finally found some stumbling words to tell them about Kathy and him. And their baby. But he rushed the words, sticking to the script he and Kathy had worked out so he didn't begin to get mixed up and maybe cry. He said he was skipping school that day and that they both needed to call in sick to work. What else could they do? David had just asked his father to be his best man.

It was a lot for them to take in so suddenly. They both pressed him. Was he sure this was the right answer? They were so young. Couldn't they wait? Couldn't the two families get together first? Work something out? Why was he rushing into this?

As difficult as it had been for David to tell his parents, their rapid-fire questions crushed the little composure he'd managed to rally.

"Because Kathy's dad is going to give away our baby!" he cried.

"He can't do that, surely," breathed his mother, grabbing her husband's hand.

The hardest thing David ever said to his parents came next.

"I really want you to be there, but if you won't come, I'll go to my wedding alone."

Then he teetered at the edge, uncertain whether he would be an orphan from that day forward.

Joe realized then why his son had been so gloomy, so withdrawn in recent weeks and why he had resisted talking about what was bothering him. And in that moment he learned that the toughest part of being a father was letting go. Letting his son make his own decisions. And supporting them. He had loved his David like the boy that he was, and now he had to begin loving him as the man he needed to become.

He helped David tie his tie then hurried into his own suit. His mother gave him a set of emerald earrings that had belonged to her mother. "They'll look nice against Kathy's red hair," she said. They met at the courthouse.

"Shouldn't we wait for your parents?" Peg had asked after Kathy rushed in. But Kathy's emphatic "No" made it clear that there was more trouble than they realized behind the hasty union. And her doubts about all of this, which had been growing the more that she thought about it, seemed validated with that one word. But she wouldn't stand in the way.

Kathy took David aside, hushed his querying eyes, and put his hand on her stomach. They stood silently for a moment, and then she whispered, "There. Did you feel that?" David understood more than ever why they were rushing into it.

After only a few minutes before the judge, it was finished. And that was that. David and Kathy, both barely eighteen, were suddenly husband and wife. It was not the Friday that Joe and Peg Clark had expected when they sat before their coffee that morning. Nor was it the wedding Kathy had always dreamed of. But if her dream was denied, so was her nightmare. For the first time in months, the two of them felt real hope.

She had left the house that morning as Kathleen O'Donnell, but she returned that afternoon as Kathleen Clark. When her mother asked her where she had gotten the emerald earrings she was wearing, Kathy said truthfully that David had given them to her.

"Kathleen! You know you are forbidden from seeing that boy."

She almost told her then. Told her that she was now that boy's lawfully wedded wife. But she checked herself, fearing a slip could jeopardize what they had done for themselves and for their child.

After a couple of weeks, David went to her parents' house one rainy evening. He had met them before, of course, but in those days he was just another anonymous high school boy that hung around their house. After what he had done to their daughter, however, he had become something far less than that. And so her parents were astonished to find him standing in their front room.

"Get the hell out of this house!" Curtis O'Donnell boomed.

Kathy stepped over by David. She had told him to expect this, or even much worse. David was trembling. But he looked her father in the eye, swallowed hard, and, after a timeless moment, spoke the simple facts that Kathy had rehearsed with him.

"Mr. and Mrs. O'Donnell. Kathy and I love each other. We're married, and we're keeping our baby."

Mrs. O'Donnell began to wail.

Mr. O'Donnell began to laugh.

"We'll see about that," he bellowed. "First you defile my daughter, and then you drag her down farther by giving her your name? What is your name, anyway?"

The two young people stood their ground. Joe had consulted one of the lawyers at his union to confirm the ironclad validity of their marriage. They had nothing to fear from Kathy's father.

They held hands. There was no point in trying to argue with him, Kathy had told David. They would just stand firm. Defiant. Certain. Terrified.

But Kathy's father knew the strength of a binding contract. He soon understood that he had been outmaneuvered. Once he realized that their marriage couldn't be torn asunder, he rationalized his defeat. This boy had gotten his daughter pregnant. Therefore, he wasn't worthy of marrying her. But, this boy had gotten his daughter pregnant. Therefore, he *had* to marry her. It stuck in his throat, but it was what he would tell everyone.

He barely considered their union valid. This scrawny high school kid, with his long hair and pimples, was now his son-in-law? Ridiculous. There would be a Catholic wedding as soon as possible, he declared. And the baby – this was the first time he hadn't used the word "bastard" – would be baptized as soon as possible.

The next day, Kathy moved in with David. It was the happiest day of his young life. He carried her through the front door of his parents' house, and they both laughed until they cried. Kathy's mother told her she was living in sin and would be until her real wedding. It didn't feel like that to Kathy though. Soon their secret was out. They told all of their friends they were married, with great smiles on their faces.

The four Clarks sorted out their lives together as well as they could in the little house with only one bathroom. Everyone held back words. Advice was given only if asked for. Groceries. Laundry. Music. Television. Alarm clocks. Doors left open or closed. Meals taken together or apart. They juggled it all, and everyone looked forward to the young couple being on their own. David was now the child of one family and the head of another. He mowed the lawn as he had as a boy, but he also went off to work as he must as a man.

The baby came along early in the morning one August day, just as expected and without much fuss, as though the boy didn't want to draw any attention to himself. David was at Kathy's side for the delivery. Proud. Happy. Terrified in a whole new way.

Curtis David Clark was perfect, and David held his boy with a swirl of new emotions. He tried not to cry, but he didn't try very hard. This was his son. The world was different now. He needed to be a good father, just like his own father.

David's parents were in the waiting room, and once the new little family had had the chance to bond, they were invited in to see their grandson. Joe was never much of a man for words, and as he saw his son now holding his own son, words left him completely. He had only emotions to steer by, but that seemed enough. Nurses bustled in and out, and boxes of tissues appeared when needed. Everyone took turns holding the baby, and David had the chance to change his first diaper. He didn't do very well, but he would learn.

Kathy's mother arrived soon after. Her disapproval of the unfortunate pregnancy and the hasty marriage had never been a secret, but even she couldn't disguise her joy at holding her first grandchild.

When Curtis was brought home, all of their friends came around to see him. Joe and Peg enjoyed having a house full of young people again. But that happy August gave way to September, and most of their friends left for college. David, who had been working for a lawn service that summer, found a job loading trucks in a warehouse at night. The hours were bad, but the pay was better, and he could get health insurance for his little family, which made him feel like a provider.

And now, ten months later, David and Joe and little Curt were sitting on the porch of the cabin. Joe had gone inside a few moments before to fetch the sun lotion and came out shirtless. Peg had slathered his back with it, and he brought it out for David and little Curt.

"We named him Curtis," David said, "after Kathy's father. She thought it would soften his heart. But he still won't hold his grandson. And he leaves the house whenever I'm there. He hates me, Dad. Kathy won't even tell me some of the things he's said. He wants to make this whole thing my fault. And I guess it is."

David's eyes were welling with tears. So were Joe's. Gone were the days when things seemed to make sense to David. When just about anything still seemed possible. Now whatever little control he thought he'd had over his life had vanished. Nothing made sense anymore, but he had to find his way through it.

"We should have named him Joseph."

A tear then escaped Joe's eye, but he pretended he was wiping lotion on his face. He cleared his throat and tried to change the mood.

"Kathy told me to make sure we keep Curt's cap and shirt on. And cover him with the sun lotion."

Their cabin once rang with little Davey's laughter. Now it could with Curt's. Joe wanted the day to be happy. They were finally at the cabin. Their whole small family. It was Curt's first trip, and that was something to celebrate, though they weren't there yet. Joe knew Davey had needed to tell him the awful stories, to get the poison out so he could heal and his father could understand. He was glad they could finally sit together on the porch and speak about it man to man. Glad that Davey could be open with him again as he had been all of his years before. Davey could mend a bit that way. And a day in their forest would do its magic too. Joe felt that he was getting his son back.

Of course, he had to disapprove of his son sneaking off to the cabin with his girlfriend to have sex, or at least to end up making a baby as they had. But there was a part of Joe Clark that felt otherwise. The two of them had shared a wonderful moment here, had begun their lives together. Where better than in this place? If he could change things, give these kids back their childhoods, he might. But then they wouldn't have little Curt, sitting there on the table, babbling his first words. Joe couldn't work it out. He didn't even want to try.

"Kathy says I can't smoke a cigar around Curt either. Just as well since I forgot to bring any. I think we're lucky she's letting us take him swimming at all."

David was still frowning.

Joe didn't think that he knew much about anything. Life had battered him no more and no less than the average, hard-working guy. He supposed he missed a lot of life's subtleties, but he thought he had done okay. Even so, it was clear to him that Curtis O'Donnell wasn't *shamed* by his daughter's "bastard child." He was *embarrassed*. There was a telling difference. And to hide his embarrassment, the man decided to focus all of his bile on Davey. To pin all blame and all shame on this boy who was now a man, though he hardly seemed ready for the job.

Joe had worked hard to raise his son with confidence, to give him growing achievements and unstinting praise. To help him prepare himself so he could stride into whatever life he met with hope and promise. And now he was doing that. His Davey did not need the shackles that Curtis O'Donnell was forging.

David pulled Curt's shirt over his head and used it to wipe some drool from his face. Then he began spreading the lotion on Curt's pale skin, over the birthmark on his right thigh. The sun would not be kind to his fair boy, he knew, but they weren't going to be in the water very long.

"Davey," his father said, breaking the brooding silence. "Here's how it is. Your father-in-law is trying to hide his own embarrassment by blaming you for a blemish on his perfect life. He's lost control of something and doesn't want to admit it. He's happy to blame you instead."

David listened but didn't respond.

"If he can't love this little boy, then there's a whole lot more wrong with him than the so-called shame of his daughter getting pregnant."

David put the lotion out of Curt's reach then began putting his little terry sun shirt on him.

"Am I making sense, Davey?"

"Maybe. I don't know. It's so hard, Dad."

Joe helped David remove Curt's diaper then handed him the boy's little swimming trunks.

"I don't know if you ever did the math, Davey, but I was thirty-nine when you were born. I thought it was too late to become a father. For you, maybe it's almost too early. But here we are. And here is Curt. He may be the finest thing you and Kathy ever do together." His voice wanted to break, and he had to pause to swallow. "If he's even half the son my son is, you will *never* feel a moment of shame or regret in your life."

"And what if he does the math someday, Dad, and figures out that we weren't married when it happened?"

"Then I suspect he'll realize it doesn't really matter. That he is loved no less because of it. And maybe more so."

David and his father had already changed into their swimsuits, and David had finished spreading the lotion on himself where he could. He turned and Joe carefully wiped the lotion on his son's back. Just as he had hundreds of times.

"Ready?" Joe said.

David lifted Curt, and the two men walked silently down the stone steps to the lake. The cove where the ground sloped gently into the water was where little Davey had first splashed about, and it was where they were taking little Curt now.

The three stood at the water's edge, and then David removed Curtis' shirt and trunks and hat. He set the boy's swimming clothes carefully on the shore, topping them with his little sun hat.

They waded into the water, and David passed Curt to his father.

"Before we had the lake, a creek used to run through this valley. That's where I brought you. And when I did this with you, Davey, you peed on me."

David laughed. "I could probably do it again, if you want."

"Well, let's see what Curt has to offer."

Joe Clark dipped his grandson into the lake up to his shoulders, and the child began to cry. Then he lifted him into the air and said, "Welcome to our family, Curtis David Clark."

PEG

"It would be a big help. It would give them a start."

"They're doing better than we were at that age."

"Maybe so, but we didn't have a toddler to feed back then."

"We didn't have anything back then."

"That's my point. We could get by with nothing. They can't."

"Think of how Davey would see it, Joe. He loves those woods. The lake. Sure, you'd be giving him something, something important, but you'd be taking away something too. Something that I think is even more important to him. Listen to how he talks about it. He wants to teach Curt how to build a fire. Catch a fish. The names of all the trees. He wants to raise his own boy there just like he was raised."

"Sometimes I think maybe we should have spent less time there. Maybe I should have taken him to the library more. Or to museums. Helped him more academically."

"He wouldn't agree with you. That forest, the little cabin. Those were his museum and library. That's where he learned his important life lessons. That's where he learned how to be a boy and now a man. More than anything he wants to be just like you, Joe. To be a father just like the one he had. He wouldn't trade a single moment you two had there for all of the book smarts in the world."

"I know. I guess I wouldn't either. But his life doesn't have to be so hard. Working all night. Not seeing his wife and son enough. Barely covering his bills. We could fix that."

"Yes, he's struggling, but Davey's not a drifter like we were. He needs this. The cabin is his anchor. There are other ways we can help them."

"Not like this. Not this one big answer to their problems."

"You need to talk to him about it before you do anything. He's involved as much as we are. It's his forest too."

Chapter Nine

Men at Work and Play

Curt knelt in the gravel before the dying fire, feeding his five-year-old curiosity by tossing bits of wood onto the embers. His eyelids heavy, head nodding, his heart resisting the sleep that was overtaking him. David sat in a chair behind him, his dad in a chair across the fire ring. The workday was nearly done. Their conversation had diminished to occasional, aimless observations. It was time to let the fire burn down. Then the three men would crawl into bed for the night.

"Come here, Curt," David said.

The boy rose and turned to his dad. David reached into the cooler beside him and fished out a can of beer.

"Give this to Grandpa."

Joe accepted the beer the boy brought to him. Curt then returned to his place on the other side of the fire ring, near his dad. He loved their campfires, but a long day of work and play and no nap because he was too stimulated to slow down made him unsteady before the flames.

David left his chair and squatted behind his son, wrapping an arm around his waist. The fingers of his other hand stroked his boy's red curls. He could smell the spicy tang of unwashed boy.

"Here," he said, handing Curt a small stick.

Curt considered briefly, then tossed the stick onto the coals. "You probably don't remember, Davey," Joe said from his chair across the fire. "But when we were building the cabin, you used to collect all of the scrap lumber and beg us to have a fire at the end of the day so we could burn it." Joe worked a toothpick in his mouth, chasing the last bits of burger from his teeth. "I guess you were a little bit younger than Curt is now, dragging two-by-fours nearly as big as you to the fire ring." He laughed, his words warm with memory. Funny, the things you remember, he thought. "I guess boys love fires. I always did."

This day's fire had been similar. Curt was delighted when this grandfather had thrown some old wicker baskets and a ratty straw hat, along with a pair of mouse-eaten leather work gloves, onto the flames, and he'd watched closely as the fire had taken them.

David liked to hear stories about his childhood – especially ones he didn't remember himself – because in them he hoped to see parallels with his own boy's life. And this could persuade him, despite all of his uncertainty, that maybe he was raising his boy right.

"Remember, Curt," David said, giving his son another stick to throw on the fire. "If the smoke blows in your face, just close your eyes softly. Not really hard. It won't sting as much."

Joe smiled, having given that bit of advice to Davey at this very fire ring maybe twenty years before. How many of his son's important memories were forged here? Joe wondered. How many hundreds of perfect nights had the two of them sat together under the stars before a fire's warmth? Too many to count. Most of them forgotten yet still remembered in some deeper way. No wonder Davey wouldn't let go. I should write down these visits, he thought, so I don't forget them. Joe drew the toothpick from his mouth and tossed it onto the coals. It was time for a cigar, for a long muse, for offering occasional words to his son and grandson. For listening to the hum of the forest. Maybe even a whippoorwill, if they were lucky, though not likely so late in the year. Sitting comfortably in their chairs with nothing more important in the world for the moment. But he'd forgotten to bring a cigar again.

"Are you cold, Curt?" David asked. Curt had only his tee shirt and jeans on.

"Where's your shirt?"

"I don't know," said Curt drowsily.

David turned and scanned the area before the cabin, hoping to see his boy's flannel shirt on the ground. But the dark had gathered beyond the fire, and he couldn't see much at all. The shirt would turn up. He held his son more tightly.

"Are you warm enough, Curt?"

"I guess."

"Do you want to sit?"

"I guess."

David eased back and let Curt slide cross-legged to the gravel. His head drooped and his shoulders slumped. He wouldn't last much longer in his race with sleep.

They had come out to the cabin that weekend to begin the periodic ritual of oiling the exterior. Every few years, Joe would seal the outside of the cabin. As little Davey grew up, he had begun to help with this work. And now little Curt was along.

Not that a five-year-old would be much help, but that wasn't important. What was important, David believed, was that Curt accompany his dad and his grandfather as they did their work and feel he was part of it.

Yet also in need of some restorative care was David's relationship with his father. Normally effortless, and apparently built to last, David's sudden flare up at his father's unreasonable suggestions about how he might lead his life, how everyone had to make sacrifices, had left both men wounded. David's words had been rushed, ill chosen. They were direct and almost harsh – surprising even him. They never quite approached what needed to be said, for his thoughts were not fully formed and his feelings were fragile and deep.

Joe had given Curt a brush and a small can of the oil and set him to work on the porch railing that morning. This was low enough for the boy to reach, while the adults worked at the eaves and porch ceiling. He wrapped Curt in one of his old flannel shirts to cover as much of him as he could, expecting the inevitable slop and splatter of a boy and a brush. The little boy was lost inside his grandfather's shirt with its rolled sleeves and the tails nearly touching the ground.

Curt soon grew bored with the repetitive work. Later, when David looked down from his ladder, he saw the brush abandoned and the boy on the ground studying an insect. He had shed the flannel shirt.

David kept one eye on his son as he continued to work. Curt wandered the open area in front of the cabin, fascinated by whatever he saw on the ground, crawling in pursuit. He'd need a tick check before bed, but that was another ritual at the cabin.

When his dad, who had kept himself on the other side of the cabin, came to claim the ladder, David wandered over to where Curt was sitting. He was staring at the lake.

"I'm bored. Can we go fishing, Dad?"

David sat beside his son and looked toward the lake. "Kind of late in the day to catch a fish, Curt. A little late in the season."

Curt didn't respond.

"Once I saw a fox on the other side of the lake. Right over there." David pointed.

But Curt was looking into the trees.

"What kind of bird is that, Dad?"

David looked where Curt's finger pointed.

"I don't know. Grandpa calls them little gray birds."

There was still some daylight left, still some work to get done, but the boy couldn't be left to wander on his own. Curt had been coming to the cabin since he was a baby, but you didn't leave a five-year-old alone in a forest. It was too late for a nap, too early to light the evening's cooking fire.

Curt was a clever child. An early talker. Walking at nine months. Reading on his own already. He got all of that from his mother. Applying a brush to the parched wood wouldn't occupy most five-year-old kids for long, David supposed, but for Curt the repetitive work lost its appeal even more quickly.

"Grandpa took my ladder," David said. "I can't reach high enough to get the ceiling on the porch. Can you help me?"

Curt looked at his dad and then back at the cabin porch. He narrowed his green eyes. David feared the boy was doing a quick calculation and would realize that his dad was fudging the facts. David *could* reach the porch ceiling with a stretch.

"If you sat on my shoulders, I'll bet you could reach it. Do you think?"

David watched as Curt then did this math. They'd both be a mess before it was over, and it would likely be over before the work was done, but it would keep Curt occupied and supervised. And they'd be together. Father and son. The rest could sort itself out later.

"C'mon, Curt. Let's get a little more work done. You and me. And then we'll go down to the lake and throw in a couple of lines."

Curt rose quickly at this prospect, and once the boy had mounted the porch steps, David scooped up Curt's discarded flannel shirt, shook it out, and put it back on him.

"See that part up there," David said, pointing to a corner of the porch ceiling. "That's where I can't reach. But you can if you sit on my shoulders. Should we get to it?"

"Sure," Curt said, though with only measured enthusiasm. He was more ready to go fishing.

David hoisted his son onto his shoulders then handed him the brush. He held the can of oil as Curt dipped too deeply into it. This was going to be a sloppy job, and David suspected he would soon be as freckled as his son. The image pleased him.

It was evident quickly that Curt's mind was not on the work.

"What's that for?" the boy asked, gesturing with his dripping brush to a hook screwed into the eaves beyond the railing.

"Grandpa used to hang a hummingbird feeder there. But it attracted ants, so he took it down many years ago. Before you were born."

"Mom likes hummingbirds."

"I know."

And so it went. Curt curious about every knothole in the wood, every spider hurrying out of the way, all but the work before them. But they were working together, even if it was only for a short while and not much work was actually getting done. He had worked alongside his own father at the cabin. Together they had laid the stone steps down to the lake. Cut up fallen limbs with handsaws until his dad thought Davey was big enough to respect the chainsaw. Spread gravel around the fire ring. Mundane chores. Simple and direct in their purpose. Enduring. And the child Davey had swelled with pride that his dad could rely on him.

Later, after he had wrung as much cooperation as he could from Curt, David grabbed two poles and the tackle box, and they headed down to the lake. Curt's mood quickly changed, and he skipped along ahead of his dad, dancing down the sandstone steps and urging him to hurry.

Since Curt hadn't mastered casting yet, David rigged his line with a bobber and a simple lure, one that had been in his dad's tackle box for as long as David could remember. Then he swung it into the deep water beyond the old dock. Maybe Curt would catch a little sunfish. For himself he tried a more ambitious set up – a pig and jig that would be needed to catch a bass, though he doubted any were biting that late in the day.

Curt's line coiled lazily in the water, and David could see the boy wasn't so much interested in fishing as in watching his dad fish. He opened the bale and grabbed the line with his finger, then cast his rig into the tea-colored water. It struck fifty feet away, and Curt gave a cheer.

"Great cast, Dad!"

The strike came on David's third cast. It hit with surprise. Curt knew what was happening instantly and turned to watch his father fight the fish.

"You got a strike, Dad. Set the hook! Reel him in!"

David played the fish as it darted about in the murky water, zigzagging the line along the surface. He was putting on a good show, pulling back on the pole then cranking the reel to draw in the line, aware that Curt was watching him.

"Don't let him jump the hook, Dad!"

David drew in more line and soon the fish was splashing at the surface before them. He leaned his pole against the rail and grabbed the line, lifting the struggling fish out of the water.

"You got it, Dad! You're the best fisherman ever."

It wasn't a keeper. Better to get it off the hook and back in the water quickly, but Curt wanted to see it. David grabbed the fish by its lip to hold it still so Curt could study it.

"What kind of fish is it, Dad?"

"Largemouth bass. Small one though."

Curt extended a tentative hand but didn't touch the fish. "Largemouth bass," he said reflectively, as though filing the information away somewhere in his head.

"We have to let it go, Curt. It's too small to eat." He knew Curt wouldn't eat it even if it was a keeper. Hamburgers and hotdogs were all he would eat when they were at the cabin. David and his dad had sometimes made dinners out of the fish they caught at the lake, Joe patiently showing him how to gut and clean a bass then how to cook it in a greasy frying pan over the coals. It tasted better because he had caught it, and he and his dad had cooked it themselves. But so far, Curt hadn't shared that interest. There was still time.

"See that stripe down its side. That's how you can tell it's a largemouth."

Curt studied the fish, its gills opening and closing slowly.

"I need to throw it back, Curt. Okay?"

The boy nodded. David worked the hook out of the fish's mouth and then knelt on the edge of the dock, leaning over the side to slip the fish back in the water. After a second, it disappeared in the murk.

"He'll be okay, Curt. He'll grow big, and maybe *you* can catch him next spring."

"That was great, Dad. You caught it!" And then more softly, "Thanks, Dad."

Curt's pole lay on the dock. They could stay and fish longer, but David doubted there would be any more strikes that late in the day. Up at the cabin he could see Joe folding the ladder. The stated work of their day was done. It was time to start the evening fire and cook their burgers.

"Let's go tell Grandpa about the fish we caught."

Curt ran across the dock and hurried up the old stone steps to the cabin, eager to tell his grandfather about their little adventure. David reeled in the rest of his line and checked the lure. Then he took Curt's pole from the dock and did the same. About time to put up the fishing gear for the season, he knew, but he was glad Curt could have this last little excitement. These keeper moments were what the cabin was for. Forever.

When David got to the top of the stone steps, Curt was at the fire ring with his grandfather, who was building the evening's fire. Joe never rested when he was at the cabin, David thought. Not until all of the chores were done anyway. But even as he sat quietly before a fire at the end of their days, his father seemed to relax with a kind of seriousness.

Curt was telling Joe about the fish, re-enacting, elaborating. He wondered how Curt would further embellish the story when they got home and he told Kathy about it.

And now that fire was dying. Joe had finished the beer Curt had brought him and gazed toward the two people opposite him. Never mind their harsh words earlier. Davey had grown to be a fine young man and had given him a beautiful grandson. Smart as a whip. And here the three of them were, he thought, sitting around the fire in the twilight. A day of work and play behind them. The sleep of the just ahead. Life sometimes gave him fleeting little rewards like this, and Joe felt it was important to recognize them when he could. To grasp them.

Curt was losing his fight against sleep. His head bobbed, and he resisted less each time. Even he knew he couldn't stay awake much longer, so he pushed himself up from the gravel, stepped over to his dad, and crawled onto David's lap. David cradled his son, wrapping his shirttails around his little boy to keep him warm. The wind in the trees overhead sighed a benediction.

After a moment, David said, "I love this place, Dad." Saying, finally, the right words.

"Amen to that."

Joe looked at his son and grandson, painted orange by the embers. Curt's head lolled on his father's arm, his body slack, his innocent mouth open. How could life be any better? Joe wondered. "You're the best dad a person could ever have."

They didn't say much for a long while. The stars wheeled above. The love songs of the tree frogs rasped in the forest around them. The coals before them slowly winked out. Their hearts were full.

"Time for bed, I guess," Joe finally said. "I can take Curt in if you want to sit out here for a while."

"No, I'll come in with you."

David rubbed Curt's shoulder. "C'mon, little man. Let's go potty before we go to bed."

Curt blinked up at his dad for a moment before realizing where he was. David set him on his unsteady legs and led him slowly across the road, where he pulled Curt's jeans and underpants down to his ankles and encouraged the boy to pee. His little round bottom glowed in the moonlight.

Curt stood silently on the side of the road, neither asleep nor awake. David unzipped his own jeans and brought forth a stream that clattered in the leaf litter. "Like this, Curt."

But the boy was too sleepy to oblige. After a minute more of waiting, David tugged up Curt's pants and carried him back to the cabin on his shoulder. The little man was asleep before they got there.

Joe was inside, turning down the quilt on the bed. David laid Curt on the end of the bed and removed his shoes and socks and pants. He searched his boy's body for ticks.

Curt mumbled what sounded like "loudmouth bass" and David smiled.

"I can't guarantee he won't wet the bed tonight, Dad."

"Won't be the first time for this old bed."

David smiled wryly at this. He supposed it was another story of his childhood he didn't know, and he supposed further that if his own boy did the same, it could be taken as another sign he was being raised right.

Joe laid a towel across the middle of the bed, and David laid Curt on the towel. The two men undressed quietly and crawled into the bed, bracketing the sleeping boy.

"Good night, Davey," Joe whispered as he pulled the quilt over the three of them.

"Good night, Dad." He could smell his father's breath. A strong, familiar smell. A good one. David found that he was more tired than he realized. He drifted, wondering how many nights he had slept in that bed beside his father. Safe beside his father. He wanted it to be that way for Curt too. Forever. Through the night their arms wrapped around each other many times.

JOE – DAVID – CURT

They're doing whatever it is they do down at the lake. I'm doing this. I found an old, paper road map in the truck that I'm using for tinder. It's brittle and tears nicely, but it's thicker than normal paper, so it might burn longer. Or maybe hotter. I've crumpled the pieces into loose wads and lined them up in the ash, mounding more in the center, and now I'm resting twigs against the paper.

I never have any trouble finding dry twigs; there are always branches falling in the forest around the cabin, and if they've fallen naturally, they've usually been dead a long time and are dry and ready to be used as kindling. Maybe I use more kindling than necessary, but after tinder, having enough kindling is the most important part of building a fire. You have to transfer the tinder's eager flames to reluctant branches and then logs, and you need enough kindling for that to happen. It this step fails, if your kindling burns out or never catches, and you have to start again, and then it's not a one-match fire.

But I've done it right. A single match to the tinder, touching as many edges as I can. The flames reach into the air. I'll add the thicker branches soon. And later seasoned logs that will take the flames and become glowing coals good for cooking and thinking.

When they get back, they'll see that I already have our dinner fire roaring in the ring, on its way to warm, orange coals we can sit around for the evening.

Someone must have taught me how to do this once. Building a fire seems like the most natural thing in the world.

Chapter Ten

A Tree Falls in the Forest

If there was any sting in Curt's barbs, David wasn't letting it show. The boy was, in some ways, growing up too fast. Still slight like his mother, just skin and bones and a bottomless stomach, but with a mind that sometimes staggered David.

David was never sure each morning, each moment even, which Curt he would face. Whether it would be the innocent ten-year-old who could often surprise him with the depth of his sweetness, or the savvy, precocious pre-teen full of cocky self-containment. It was as though there were another Curt nestled inside the Curt he could see. Another person who maybe didn't like David very much and was ready to hasten down a different path.

"You're strong, Dad," Curt had quipped as David sweated past him, lugging two coolers, one atop the other, from the car and into the cabin. "But when we get back home you can put some deodorant on to fix that."

They'd intended the weekend trip to be a larger affair. Kathy had said she might come, but then demurred the night before. Joe had forgotten all about it when David had called him and told them to go on without him and Peg. So that left only David and Curt to joust this time. But it was time in the woods, which generally set its own level for both of them.

And there was work for them to do. An old oak, too near the cabin, was dying, shedding large limbs with each spring storm, and David worried that if pushed the wrong way, the substantial remains of the old tree could come down on his dad's cabin, and who knew what damage that might cause. His plan for their visit was to fell the oak in a safe direction. He regretted that his father hadn't joined them since his woodcraft was better, but David had a cut down many trees following his father's example and believed he could bring down this tree safely as well.

David had explained his plan to Curt on the drive to the cabin. Curt was skeptical. The tree wasn't *that* close to the cabin, he'd contested. "I think your fear is unfounded, Dad."

Yet the idea of breaking out the chainsaw had secretly excited the boy, so after they had unpacked the car, Curt stepped around the back of the cabin to have a look at the tree. And there he found another large limb on the ground, fallen within a few feet of the cabin itself. Curt looked into the branches of the old oak, calculating their height in relation to the cabin and how the slope of the ground could, quite possibly, cause the tree to fall the wrong way after all. Maybe, his dad was right. This time. That thought made the dying tree look enormous. Dangerous. They had to take it down. Or, his dad had to, because Curt was not allowed to touch the chainsaw.

Curt hadn't heard his father come around the cabin after him and jumped a little when he spoke.

"Don't like the look of that old thing."

"I think maybe you're right, Dad." Curt began dragging the fallen limb through the gravel toward the fire ring.

When Curt had returned from the fire ring, he found his father standing in the same place, still looking at the tree.

"What do you see, Dad?"

"Just studying it. There's a lot of weight up there. A lot of trees around it. We have to figure out how we can bring it down without having it twist and fall toward the cabin. Fortunately, it looks like most of the weight is on the far side. See?" He pointed into the branches. "I'm feeling a little better about that."

David stepped up to the tree and ran his hand down its bark. Curt was beside him. They stood there for several minutes as David looked into the branches again and then to the area around the tree. Curt guessed his father was seeing things he wasn't, but he thought he shouldn't interrupt him to ask.

David walked away from the cabin, into an area of scrub and large rocks rising from the ground. He turned and looked back at the tree, at the cabin. He toed a couple of rocks loose.

"We should probably clear some of the scrub around the base of the tree before we start. I'll need an open area to work."

"I'll get the loppers," Curt said, darting to the cabin to fetch the tools. When he returned, he handed the larger, heavier pair to his father, and then the two of them began cutting the scrubby plants and tiny cedars at ground level.

They worked on the scrub for a while, but David was more thorough than Curt, who was eager to get to the big job of the day. It seemed to him that they had cleared more area around the tree than they needed to, but he could see that his dad was not going to be rushed.

"I think we should just keep cutting the scrub, Dad, until we have the whole forest cleared. Don't you?"

David recognized Curt's sarcasm; he seemed to resort to it almost constantly. David wasn't sure why. He supposed Curt picked it up from his friends at school, and he wondered how many other parents were getting their doses. But then he corrected his thought. He'd never heard Curt say a single sarcastic word to Kathy. Curt was reserving all of it for him. Yet it seemed good natured, or at least not intentionally mean.

"I guess we've cleared enough, Curt. But you're going to stay well back," he said, looking directly at his son. "And when that tree comes down, be ready to run if something goes wrong. Got it?"

The boy nodded. This part was not to be joked about.

The two of them walked back into the cabin, putting the loppers on the shelf where they were kept. And then David pulled two cans of 7 UP from the cooler, handing one to Curt.

"So, let's think this through," David said, opening his can and taking a sip. "We'll do our wedge cut on the far side of the tree from the cabin." He made a slow, slashing gesture with his hand. "It's a red oak, so I hope it isn't hollow. We'll cut it high enough so that when we're done, we'll have some decent stump left for sitting on."

"And ruminating!" He had heard "we" in his father's words.

"Yeah. That." David was pretty sure Curt wasn't suggesting something nasty. He was still only ten years old, after all, even if he was ahead of just about every development curve, except growth.

And in that he was perfectly average. A perfect boy in every way. "Given the spread of the branches still left up there, if we cut the wedge right, I'm pretty sure their weight will bring it down away from the cabin."

"Pretty sure, Dad?"

"Confident. And then, problem solved."

"That remains to be seen, Dad." There was a lilt in his voice, but the words hung in the air between them.

David put down his pop can and walked over to the tool corner where the chainsaw rested. Curt quickly set aside his own can and joined his father. The serious stuff was about to start.

David took the chainsaw onto the porch and set it down. then turned to go back into the cabin. But he faced Curt coming out, with the tool kit and a container of chain oil.

"Hey, thanks. Just what I needed." Before taking the items, he ran his hand through Curt's red curls. Curt didn't seem to mind.

The two of them sat on the porch steps with the chainsaw between them. David carefully filled the oil reservoir and checked the tension on the chain, turning the tightening screw and checking the tension again. Satisfied, he rose to get the can of gasoline, but Curt was quicker, running to the car where they had left it, bringing it to his dad.

"We'll fill the saw out by the tree. In case we spill any gasoline. It won't stink up the cabin that way."

David carried the saw while Curt trotted beside him with the fuel, his father's stride longer than his. They stopped before the tree.

"So here's where I plan to start the wedge cut." He drew his finger across the bark at a downward angle. Curt was paying close attention, but he didn't hear "we" this time.

"And I'll complete it here. Before that happens, I want you standing over by the car. Understand?"

"Yes, sir."

"Then I'll make the back cut here, and when I start to see the trunk leaning, I'm going to cut the engine on the saw and run over to join you. If I do it right, the tree will fall right on that big rock over there." He pointed. "Probably be really loud too, so don't be startled, okay, Curt?"

"If a tree falls in the forest, and no one is around to hear it, does it make a sound?"

"What?"

"It's a thought experiment, Dad. If no one is around to hear it, does it make a sound?"

A thought experiment? David wondered. That Catholic school was certainly bringing him along.

"Well, of course it does. It crashes to the ground."

"But if the crash doesn't reach an ear, is it a sound?"

"I guess the birds and raccoons would think so."

"Oh, good point, Dad!"

David smiled inwardly and accepted what sounded like an unguarded concession from his son. "Okay. Time for you to get over by the car. It's going to be okay. I'm sure of that. And one of the ways I am sure is because you're going to be safe over by the car."

Curt hurried to where he was instructed. He watched as David put the saw on the ground then put the toe of his boot into the grip to hold it in place as he started it.

"Wait, Dad!"

David turned.

"You don't have the safety glasses on. I'll get them. Don't start."

Curt ran into the cabin, emerging a few moments later with the glasses. David was alarmed that he'd forgotten them, especially in front of Curt, but he was glad his boy hadn't. It told him Curt paid attention.

David slid the glasses onto his face and tousled Curt's hair again. "You know you're the best son in the whole world, right, Curt?" The boy returned to his vantage near the car.

David repeated his earlier steps and had even grabbed the handle of the pull cord, but then he stopped.

He was thinking about Curt. He realized that his son wasn't going to be a boy much longer, and though part of him wished he could keep Curt that way, he knew his wish wasn't right, wasn't fair, and wasn't going to happen regardless. He pictured Curt and his buddies – Luis, Sean, Matt – wearing their honest smiles and adventuring around the neighborhood on their bikes. Curt laughing at the television or at some joke he would hurl at his parents. His fleeting moments of spontaneous, unguarded affection. It would all be ending soon. Too soon. Curt, it seemed, wanted to sprint into adulthood. The boy had no idea what difficulties waited for him there. His pockets were still innocent of a ring of keys or a wallet, yet even the normal challenges of a boy his age, his schoolwork, was easy for him. Not a challenge. Almost a frolic. What could David do to prepare his boy for the other challenges ahead? To give him a little direction? A little confidence? What could he teach him?

"Curt, come here."

Curt hustled over, worried that something was wrong. Had his dad decided he wasn't going to cut down the tree?

"We're going to make the wedge cut together, Curt."

Curt suddenly found himself both thrilled and terrified. He had never even *carried* the chainsaw for his dad, but now he was actually going to use it?

David removed the safety glasses and carefully slid them onto his son. Curt didn't move, paralyzed. His father considered him big enough, man enough to take this huge, frightening step. Curt felt uncertain whether he was ready, certain he wasn't. Wanting to do it. Afraid to do it. Pull yourself together, Curt urged himself. You can't back out now. Not in front of Dad.

David had started the chainsaw, and the noise made Curt jump. He set it on the ground before his boy, and after a moment of hesitation, Curt lifted the idling saw. The vibration seemed to make his whole body shake; its grumble filled his ears. The saw was too heavy for him. He could barely get it off the ground. He knew he wouldn't be able to hold it long enough to make even the first part of the wedge cut.

But then his father reached around him.

"Switch hands, Curt," David spoke in his ear. "You're a lefty, so you're holding it wrong."

David held the front handle of the saw as Curt inverted his hands, putting his right on the trigger grip and his left on the front handle. This worked better, but it was still too heavy. He didn't want to tell his father this, but he knew he had to.

Except that he didn't. David had kept his arms around his son and held the saw. They would make this cut together.

"Okay," David said over the noise of the idling engine. "It's going to be really loud, so if anything goes wrong, I won't be able to explain. I'm just going to pull you away. Got that, Curt? I won't be angry. We're going to be safe and smart about this."

Curt nodded his head. They were going to be safe and smart. His dad was going to make sure of it.

"Give the trigger a pull just to hear how loud it's going to get. Once we start the cut, we need to stay with it until we're done. I want you to understand what it's going to be like."

Curt barely pulled the trigger, and the idling engine growled a little louder. Then he pulled more, and its scream filled the forest. It never sounded this bad when he would watch his dad or his grandfather. He released the trigger.

"Remember how I showed you where we'd make the first cut?" David shouted above the grumbling of the saw.

Curt again nodded his head.

"Well, let's do it."

Curt could tell that it was his dad who was really lifting the heavy saw, really directing the blade to the correct angle. But his dad's hands were right beside his, so they *were* doing it together.

The slightest pressure from his dad's right hand told Curt that he needed to pull the trigger, which he did. The machine screamed again. Then they touched the whirling chain to the tree and began the first cut. Bits of old bark flew free before the chain bit into the wood itself. Sawdust began powdering Curt's jeans. His father directed the saw as it cut into the tree, while Curt held on, a part of it. The noise was painful. The sawdust was already tickling his nose. He could smell the hot chain oil. The vibration was hurting his arms.

But his dad's arms stayed wrapped around him. Huge arms that looked so powerful against his skinny ones. His dad was right behind him. He could feel his father's chest against his back. His dad was holding the saw for him, and with him. They were making the cut. How could something so frightening feel so good?

And after what seemed like forever, he could feel his father lifting the saw free from the cut. Curt let the engine idle.

"Okay," David said above the noise. "First cut done. Ready to complete the wedge?"

Curt wanted to step away. He wanted to blow his nose, wipe his face, brush the sawdust from his clothes, stop the ringing in his ears. He hadn't realized he would be making the second cut of the wedge.

"Yeah, Dad," he breathed, hoping his father heard the words but not the fear within them.

David tilted the saw so that it was perpendicular to the trunk and then guided it toward the tree. Curt pulled the trigger again, and the chain bit in. This cut was easier because it was shorter. They were going directly across the tree rather than through it at an angle. In no time, the second cut had met the first, and with a quick flourish, they popped the wedge from the tree. It landed at their feet. David then cut the saw's engine and hurried Curt away.

"That tree is unstable now," he said, looking back. "So, that's a good wedge we've cut. Now's the hard part. I'm going to make the back cut alone, and you're going to stand over by the car again. This is serious, dangerous work, and I want you safe. Understand?"

"Yes, sir."

His arms were still tingling from the buzz of the saw, his ears ringing. It was a bigger moment than he had expected; and he was ready to step back for a while.

David slid the glasses from Curt's face, placing them on his own. Curt ran over to the car. Once David was satisfied his son was safe, he returned to the tree.

Curt could not take his eyes off his father. He couldn't see exactly where David was directing the screaming saw this time, but he could see David, and that was enough.

David bent, leaning toward the tree with the saw in his hands. Curt could hear as its whine increased, as it bit into the wood a third time. And after his father had barely started, Curt saw him pull the saw back, shut off the engine, and hurry away from the tree. David stood halfway between the tree and Curt, and Curt wanted to go to where his father was standing but knew he could not. Curt could see the tree beginning to lean. He could even hear wood snapping rapidly in what was left of the trunk. But only for a second before the whole tree smashed onto the leaf-covered ground with an almighty boom that filled the forest. He felt the impact in his stomach, in his groin.

David turned to Curt with a smile on his face. "I think *that* tree made a sound when it fell!"

Curt wasn't ready to speak yet. The scream of the saw. The violent crash. His ears ringing and arms buzzing. His dad's strong, strong arms had been wrapped around him. Not like one of his hugs either.

Curt looked at the fallen tree, broken across the large rock. Directly across the large rock, just as his father had said. He looked at that break. And then he looked at his father. And he felt a smile forming on his face. His dad had done it. He didn't know what to think.

"Right where I told you it would fall," David said, as though reading his son's mind, pointing to the rock.

"Even a broken clock is right twice a day, Dad." Curt grinned.

David had Curt use the chainsaw to cut the smaller branches of the fallen tree, now parallel to the ground. He only had to lift it a foot or two and then let its weight press it against the wood. David stood two steps behind his son as he worked his way through a few of the branches, showing him where to make each cut so they had decent pieces of firewood and some that they would split later with the sledge and wedge for the potbellied stove inside the cabin. Although Curt grew more confident with each cut, the weight of the saw wore him down. David urged him to give it more gas, that he needed to tear into the wood. "You'll be at it all day at that rate, Curt!"

Curt knew his father could have ripped through all of the branches in the time it had taken him to do his half dozen cuts. But the saw was heavy, and loud, and the vibration was really starting to hurt.

Curt thumbed the off switch then turned to his dad. "It's making my arms buzz, Dad."

"Just a second."

David went into the cabin and reappeared a moment later with a pair of gloves.

"These are padded, Curt. They should reduce some of the vibration." He handed the gloves to his son. "Do you want me to start the saw?"

He didn't, but he stepped aside so his father could. Curt pulled on the old, grease-spattered gloves. He could feel the padding inside worn through at the fingertips. He took them off to shake out the twigs and bits of leaf and maybe dead spiders in them. They belonged in the fire, not on his hands.

The work was actually harder after that with the too-big gloves on. Curt thought that he'd had enough of his dad's lessons in manliness for the day, so he put on a masquerade, cutting slowly, pausing longer between each cut, heaving noticeably as he breathed, wiping his brow. It worked. After a few more cuts, David decided their work was done. The remains of the fallen tree could wait.

Together, David and Curt cleaned the saw and then put it away. After that they straightened up the ravaged area behind the cabin, but they moved slowly and only did what seemed necessary. They worked but spoke little, David only giving a few simple directions. Curt said nothing much at all.

Dark, steel-colored clouds had rolled in and threatened rain. Night would fall quickly that early spring day, and after a can of pop on the porch, Curt began building their evening fire – another successful one-match fire, made with wood he had cut himself. They had their dinner early: burgers and chips and pop. They ate the chocolate bars but didn't make the S'mores that were Kathy's favorite because she hadn't come. Then they sat together, mostly in silence, as they watched the fire burn down and the orange embers snap and glow. Had Joe come with them, he would have been smoking his cigar then, adding his own reflective silence to their mostly silent conversation. Quieter now because, David noticed, Curt was more withdrawn than his usual. Looking back on the day, he worried that Curt might not have been ready for the saw, that he may have forced his son to it too soon. How can you know these things?

Ahead of the storm, strong gusts of wind blew through the bare trees above them, filling the forest with creaking and sighing, and Curt realized that his dad had been wise to take down the old oak. In his lap he held the wedge they'd cut, reluctant to throw it on the fire as his dad had suggested. He had made that wedge. Or at least been a part of making it. That was good. But he feared – knew -- that he had disappointed his father when he complained about cutting the branches. It *had* been too hard. The saw was too much. He *knew* that. He wasn't strong like his dad, and his dad knew that, too. But when his dad brought out the gloves, how could he stop? His exhaustion performance worked, but he hated that he had to do it. He'd wanted to stop. He couldn't keep working, but to stop he had to deceive his father. So he wasn't – what? – strong enough? man enough? to work beside his dad in the forest? He didn't know, and it burned in him that he didn't know.

The clouds had held off, allowing them their dinner and musings before the fire. But now the fat, cold drops pelted them. In the dying light, David spread the remaining embers so the rain could quench them. Curt had already retreated to the cabin porch, the wedge still in his hand. David joined him.

"You did good work today, Curt. You can tell Mom all about it when we get home. Tell her what a man you're becoming. I'm proud of you." David hoped that was the right thing to say.

Curt was more tired than he expected, not only from his work with the heavy saw and carrying and stacking all of the logs his father had directed him to make, but also with the raw excitement of his day. With being trusted by his father and then with his own inability to dismiss this, to make a joke of it.

David offered to show Curt how to lay a fire in the wood stove; it would be cool that night and they needed one. But Curt declined the lesson and later declined the chance to play a few hands of Gin Rummy by lantern light. Instead, he stripped to his briefs and searched his body for ticks but didn't find any hiding among his freckles.

By the time David was ready for bed, having stoked the stove and straightened a few things in the cabin, Curt was already in the deep sleep that only bone tired and blameless boys can achieve. David undressed and joined his son in the bed. He lay on his back with his hands behind his head and stared into the darkness above him. The rain was drumming on the metal roof. Steady and monotonous, soothing.

"If I tell Curt that I will always love him," David whispered to the universe, "but he isn't awake to hear me, will he still know it in his heart?"

The universe answered, for Curt stirred in his sleep and rolled over, throwing his arm across his father's stomach and resting his head on his father's shoulder. David wrapped his arm about his boy and pulled the quilt over both of them.

DAVID

Curt is still just a boy. He thinks he's really clever, and he is in many ways, but there's a lot he doesn't know about the world. And like Kathy says, that's the way it should be. Let him be a boy for as long as he can. Save the hard choices, the adult choices for later.

He has his friends at school, but I can see how he's smarter than them. He laughs at jokes they don't get and says things that go over their heads. Kathy gives me a wink when he does so I don't miss it too. But a lot of the time he just wants to be by himself. Sit in his room after dinner, sometimes all evening before I go to work, usually with the door closed. Homework or reading, I guess. Or whatever ten-year-olds do inside their heads. I can barely remember those days. I pop my head in before I go, and he'll look up and say something like "See you later, Dad," and go back to whatever he was doing.

He seems content. Doesn't seem lonely at all. I don't know what he would have thought of a younger brother or sister. Whether he might have even wanted a one or not. He's never said. But there's no going back now. Kathy said I didn't have to, but I knew I did. It's a frightening thing, being a dad. Having someone depending on you for everything. I put on a smile, but I'm scared all the time.

I'm not sure I can do it right. That's why we stopped at one.

Chapter Eleven

Meet the Teacher Night

The sidewalk before them was cracked and heaved, even crumbled to gravel in places. Gone altogether. Littered with trash and leaves and weeds and broken glass. The streetlight above them was out, and the one beyond was flickering. David kept his eyes down to make sure they didn't trip, still secretly wounded from the "good laugh" they'd had at Curt's school that evening.

They lived in an older neighborhood. A little on the tough side, but it was what they could afford, and Angelus Parish seemed vibrant, with a good school that challenged their boy. For the present, they were okay, but they had begun talking about somehow finding their way to the suburbs, how that might be a better environment for Curt. Make him want to strive for something more.

David and Kathy were returning home after Meet the Teacher Night. Curt had stayed by himself in the apartment for the evening, an arrangement they were all a little nervous about, though Mrs. Washington across the hall said she would keep her door open for him. Curt had started fifth grade that year. A big boy now, and, as David and Kathy were just told but had already guessed, a clever boy. A gifted boy. Kathy's mother would be delighted with the news. David's parents would not be surprised.

"It's good to see that more than just his parents think he's smart," Kathy said. She held the folder with her boy's scores and evaluations to her chest with both hands. "I think the gifted program will be good for him. Help focus that busy little brain of his. Don't you think?"

Curt's teacher had said all manner of nice things about him. A top student. Well behaved and respectful. A good influence in the classroom. Lots of friends. Always eager. Always positive. Articulate, which David reminded himself to look up when they got home. Kathy and David had much to be proud of, the woman had said. This official stamp on it made David's head spin with pride, and worry.

As they walked, David was remembering when his parents had come home from a similar conference with one of his teachers, long ago. "I can still hear what Dad told me that night," continuing aloud the wistful thoughts in his head. It was a mannerism Kathy had grown used to in their years together, so she soon followed the path of his thoughts. "He said I should never forget that I had advantages the other kids didn't. A good attitude, he said. Good looks. Good personality. I loved hearing that from Dad." They walked a few more steps. "It's only occurred to me just now that he never said anything about me being smart. Not a word." As hard as he had tried, and sometimes he *had* tried, he rarely managed to rise any higher than a C student. He saw then, as they moved down the crumbled sidewalk in the gathering dark, that he'd always known this about himself yet had managed to ignore it. Or to accept it, because that had seemed sufficient, even after he'd met Kathy, who was so much smarter than he ever was. But now there was Curt.

They passed beneath a dying elm tree; its fallen twigs lay scattered on the sidewalk before them. David kicked a larger one aside, the toe of his work boot scuffing the gravel.

"I never got to teach Curt how to build a one-match fire. Did you know that? He just did it all on his own one day down at the cabin. Didn't need my help at all."

"He could do it because he watches you, Davey. He told me. Every single thing you do is a lesson for him."

"Sure. I guess it is. But I don't think whatever skills or knowledge I have is what Curt really needs. Or even wants. Not anymore. He's going to be too smart for me pretty soon, Kathy. Did I tell you what he said the other day? 'Did you ever notice that your smallest finger corresponds to your biggest toe?' And when we were at the cabin, sitting around the fire, he said 'There is no day or night in space.'

I can't keep up with him, Kathy. The day is coming when I won't impress him anymore. When I won't be what he needs. Already I can't help with his math homework. Fifth grade!"

Kathy considered David's words. There were qualities more important in a father than book smarts. Like steadfastness. Hard work. Unceasing love. And a sweet kind of innocence a man can maintain despite the hard knocks he's had in his life. Her husband had a good, good heart.

Had Kathy listened to her head rather than her heart, she wouldn't have gotten pregnant at seventeen. Or married and become a mother at eighteen. But she'd never regretted the choices of her heart, and she knew Davey was being a good father by listening to his heart as well. Curt could learn from that kind of teacher too. Especially the important lessons that weren't in books.

"Don't overthink this, Davey. Cleverness can get a boy into trouble. What Curt will need most of all in the years ahead is a lot of love and a good example. In all the world you're the teacher who is best at both of those."

But the dam in David against self-doubt had already broken. "What kind of example does he think I am? He tells everyone that his dad is a zookeeper so he doesn't have to say that I really load trucks in a warehouse! He's embarrassed by me, Kathy. He's telling a story he *wishes* was true about me."

The students' essays were taped to the wall of the classroom. David and Kathy eagerly sought Curt's, and they had a good laugh about what he wrote. David pretended to be amused by it but was not sure how well he had pulled it off. "Curt is such a storyteller," he chuckled. Then, stung, David took the chance to read some of the others. He should have stopped himself; it had been a salvageable evening until then. One little essay, by a girl who wrote about her fireman father, kept coming back to him. Maybe if I were a firefighter, David thought, Curt would see me as a hero rather than just as an embarrassment. But the fact was that David never could bring himself to give Curt many details about his job. After a while, the questions stopped coming. And David knew it wasn't much to be proud of: grunt labor, just his way to pay their bills. So what did that leave Curt for his essay?

"Curt needs a doctor or a bank president for a dad, Kathy. Somebody that can open doors for him. Curt doesn't think very much of me." Nor, sometimes, did David himself.

She slipped her hand in his and squeezed it.

"Of course he does, Davey. He listens to every word you say. He watches you constantly."

Several cars rumbled down the street beside them.

"I'm not going to be loading trucks forever, Kathy!" How much he wanted to say that to Curt, too. But if he dared to, he feared the boy would just scoff or roll his eyes.

Yet the truth was that moving up didn't seem like it was going to happen for David. Not any time soon. There was no path he could see before him. Kathy had to notice. Ten years of doing the same work night after night. A raise once a year, but no promotion. No real change in responsibilities. But if Kathy did notice, she never said anything. Never pushed him. Never questioned him. Maybe she was waiting for him to finish college. "I'm going to get my four-year degree in ten years at night," he joked when people asked, though it wasn't funny to him. Or maybe she was beginning to guess what he already knew, that there was little point in someone like him being ambitious.

There weren't many opportunities to get promoted at the warehouse since nobody above him was moving on. After ten years at it he finally allowed himself to feel competent and did help supervise the other loaders informally, but they couldn't give him the title because, technically, they didn't need two supervisors on his shift. So when an area manager position opened, he had applied, with a small measure of actual confidence that he'd scraped together somehow, mostly from his dad's encouragement. It felt like the biggest risk he had ever taken in his life. On the face of it, there was nothing to lose – his own job was secure – and there was even the remote possibility of something to gain. Yet it felt maybe too ambitious for someone like him, even dangerous or forbidden, putting his ego on the line like that. His doubts were confirmed; the job went to the woman who had been his supervisor when he'd started there years before. She deserved it, of course. He knew that. She had more tenure there than he had. Plus, she had a degree;

David was *still* working on his. He would have been in accounting class that evening had he not skipped it for Meet the Teacher Night. "You know what Jon calls Wyandot University?" he began again. "The little college at the end of the alphabet. Why Not University, for people with nothing better to do."

"Davey."

"He's right. The only reason we can afford it is because it's a third-rate school."

"Davey, stop!"

He hadn't told Kathy that he didn't get the promotion because he hadn't told her that he'd even applied, contrary to what his father had suggested when David had gone to him for advice. Why get her hopes up when there was nothing certain? Nothing even likely. Why set her up just to let her down in this way too? It was hard enough doing that to himself. Because somewhere inside he knew all along he wouldn't get it. Just imagining the conversation he'd have with her when it didn't happen was enough to keep him silent. Worse, maybe, would be disappointing Curt, who David feared could already see through him with the same penetrating green eyes his mother had.

But a perverse part of him was relieved that he didn't get the promotion. He wasn't sure just how well he could manage people anyway. He had always felt more comfortable *among* the crew than above them when he did his informal supervision work. Wasn't that wrong though? Wasn't he supposed to move up and be a better provider? Were they ever going to make it to a decent neighborhood, have a decent life, if he didn't? Yet he thought about Curt. Too smart for him already. Wasn't that another sign that he didn't have any business being a boss, if he couldn't even be a dad his own clever boy could respect? Nothing made sense.

"Remember when Curt was just a little guy? When we first moved to the apartment? And I used to hold him up so he could touch the ceiling? Remember how that made him feel so big?" He scuffed along a few strides, his heel spurs stabbing him with each step. "It made me feel big, too, Kathy. And the way he used to rub his fingers on my cheek to feel the stubble. It was easier being a dad then." David figured that his brief days of being a hero in his boy's eyes were gone forever. Curt was comparing him with other adults now. And finding him lacking. His essay showed that. David knew he would soon be just the one in the family who worked in a warehouse loading trucks. Just the guy who paid their bills. Curt was going to have to be satisfied with that. They all were.

"Let's get some ice cream to celebrate," Kathy said.

"I don't have any cash on me. And I'm going to have to get to work pretty soon."

He missed her point, which was just as well. She wanted to divert his thoughts, thoughts she had grown able to read. Get him away from the spiral of defeat he so easily fell into. Get his head and his heart focused on the three of them together. Being a family. The biggest thing in the world. The best thing they had ever done together.

"I have a little cash. The Quik Trip is only a couple blocks out of our way. It won't take long."

Of course she had cash. She always had cash because, David was certain, her mother gave her money all the time. Just like her mother was paying to send Curt to the Catholic school, which the two of them couldn't possibly afford on their wages.

From several blocks over, in the direction of their apartment, came the sudden, harsh wail of a police siren. They held their words as each calculated where it was and whether it would just keep going and not stop where it shouldn't. When they reached the corner, where they could turn toward home or press on to the convenience store, they waited silently for the sound to tell them which way they would go. The siren wailed into the gloaming, well beyond their apartment and still onward. After taking a breath, David and Kathy crossed the street and continued down the block to the Quik Trip.

The store sat brightly lit across the street. Cars pulled in. People stepped out of their cars and walked into the store. Others left. And on the side of the building, beside the greasy dumpster, in the orange cone cast by the security light were two boys about Curt's age. David had seen them around the neighborhood but didn't know their names. They were smoking. Even from across the street, David could see the contempt in their eyes. Not for him, he knew.

Or not *just* for him. It was the sneer they'd already acquired for life and its false promises. For every adult and every word of advice or admonishment that dared enter their sphere.

How had he escaped this? David wondered. His parents, and the decent, steady life they had given him obviously. And then Kathy. His buddy Jon didn't know it, but he had saved David's life that day when they were sophomores. When he'd pushed timid Davey toward that unattainable girl named Kathy, so he had to say something, anything, to her finally. His life seemed to open before him then.

The smoking boys seemed to be taunting him, daring a confrontation, but David tried not to look at them as they crossed the parking lot and went into the store. It hardly seemed possible to him that boys that age could already be racing toward the cliff, and the idea of losing Curt that way left him breathless. Was a decent, steady life enough anymore?

He hung back as Kathy selected the ice cream from the freezer – mint chip that she knew he liked best – and flipped through the sheaf of papers about their son as she paid at the register. All very impressive he supposed. The words he didn't understand and the charts he couldn't read, most of it just a fog of details, not making any sense to him, except that it was all supposed to be good news. When she returned, David exchanged the folder for the bag with the ice cream. She was a better keeper of the evidence of their clever child.

Their diversion to the store brought them the few blocks home by a different path.

"Next free weekend you have, you should take Curt out to your dad's cabin. You haven't been out there for a while, and I know Curt would love to go. Just the two of you."

This suggestion brightened David's mood a bit, which was also part of Kathy's diversion. "Yeah. That *would* be good. I'll look at my schedule and find a time."

David fumbled the key into the lock of the back door to their building, and they were both silent as they climbed the stairs to their second-floor apartment. TV sounds drifted into the hallway. The smells of dinners being cooked. A mellow evening of people living their lives, but their boy was waiting for them above. Alone, but fine. Surely fine. He was eleven years old after all. And well behaved. And Mrs. Washington was just across the hall, with her door open. And they had ice cream to celebrate their gifted little boy.

Curt had left the door to their apartment locked, just as they had instructed him. Just as they knew he would. But when they entered, Curt came running from the front window. He'd sat on his bed there, in the old sleeping porch that served as his room, watching for their return. Perhaps for the whole time they were gone, David realized. His schoolbooks looked untouched on the kitchen table. Yet they had come from the Quik Trip, from the wrong direction, and Curt hadn't seen them approach. His green eyes were wide. They had left him on his own for nearly two hours. Nothing had happened, but what if it had? What would he have done without them there?

And so when he had heard the key in the door, he sprang from his bed and raced toward his parents. Raced toward them both and pushed past his mother to throw his arms around his dad's waist. Pressed his face into his dad's flannel shirt and closed his eyes tight for a moment until he felt his world was back in balance.

"I'm so glad you're back!"

David bent to kiss Curt's forehead. This, he thought. For now, this is right.

KATHY

Sometimes Davey and Curt come along, and he takes Curt to the playground while I run the figure eight path a few times. He doesn't like me running around our neighborhood alone, and he's probably right. So we come here a few nights a week, before he goes to work and Curt goes to bed.

I think Curt would rather be home, reading a book or watching something stupid on television. But he needs to get out and get some fresh air. Get out of his busy little brain and get active. And Davey needs to be out too, so he doesn't sit there and brood. He needs to stop being that way in front of Curt. He thinks he's a failure, and I've learned to stop contradicting him because he'll pull out a half dozen examples of how he doesn't measure up to this or that ridiculous standard. That he loads trucks. That he's not smart enough to help Curt with his homework any longer. That everyone else seems to have life figured out and to him it's just a big muddle. But the thing is, life is just a big muddle. We're all feeling our way along. Our difference is we have each other. The three of us have each other in this big muddle. And nothing's more powerful than that.

I think Davey knows this. Deep down. I actually think it's what really drives him. And even Curt, so aloof sometimes, knows what home and family mean in this world.

I'm nearly done. I come around the last turn and see them at the playground. Davey is chasing Curt around the equipment. Or Curt is chasing Davey. They're laughing, calling to each other. They're playing together.

I think I have another lap left in my legs.

Chapter Twelve

Runaway

Little Curt. Not so little anymore, David understood, but it was still a jolt. Soon after they'd gotten to the start, where thousands of other runners were standing about and the energy of the crowd was palpable, Curt had spotted some high school boys with their bibs pinned to their shorts so they could run without shirts, and he began messing with his own shirt. Lifting it, testing whether it was too cool to go without, whether he was too scrawny to run shirtless as they would. Still just a kid compared with those bigger boys with their athlete bodies. Their muscles. Their cockiness.

Kathy, talking to a friend, was wearing a shirt, though David noticed a few women in only sports bras. He felt distracted, seeing women dressed in their underwear, but he supposed it wouldn't be long before Curt would start showing an interest in them.

Since his dad wasn't running, Curt studied the bigger boys. How they grabbed their ankles to stretch their muscles or bounced on their toes. How they joked and laughed and jabbed each other in the stomach. Showing easy impatience before the run. Fully in their worlds. In the end, he whipped off his own shirt and tossed it to David. The milky white skin of his freckled chest betrayed a winter indoors, and this drizzly, late April morning was only just warm enough for him to stand outside half naked, waiting for the run to start.

David helped him move the bib, sliding his hand up the inside of Curt's shorts so he could direct the pins through the wispy fabric. The compression shorts he wore underneath hanging loose against his skinny thighs. His new shoes still looking clean. With the transfer made, David's boy had grown up a bit. They both sensed it.

But when Curt threw his head back to pull on his bottle of Gatorade, David was struck by a memory. Just a flash, but vivid nonetheless. Curt was a toddler again, stumbling around in his droopy diaper. Somehow, he had managed to slip his feet into his mother's running shoes and stood before them, unsteady but proud of himself. "Momma's little running boy," Kathy had cheered. And Curt had tilted his head back to pull on his bottle of milk. David could still see that sweet moment, and he supposed he should have guessed then that Curt would follow his mother down the running trail.

"Can I have a hug, Curt?" David said, stuffing the discarded shirt into his pocket. Curt's running shirt. It weighed next to nothing, and it hadn't been cheap, but Curt said the shirt was perfect for all of the miles he'd run in it. And now he'd be running without it.

Curt turned to his dad and the two of them embraced for a moment, but Curt was too anxious to linger.

"I'll be watching for you at the finish, Curt. Have a good run."

This was Kathy's third Trolley Run, so David knew the right things to say, the right places to be at the right times. And because it was Curt's first time running it, he was now an insider, no longer a spectator with Dad but a runner with Mom. A new distance, but David had little doubt that his boy could complete the four miles, especially with Kathy beside him, encouraging him and helping him control his pace so he didn't burn out too soon. Kathy would talk to him as they covered the miles, get him to talk to her and help keep his breathing even, his mind off the agony she knew would come.

"What do you talk about when you and Curt run?" David had asked her once, hoping to get a glimpse inside his boy's head.

"Oh, anything. Nothing in particular." She answered as though she had never considered the subject before. "All kinds of stuff. We just talk."

This left David envious, and a little sad. Curt was finally moving beyond the stage where he would merely grunt answers to his father's questions about this or that. But now it was sarcasm, joking, not taking seriously anything David said. A conversation about nothing at all would be nice. He thought he was entitled to at least that much.

So mother and son would chatter on the run. Miles and miles. Side by side, all the way to the finish. He'd keep her from running the race she could, but she'd prevent him from running the race he shouldn't.

They had to get into their wave, so David stepped back to let them go. Kathy and Curt headed off, but Kathy turned to give David a smile. Her red ponytail stuck out of the back of her running cap, sweeping the air as she turned. He'd always liked that. Then they were swallowed by the crowd of waiting runners, and David hobbled to his car a few blocks away so he could drive to the finish and find a decent spot to watch for them as they came blazing in.

His mother's running had always been a part of Curt's life, and he never objected, until he did. "Why does Mom have to go running all the time?" Curt had complained only the summer before. He'd been surprisingly whiny about it. Curt was a boy who always seemed subdued, in control of himself, and David guessed some kind of tension had been building about this. David was drying the dinner dishes, and he slung the towel over his shoulder, only a little insulted that his son considered an hour alone with his dad to suddenly be intolerable. Yet from somewhere, David had summoned the perfect response.

"You have your sneakers on. Go with her! She'd love to have you along. If you hurry, you can catch her before the bus comes." He grabbed some change from the bowl by the front door and poured it in Curt's pocket. "That should cover your fare. Now go. Hurry."

David's suggestion had found exactly the right place in Curt's fertile mind, and the boy pounded down the hall stairs and out the front door of their building. David watched from the window as Curt pelted across the crumbling sidewalk after his mother. He could see from her quick clapping how delighted she was when Curt reached her. That was the first of their runs together.

Before they'd moved to the apartment, when they were still living with David's parents, Kathy had started running to get back in shape after Curt was born. Sunnyside Park was only a couple of blocks away, and it had a nice path for running, with lots of people around in the evenings. David had tried going out with her a few times back then, but his feet hurt too much. Standing all those nights in a warehouse in sneakers had taken its toll. His heels gave him stabs of pain; it hurt to walk sometimes. Now steel-toed work boots were required in the warehouse, but the damage was done.

Once they moved to their apartment, and their new neighborhood was maybe not quite safe enough for a woman running alone, Kathy began taking the bus back to the park to get her miles in.

For a long time it was simply what his mother did most evenings; Curt took no special notice of it. But something had changed in him, and he began to miss her when she left for her runs. Then David had shoved him out the door after her that one time, and what had been Curt's adversary, taking his mom away from him, soon became his own little passion. Running with his mom. Then, just running.

Curt would come home glowing from those early runs with Kathy. Sweaty, exhausted, and glowing. His coppery red curls would be pasted to his forehead. His green eyes wide with excitement. Kathy said it was runner's high. A rush of endorphins. David didn't know what endorphins were, but if they made his boy happy, he was happy too. Soon Curt wanted to go running on his own, but they both thought he was still too young for that. So David would sometimes walk with him to Curt's school and watch as his boy ran laps around the playground. At dinner Kathy and Curt would talk about running. About pacing and hydration and quads and glutes, and mysterious things like pronation. David was learning the lingo, but Curt was learning it faster. David listened, contributed a word when he could, and wondered how this transformation had come over his son so quickly. And how he had missed seeing it coming.

For too short a time, David felt he had been Curt's whole world. The face he saw every morning, the lips that kissed him, the arms that held him, the hands that changed his diapers and tied his shoes and dried his tears. That held his hands as he took his first steps. But now his boy was outrunning that.

Crowds were already gathering near the finish as David got there, and he had to park several blocks away then hurry over to the finish arch, his heels giving him the pain they always did when he walked too far or too fast.

The chute after the finish arch was blocked by temporary fencing so that when the runners came hurtling across the line, they wouldn't have crowds of people in their way. David wouldn't be able to hold out his arms for Curt or Kathy to collapse into as he sometimes did when they went running in the park, so he tried to find a spot near the finish where he could at least see them as they came in.

Everyone else had the same idea. It would take Kathy and Curt most of an hour to run the four miles, and in that time thousands of people would gather at the finish, all jostling for a chance to see loved ones come running in. All eager to take photos or cheer or wipe away tears.

When it became obvious that Curt was going to be serious about running, that he was going to stick with it, Kathy had told David that their boy needed some decent running shoes. Maybe some good socks, too. And David, who had never been any more of an athlete than what was required in high school gym class, supposed that his growing boy would probably be needing a jockstrap pretty soon too. Kathy might know about running shoes, but this was something a father would know about.

So outfitting his boy with a running kit could be father and son time, a chance for David to participate a little in Curt's new passion, and the two of them took a trip to the mall one Saturday afternoon to do that.

The young man at the sporting goods store quickly sized them up and, after slipping an expensive pair of Nikes on Curt's feet, assured him that he would run much better if he also had running shorts and a shirt spun from a new, lightweight fabric. "It's like dressing yourself in air," the man had said. "All the runners wear it now. The *serious* runners." Curt was so obviously enthused by their trip, by the indulgence being given to him, that David decided to splurge and suggested a bright green shirt that would go well with Curt's red hair. Then he brought up the jockstrap, and he got the surprised look that he expected from Curt, but it was for the wrong reason.

"A jockstrap? Dad, nobody wears those things anymore!"

David wasn't sure how Curt had come upon this bit of knowledge, but the salesclerk confirmed it, saying most guys wore compression shorts now. "They hold your quads in place," he said, squeezing Curt's thigh. "Give you better performance and less fatigue." David had never heard of compression shorts. Curt evidently had, though, and got to browse through a selection of these, picking out a pair small enough for his skinny legs and nonexistent hips.

"Thanks for buying me all of this stuff, Dad." Curt had wanted to wear the running shorts, and especially the compression shorts, out of the store but they didn't have a changing room, so he settled for running his hand over the smooth fabric of the green shirt he did wear as they sat in the food court and sipped a couple of pops. He had also worn his new shoes.

"It's like Grandpa says. The right tool for the job at hand."

"Or at foot," Curt corrected, pleased with his little observation. He held his feet out to admire his new shoes.

When they got home, Curt immediately went into the bathroom and tried on all of his new gear. Kathy and David had sat in the kitchen, going over the significant cost of the purchases. "It made him so happy, Kathy," David said. The shoes really weren't much more than what decent hiking boots would have cost, David noted, though he'd been wise enough to stop suggesting those once Curt's other interest took hold. And Kathy in turn admitted that cotton shirts really did get heavy with sweat, especially with summer coming. Then Curt came into the kitchen with his new gear on, the price tags still dangling, and stood before his mom.

"Well, look at my running boy!" She pinched the fabric of his shirt and flicked at the hem of his shorts, finally pulling them up slightly to examine the compression shorts he wore underneath. "Those should help you."

Curt had run in his new shoes a couple of times since then, but he wanted to keep them clean for the Trolley Run, so he laced up more often in his old sneakers. He wore the shorts and his new shirt every chance he could though. They were letting him try a few solo runs, but only around their neighborhood. And they would watch from the window when they expected him back, releasing the tension they didn't even realize they felt when he turned the corner at the block and came trotting their way. Then he would come in and tell his mom how good he felt. How the right gear really did make a difference. David would stand to the side and listen as Curt and Kathy discussed details, happy that his quiet son was so outwardly excited about something.

David had picked his spot near the finish arch. If the run started on time, and if Kathy and Curt had been at the front of their wave as they'd intended, then David thought he would see them in another half hour. He had planned to watch for Curt's bright green shirt in the crowd of runners, but that was stuffed in his pocket now. He'd have to look for their two red heads instead. And now for Curt's milky white chest. David hoped his skinny, barely dressed boy wasn't cold.

The swiftest runners came to the finish line about twenty minutes after the official start, but David didn't expect Kathy to be among them, especially if she was pacing Curt. The crowd cheered for these first finishers. And then there was a gap before more runners came blazing in. Individuals in the crowd cheered individual runners, and once they made their way past the finish line and out of the chute, into the open area beyond, family and friends would huddle around them, slapping them on the back and handing them bottles of water.

David watched as runners poured in by the hundreds now, wishing he could see farther up the road so he had more chance to spot Kathy and Curt, worried that he would miss them, miss Curt crossing his first finish line with a big smile on his face. Or maybe tears. Either way, Curt would be victorious, and David understood this run was a kind of hurdle his son needed to get over. He would be different after he crossed that line.

Masses of runners were flowing under the finish arch, bearing looks of euphoria or pain, dripping with sweat or blissfully untroubled, gasping or laughing or doggedly serious. Adults. Children. Old timers who belied their age. High schoolers who ran in packs. David scanned them all, watching for Kathy and Curt. Still a little too early, but in the crowd of runners it would be easy to miss them.

And when the two of them turned the last corner and came into the straightaway before the finish arch, David did spot them. They were too far away for him to see their faces clearly, but Curt, he could tell, was struggling. The bounce was out of his step, the boyish way he made running look effortless. His stride was ragged, his arms floppy. He thought Curt might be crying, but he was too far away to be sure.

Kathy urged a final burst of speed from the boy as the two of them covered the last fifty feet, and then they were done. Curt fell into Kathy's arms, beat but not beaten. David could see Kathy saying something. "You did it, Curt!" Or "I'm so proud of you!"

Words David wished he could be saying to his boy at that moment.

PEG

Life has its rhythms. Birth and growth and death. Meetings and partings. Comings and goings.

My little Davey, my magical boy, my Dandelion, is moving away. You raise your children to fly. And when they do you know in your mind that it's what you strived for all their lives, what they must do, as inevitable as the seasons, but in your heart you know something different. It's hard to let go because you come to understand there will always be a hole inside you, one that will never be filled.

I can't help but wonder if this might be the last time I'll see him. The last time I'll caress his cheek or tease out his smile. I try to remember all of the tears I dried and the songs I sang with him in the bath and the hands I held crossing the street and the little secrets I listened to. His struggles with homework. With friendships. With all of the pains of growing up.

And that's what I want to keep. The snapshots I shall choose. The moments I'll decide to remember. Maybe it's because Davey had to grow up too fast, before he was ready, that I cling to the little boy he was. Timid and uncertain, needing his confidence boosted, adoring his dad but loving me too in the subtler ways mothers come to see.

He's not going far. Just across the state. And it's my job not to stand in his way. Not to hinder him with problems he can't solve, patterns he can't change, because he has his own problems to solve. He has his own life to live now.

Chapter Thirteen

The Saddest Casualty

"I never knew Dad had a ponytail!"

"Oh, yes. A fine one that went halfway down his back. That was in the Sixties, of course. Before you were born, Davey." She smiled through the gray mists that were overtaking her, spoiling his visit.

"So you guys were really Hippies?"

"Yes, we were Hippies."

David held her hand, the one that ached because that arm had the IV in it, but she gripped his as hard as she could; she didn't want to let him go. She didn't want to let any of it go, though she knew she must. She opened her eyes and looked at her son with a soft smile, blending memory and imagination. The Summer of Love. It certainly had been. The proof was sitting beside her, holding her hand.

"Groovy, and all that?"

Peg closed her eyes and smiled softly again. "Yes, Davey. Your parents were once groovy."

Days long gone, she mused. They learned they had a baby on the way, so Joe cut his hair and joined the union. And they decided to get married.

"Dad had a ponytail!" David shook his head, trying to picture such an unlikely image.

It wasn't that Davey had never been curious as a boy, Peg reflected. Rather, his love for his father was his steady state, his favored parent, and he became incapable of seeing the man any other way than as he saw him each day. That left gaps in his knowledge. To him, his parents had no past lives that were ever any different, and no changes in their future. She wished that part were true. But that was why he was there.

"I see most of *your* hair is gone now too, Davey. Your beautiful golden curls." A scarf covered her head, all of her own hair gone. She reached across the bed with her free hand and stroked her son's short, tight curls. "My little Dandelion is all grown up." On the bedside table was a framed photo of Davey as a boy of three or four. Shirtless, his fists on his hips, peeking up at the camera through long, shaggy curls that hung over his forehead, like the cocky boy he must have once been. David didn't remember having that picture taken. Had he ever been that little? Part of him wished he could be again, when life didn't seem to have any worries. When it all had made sense.

"Things change," he said, his hand touching hers touching him. "I'm in management now, Mom. I have to look the part. It's weird. I even wear a tie."

Peg laughed. "So you finally mastered those horrid things?"

"Well, Kathy helps me." He looked down at his feet to hide his blush. He could tie a necktie, but he liked when Kathy did it for him, standing behind him, reaching around his chest. "She's the best thing that's ever happened to me, Mom." He could feel his mother's hand press his weakly.

"And a wedding band too," she said.

"Kathy surprised me with it. Now that I'm not actually loading the trucks anymore, I can wear one. Still getting used to it. The ring, I mean. Not being married."

"Kathy will give you a good life, Davey. A long, happy life."

Peg let her hand fall from his head and closed her eyes. Let the beeping monitor fill the silence. It was easier to do that, but her boy had come to town and was with her, and she wanted to drink in his face as much as she still could. She and Joe had had lives full of twists and turns that they met together, and when Davey came along in their later years, she hadn't yet learned how happy it all could be. Someone had once told her that nothing was more pure, or more intense, than the love of a child. And even now she could still feel Davey's childlike love.

But then her boy had moved across the state, and she grew sick, and he was too far away to do anything about it except come back on his first free weekend. His dad had called and said he needed to come see her, so he did. David knew moving hadn't made her sick, but he felt guilty nonetheless. As though his move had somehow made it worse. As though he were abandoning her when she needed him. He felt horrible, like an unloving son, but he didn't want her to know.

"I'm sorry Kathy and Curt couldn't come, Mom. He's so busy already. He wants to run cross-country at his new high school. He's already making friends. I think he'll fit in okay."

"A *Jesuit* high school. I hope he gives those teachers some fits."

When Kathy's mother learned that David had taken the promotion that would move them to St. Louis, she promptly instructed them to settle in the western suburbs where the public schools were, she said, decent. But they couldn't afford any houses out there, and when they chose one in Richmond Heights, her mother shook her head then said she would pay to have Curt attend the Catholic high school nearby. David knew that his clever boy needed to be kept challenged, so he went along with it. Not that he had a choice.

Curt could already talk him into a corner, win every argument. Give him a hundred reasons why this or that should or shouldn't be. How his poor old father hadn't quite thought something through all the way. It had gotten so easy that Curt had apparently stopped trying. David thought his boy had grown more agreeable, more cooperative, in recent weeks. Maybe the move, and soon starting high school, had left Curt a little uncertain too. And likely there were matters about Curt he didn't know, that the boy only shared with his mom.

David couldn't recall any more than a few times in all of his life when he didn't readily agree with his dad, with his suggestions, his decisions, his advice. His dad always seemed to make perfect sense, and David liked the simplicity of it. The certainty of it. That was the kind of father David wanted to be with Curt, but the clever boy had already outrun him, just as he was running cross-country now.

"Curt's a good boy, Mom. He's smart. And he really is well behaved. If he gets into arguments with his teachers, he'll be respectful. He still minds me, even though we both know he can outsmart me. He'll behave with his teachers, too."

Peg looked at David through half-closed eyes. Her poor boy.

He'd had to grow up too fast, and parts of him never did. He still had blind spots. A naiveté that came across as boyish innocence in her boy who was now a man. But Kathy was there to guide him. He was right about her. She was the best thing. And the two of them had produced Curt. Her boy's boy. As curious and questioning as his father had never been. And now taking his own first racing steps toward manhood. Life sometimes gave these compensations, if a bit late. Her thoughts were drifting, the medicine was taking her away, but she had a point to make. After a few moments, she found it.

"A little misbehavior is a good thing, Davey."

"Is that the Hippie talking, Mom?" Peg mustered another smile. "Perhaps. Maybe it's just the grandmother in me. I wish I could have seen Curt."

"I'll bring him next time I come. His voice is changing. He's growing so much lately. Kathy says she has mending Curt has outgrown. He's becoming a young man, Mom. When you get better you can come to St. Louis and see our house. Curt has his own room now. A real bedroom. Not a drafty old sleeping porch like he had in that apartment. I always hated that."

She thought she needed to correct him then, but her thoughts were fuzzy. It had been hard work paying attention this long. She needed to sleep, but her time with Davey was too short as it was. He was saying something about their mortgage, how he didn't like being in debt to Kathy's mother. Paying interest even.

Despite her wish, she closed her eyes again. She was drifting among the memories of that baby of hers. That naked little boy they'd handed her. Ten fingers and ten toes, and two lusty lungs. The baby that soon after was almost taken from her. Her visiting him in a hospital then as he was visiting her now. But with two very different endings. It seemed so long ago, as though it might have been some other woman's life she was remembering. Someone else's baby. Someone else's story being told. But she felt Davey's hand holding hers and knew it was her story. Her story nearing its end. She was soon going to be taken from him. She needed to keep talking, to stay awake while her boy was with her. To have all of the conversations she never seemed to have with him as he was growing up.

"Nothing last forever, Davey."

"Yeah, I know. It's just going to be a long time with her mother's nose in our business."

What were parents, after all? How much was too much, she wondered. And how much too little? What was the balance between guidance and letting go? Letting go.

"What did you two talk about? All those weekends you and Dad spent at the cabin?"

She caught him off guard. It took him a moment to catch up with how the conversation had changed.

"I don't know. Stuff. Nothing special."

No deep, man-to-man talks? she wondered. She doubted that. "You and Dad should go down there tomorrow. He'd like that."

"Mom! I came here to see you."

"We were going to move there someday. That had been Dad's plan. Add on to the cabin and then live there. Take him tomorrow, Davey."

"How about when I come back with Kathy and Curt, we can all go together? Maybe next month. It will be like the old days. When's the last time we were all there?"

Through the mist Peg finally realized, with a stab of horror, that Davey did not know. Joe had not told his son. Could not tell him. She'd been sick that spring, yes. But Davey was moving his family to St. Louis, starting his new job, and she didn't want to burden him with that too. But as the news grew worse, they realized that he had to be told; Joe said he would do it. Then evidently couldn't bring himself to. That was why Kathy and Curt hadn't come. Why Davey seemed almost lighthearted. Because this was something these two men in her life could not talk about. Maybe because Joe had never had such man-to-man talks with his own father. Because Joe had never known his father, who had run off soon after he was born. Joe's older brother disappearing not much later. Shames that left a hole in him. Shames Joe never wanted his Davey to know about – which Davey obliged by never showing an interest – so he held them in and compensated by being the only kind of father he could picture: a buddy, a big brother, a best friend.

David had chattered on. Something about how they could still move to the cabin once she got better.

He didn't know. The biggest thing of all, and he didn't know. Innocence is always the saddest casualty, she realized. It was going to be cruel to tell him, just as it would be cruel not to.

Peg stifled a sob.

"Does it hurt?"

She nodded, unable to speak in fear of what she had to say.

"Should I get the nurse?"

"No. I can manage." Her words were husky. "Just stay here with me, Davey. Let me hear your voice. Look at your beautiful face."

He blushed again. Her boy was grown now, but he still blushed for her. She wanted to hold him to her chest, once again to the breasts that had fed him and that now were betraying her. The boy whose diapers she had changed, whose hurts she had soothed. The little boy who had cried over his homework and the bigger boy who had cried when his dog died. Who went to his father with his little confidences and questions but who always had a hug and a kiss for her when he got home from school each day. Who later turned to her for advice when it was his time to change diapers and console a crying boy of his own.

And now the very hardest moment between a mother and a son. She fought the medicine that was blurring her thoughts, the tears that were stinging her eyes.

She said, "Davey. There's one more thing we need to talk about."

DAVID

I don't know how that family fit five kids and a dog in this house. They must have raised them in the yard. There's hardly a blade of grass left. And this old fence probably didn't keep any of them in either. When I finished taking apart the rotting pieces, the few remaining sections looked stupid, so instead of repairing it, I'm taking all of it down. Curt doesn't need keeping in anyway.

It's a luxury, doing chores in the daylight. Curt calls me "Diurnal Man," like I'm a superhero. I had to look it up. I think he was ribbing me. Even so, I'm only slowly adjusting to working during the day and sleeping during the night. I'm still tempted to go in and see how the night crew is doing in the warehouse, and Kathy has to remind me to give it a rest. Give myself a rest. Then she takes me to bed and sees to it.

Curt is at cross-country tryouts. Kathy says usually no one gets cut from cross country, so it isn't really a tryout, but we took him to his new school all summer to practice informally with the other boys, and I guess since he's a freshman, he has to go through the paces. No one could say when tryouts would be over, so I'm waiting for him to call to pick him up.

We're doing our best to make life normal for Curt. We moved him across the state. He's starting high school with none of his old friends. And in the middle of it, Mom died. So whatever Curt needs us to do to give him stability and routine, we're doing it.

Out front I see a black Mercedes drive past and then stop. After a moment, it reverses and idles in front of our house. And then out pops Curt, his gym bag in hand. "Thanks!" he shouts as he slams the door; then he trots into the house.

Chapter Fourteen

The Most Natural Thing in the World

Their long Saturday was nearly done. The fire was out. The boys were in the cabin, and they'd promised David they wouldn't sneak out after he was asleep to get into trouble.

Curt seemed to have a fine day, though it had been getting harder for David to read him anymore. He'd turned fourteen on Thursday, and Kathy made sure that this party was better than the thirteen that had come before, even if, David thought, the boy maybe wasn't all that interested in a family party any longer. It had been a time of change for all of them. A new job for David. A new city. An actual house in Richmond Heights. No more apartment. High school starting for Curt in a week. New friends. The cross-country team. If any of that was bothering Curt, he was not giving any signs that his father could read.

Kathy's party had to compete with a boys-only trip to the cabin. With the move, they'd only gotten out to the cabin once that summer, and David had promised Curt they would make another trip, that he could bring a friend. It had to be an overnight since the cabin was farther from St. Louis. The drive was longer now.

Curt brought his new buddy, Brooke, a boy he met at cross-country practice over the summer. David was glad Curt was able to find a new friend so quickly. Getting uprooted like that had to be hard for him. Curt had promised Brooke lots of guy stuff, lots of swimming, a campfire. David had to draw the line at some of the guy stuff. They could howl at the moon all they liked and scratch themselves anywhere they wanted, but they were not going to swing axes or use Grandpa's chainsaw. He figured that still left plenty of fun for two big boys.

They had picked up Brooke early that morning and began the long drive west to the cabin. David had a box of donuts and some orange juice to throw at them, and in the trunk were the two coolers with what he hoped was enough food for a pair of growing boys for the weekend. Curt and Brooke slept in a heap on the back seat most of the way. Coming from this new direction, David had missed the sign for his exit and had to backtrack a little, but when they left the highway and got on the winding Ozark roads, Curt stirred and began to recognize landmarks. His grunts stretched into words and then whole sentences. After he elbowed Brooke awake, the two of them began a chatter that hadn't stopped all day.

When they arrived, the boys shot from the car. Curt raced Brooke all around the cabin and then down to the lake. So much energy. They left David to unpack the car and open the cabin, but it was a routine he knew, even if he didn't get to do it as much since they'd moved. He went where a good job was offered, and he didn't regret that, but he did miss seeing his dad as much as he used to, especially now that his mother was gone. And he missed easy access to the cabin where so many good moments of his life had occurred.

He'd barely humped the gear inside before the boys were tearing into their bags, throwing their spare clothes about to find their swimsuits. Brooke disappeared into the bedroom to change, but Curt simply slipped out of his clothes and kicked them into the corner then pulled on his trunks.

"Hold on," David said. "Let me get changed. Brooke has to pass the swimming test before I can leave you boys on your own in the lake."

Soon after David's father had built the cabin thirty years before, he'd had the lake carved out of the Ozark valley. His dad said David had to be able to swim all the way across the lake and back without resting before he'd be let in on his own. It was only a two-acre lake. Not that big, really. But that was their test now. Curt assured him that Brooke was an excellent swimmer, but David was responsible for the boy over the weekend, so he took this bit seriously.

They fidgeted on the porch, supposedly rubbing each other with sunscreen, while David went into the bedroom to change. When he stepped onto the porch, the boys raced down the stone steps to the lake, threw their towels on the dock, and hollered at David to get his "decrepit self" down there. He was hardly decrepit. He was thirty-three years old, and for most of the last fifteen years, he had loaded trucks for a living. He was in pretty good shape, but he'd come to see that Curt needed to keep a wall of sarcasm between them. Although not sure why, he was happy that his son was not moody like so many other boys his age.

David stationed himself at the end of the dock so he could watch Brooke. The boy waded out from the shore and then began paddling across the lake. Curt swam alongside him, and the two kept up their chatter as they went. The test was effortless for them, which was fine with David. He'd confirmed that Brooke was capable in the water, and he already knew that Curt was. Despite the arm's length that Curt held him to, with arms that seemed to grow longer every day, David was pretty sure his son loved him and understood his need to keep him safe.

After that, he felt free to go back to the cabin to finish unpacking and get some lunch ready for the boys. David could see most of the lake from the porch, and he told Curt he would call to them every now and then, expecting their shouts of assurance that they were still alive. He figured after lunch he would go down to the lake and join them.

When David was a little guy, his dad had told him that before he had learned to swim, he would paddle David all around the lake on his back. David had tried that with Curt when he was younger, but that boy would have none of it, jumping off and splashing about on his own. Even this was going to be different for him, and David guessed that was fine. He had to go his own way. But so much of David's life had happened at this cabin, so many important moments, and he was sorry that it wouldn't be the same for Curt now that they'd moved farther away.

Happily, Curt still seemed drawn to the cabin. He begged all summer to go, and since Kathy wasn't as in love with the place as David was, she said that Curt and David could make as many boys-only trips out there as they wanted. He was just sorry it took until August to do it again.

Lunch was messy. Salami sandwiches, which were Brooke's favorite, Curt told him. Chips they shoveled into their mouths. The last of the donuts. And more cans of pop than David wanted to count. At one point, Brooke said that Coach Rice had told him the carbonation in pop slowed them down, and Curt listened carefully, but then both of them just kept drinking it. They were supposed to be carefree boys this weekend, David thought. They could worry about stuff like that later.

They used paper towels for napkins, but that was mostly for show. Their wet swimming suits were more effective for cleaning their greasy fingers. They ate with frenzy, sitting on the edge of the camp chairs. Their swimsuits dripping into the gravel. Their boy hearts racing with their weekend of fun ahead, their bodies eager to get back into the water. They ate around the old fire ring, but they left having an actual fire until dinner when they cooked burgers and made a dump cake in the Dutch oven to celebrate Curt's birthday once again.

Curt inherited his fair skin from his mom, and David could already see at lunch how the sun had found his shoulders, the bridge of his freckled nose, and the tops of his ears. Brooke wasn't as fair. He didn't seem to be getting burned, but David was responsible for them both. As they darted back to the lake after lunch, he shouted for Curt to take the sunscreen with them. "And use it!"

After they were gone, David cleaned up around the ring and spent a little time collecting kindling for a fire that evening. He was going to let the boys build it, throwing down the manly challenge of getting it started with just one match. Curt usually scoffed at David's one-match challenges, but he was always able to do it.

Curt, he was slowly admitting, wasn't the same. David guessed that was fine. He was more like Kathy. Much more clever than David at that age. Certainly better in school. An athlete. Better at making friends. Understanding stuff. Better at it all, it seemed. What father wouldn't want that for his son, right?

With the sun high in the August sky, and the boys alternately shouting and growing mysteriously quiet down at the lake, David thought it was time to take a dip as well. He wanted to cool off and wash away some of the day's grime. Since he was still in his trunks from before, he walked down the stone steps to the dock.

As he reached the dock – the boys were across the lake, splashing each other – he saw their towels on the boards. But when he looked again, he saw it wasn't only their towels but their swimming suits as well. Curt and Brooke were skinny-dipping.

How had he convinced Brooke to do that? When it was just their family at the cabin, Curt usually swam naked. So did David most of the time. Skinny-dipping was the most natural thing in the world, and his birthday boy was in his birthday suit. But a school buddy?

He looked across the lake again. The boys were swimming now, and he could see their milky white bottoms break the surface. David was glad they were comfortable with it, but it made him worry about when Curt started asking to bring girls on these trips. He hoped they put on plenty of sunscreen.

Had it only been Curt in the water, David would have stripped down and joined him. But with Brooke there, and naked as he was, he didn't think it was right for him to get in the water at all. Even watching them from across the lake felt a little creepy. So he caught Curt's eye and he waved, then trudged back up to the cabin. There was enough to do up there to keep him busy. He could discover whatever new tool his dad had added to his woodland arsenal, as he called it. Or split more logs for the fire; they would need coals for the Dutch oven. Or he could clear more scrub that was always creeping toward the cabin.

Hunger would eventually drive the boys back, and David would throw more chips at them to hold them off until he got the burgers cooked.

That was hours before. The boys were in the other room now, fed and tired but not ready to sleep. Reclining on sleeping bags spread on the floor. He could hear the rise and fall of their chatter above the forest sounds outside. David was listening for a whippoorwill, but he hadn't heard one yet. It was probably too late in the summer for them anymore he admitted, but the call was part of his boyhood, and he never tired of hearing it.

After their dinner of burgers and more chips, and birthday dump cake, the boys had horsed around the campfire, throwing more logs on until it blazed so high David feared it would burn through the night. Brooke said he wished he had brought his guitar, and Curt quickly agreed, telling David that his new friend could play well. It had been a good birthday trip for Curt, but as David watched these two cocky boys all day, he felt a little bit like an outsider. He remembered feeling like that at their age, but not so much anymore.

After the sun had gone down and the fire was burning itself to coals, the boys had returned to the lake to swim in the moonlight. "To wash off the ticks, Dad." David had done this many times over the years, and he knew two tadpoles like them were safe, but he didn't join them this time either. He supposed they were naked again, under cover of darkness, so it would be still an inappropriate place for him. At least he didn't need to bother them about sunscreen he thought. Later he hadn't even dared go out on the porch as the boys sat there, eating more chips and air drying themselves in the chairs. They had draped their colorful swimsuits over the porch rail, and David understood this to be Curt's flag for him to keep away.

"So it's a good dam," he heard Curt say. "Not a dam problem with it."

"No dam work to keep it up?" answered Brooke.

"Keep it up?" Curt giggled.

"Dam, that's big!"

"Dam big." He giggled again.

"Dam!"

The boys were pleased with their naughty talk. More guy stuff, David supposed.

"Hey, Dad. We need a couple of Grandpa's cigars out here!"

"That's not going to happen," he shouted through the window. "You're both supposed to be cross-country runners, remember?"

That seemed to settle it for them, and David got back to straightening things in the cabin. He was not sure how long they stayed out there. He'd finally gone to bed.

A little bit before, Curt had come into the bedroom. He was wrapped in his towel and began messing around in the closet, looking for the baby oil to put on his sunburn. Once he found it, though, he was gone as quickly as he came. Back to Brooke.

Early on David began to see that Curt was going to live a different life. He had denied the signs for a long time. For David, being as much like his dad as he could was the best way to figure out life. But Curt had drifted away. He was growing up, and sometimes David could see the uncertainty in his boy's green eyes as he faced new challenges. Yet he took his troubles to his mother more than to David. Confessed his little secrets to her. Shared his triumphs and his sorrows with her first. David didn't know if he was sad about this or not and tried not to think about it too much. All he could seem to do any longer was try to keep the door open with his son, take him on trips to the cabin, support his running, have little talks about this or that when Curt let him, and just try to live as much like a decent man as he could. Then accept whatever his boy would share with him. Throughout his life, David was constantly finding that the world was a bigger place than he knew, so he eventually resigned himself to expanding his thoughts to accommodate it, and this included his accommodating his son's separate life.

David loved his father, and he loved his son. Curt would start high school in a week. Off to new adventures. Whatever way he took his precious life, David hoped there would still be some small space in it for a man like him.

CURT

You could fit five of my house inside Brooke's. This place is more immense than my grandmother's even. His dad does some grandiose thing at Washington University, so they live nearby. There's a whole top floor that used to be for servants. And an apartment above the garage. If I ever run away, that's where I'll hide out.

Brooke's sister brought us home from practice. She used to run cross-country too, but she wanted to spend more time with her boyfriend, which irritated Brooke's parents, so they said she still had to pick him up after practice. I met her boyfriend once. He called me Brooke's special little friend, like it was nasty or something.

I come here a lot after practice. Brooke says the showers at school are unsanitary, and there's never enough hot water at home, so I shower here. After a few times, he said we should just shower together. We would at school with the whole team, he argued, so why not at his house. That made sense. That way he could scrub my back, he said, and I could scrub his. Sure couldn't do that in the school showers. And then he said he could wash my hair for me, too. He said I have so much curly hair that maybe I could use the help. So I let him. Brooke takes a long time lathering my hair, rubbing my scalp with his fingers, and then rinsing out the shampoo, reminding me gently to keep my eyes closed, tilt my head back. He has to stand really close to me in his small shower, and he bumps me a few times, but I don't mind. Anyway, it feels good, letting someone wash me.

Chapter Fifteen

Moving Day

Curt thought that something bad was beginning. Or rather, he was coming to see, that something had been underway, so slowly at first that no one noticed it – certainly not his obtuse dad – and was now starting to manifest itself in ways that could no longer be dismissed. And then he thought, no, that wasn't quite right either. Something was also ending.

The not-so-subtle signs were there, but with all of the weekend's hustle, with so many uncomfortable decisions that had to be made so quickly, his distracted father was missing the signs. His clueless father who could only seem to hold one thought in his head at a time.

Moving day had finally come. Talked about for a long time. Planned for a shorter time. Dreaded the entire time. It was the day to pluck Joe from his tiny, too big house in Waldo and settle him into a more sensible apartment a little farther down the road. He didn't need, could no longer manage, all of the care and worry of a house and a yard, so they'd all agreed an apartment was better. Still the same neighborhood, so his touchstones were at hand: the familiar streets and stores, the few remaining friends, the memories. David had taken another load of boxes and some furniture over to the apartment while Curt had been tasked with staying behind to help his grandfather sort and throw out and somehow chip away the casual accumulations of the old man's lifetime. Sediment in that small house that had no place in the smaller apartment. "Be merciless," David had told his son. But Curt found that he couldn't.

"I'd forgotten I had these," Joe said, drawing a crinkly manila envelope from the box before them. They sat in the front room, stacks of boxes beside them to be worked through, a roll of trash bags waiting to receive all of the things that could be discarded. Boxes of tax papers, insurance papers, old bank statements. Who knew what else they would unearth. Comfortable silence surrounded grandfather and grandson in the old house, punctuated by the occasional drone of a passing car, the bark of a neighborhood dog. "Your dad's old grade cards."

Joe's fingers pushed back the flap and his mottled hand dipped into the envelope. He drew out the cards and let the envelope fall to the floor. Curt picked it up.

"Look at these," Joe said, mostly to himself. The corners of his lips turned up in a wistful smile. He drew on his cigar and let the smoke roll slowly from his mouth. "My wonderful boy." Joe studied each card, pausing to recollect what stories it told him, tracing a finger across the faded ink and yellowed paper, before slipping the next to the top of the stack. Curt watched, knowing he was unable to fathom the full richness of the memories these handwritten cards were summoning in his grandfather. There were stories his grandfather might gladly tell him about his dad, but Curt did not want to ask to hear them because of his dad's instruction to get the work done, get the boxes sorted. It couldn't all be done in a weekend, but as much as they could do had to be done.

Joe handed the cards to his grandson.

"Your father was a good boy, Chris."

"Curt," he said. "My name is Curt. Remember, Grandpa?"

But Joe was already reaching into the box for the next memory.

Curt quickly reviewed a few of the grade cards. No surprises there, though this was the first time he had seen them. A "C" student. Consistently unremarkable. A not-really-all-that-bright kid. Validation of exactly what Curt believed he already knew about his father. Knew so well. Didn't need to be told. But there it was. Poor man.

"Keep? Or throw away, Grandpa?" He slipped them into the envelope that read "Davey's Grade Cards." Curt knew which choice he hoped for.

"Don't suppose I'll need them where I'm going. Maybe your mother would like to have them. Maybe you should hang on to them for now."

And so another thing not thrown away, but at least this one slim envelope wouldn't be going to the small apartment to take up space and be forgotten once again. Not much, but something to add to the pile of not much. Curt supposed his dad would not want him to have his grade cards, certainly not want him to see what a plodding student he had been and all that could be inferred from that. Which is why Curt wanted to keep them. The cards confirmed, or maybe justified, feelings he could not quite put into words about his father. Not pity, certainly. Not disappointment, though there was that. Not yet contempt. Nor disgust. Shame, maybe? he wondered. Embarrassment? Wrong feelings a boy should hold for his father, he knew, but there they were. So why not keep the grade cards and feel some – what? – permission for how he felt? He wasn't sure.

They were making painstakingly slow progress through the boxes, the trash bag woefully lean. Whatever boxes they didn't get done, someone would have to go through later to figure out what was there and decide what to do with it. This would give his father legitimate cause to complain when he returned. Curt realized that, and he thought, you try doing this, Father! How can I be expected to steal from Grandpa? He has the right to live in his memories, his stories, maybe for the last time for some of them. What else does he have anymore?

It had to be hard, moving out of his home after so many years. Being alone and then being pushed into a new place where nothing was familiar. And still being alone. Curt could see that his grandfather would be living out of boxes – or more likely doing without because how could he find anything in all of this mess? – until they could come back to town again and sort through more of it for him.

Curt knew his dad was missing a key fact. David's father was slipping. They both were, just in different ways. His grandfather was losing his grip while his father, in a way, was trying to tighten his and thereby losing it. Maybe he did see it, even with his C-student mind, and was just trying to deny it for as long as he could. Maybe by pretending to be authoritative and decisive, qualities Curt knew weren't even remotely in his dad's make up, the man could ignore for a little longer the painful inevitability that Curt could already see. It had to hurt. Poor man. For a moment, Curt felt something odd, something like tenderness for his father, but he shook it off.

Joe had pulled another large envelope from the box and was scanning the contents. The cigar smoldered in his hand.

"Trash," he said, giving the sheaf to Curt. Yet when the boy glanced at the papers he saw they were certificates for something. Insurance? Stocks? The kind of stuff his mom would know about. Maybe not trash. Not yet. He added them to the pile he was accumulating that he would show her when they got home. His father wasn't going to like that with his simplistic, binary view to either keep or throw out. No gray area to challenge his idea of how they needed to get the job done. Be merciless? It's not all socks and underwear, Father!

A dozen photographs spilled from the next envelope Joe had pulled from the box. Curt helped him collect them then watched silently as his grandfather placed each individually on the coffee table, sorting them into two categories. He puffed thoughtfully on his cigar. Joe puzzled over several before dropping them in what Curt guessed was the discard pile.

"I have no idea who these people are."

"Do they say anything on the back?"
Curt picked up the first of the discards. The photo of a man standing beside a car. On the back was the word "Simmons."

"Do you know someone named Simmons?"

"That jerk! Throw it away."
Most of the photos had no notation on them and whatever stories they might have told were lost forever. But amidst the discards was a black and white one of a baby. Maybe six or seven months old. Curt knew instantly who the child was, incipient blond curls already collecting on his head. A weak, innocent smile painted on his lean, pallid face. On the back it read "Our Davey. Healthy again!"

What did that mean? Had his father been sick enough when he was a baby to warrant a caption like this on what should have been a routine photo? Babies shouldn't get sick like that.

"Was Dad seriously sick when he was a little baby, Grandpa?"

"Your dad?" Joe said, not lifting his eyes from the other photos. "Not that I recall. Always healthy as a horse. Ate like one too." He laughed.

That didn't add up. But how would he ever find out? Curt wondered. How could he ever learn something as remote as this about his father? At the age of that baby, his dad couldn't possibly remember himself. Did he even know this fact about himself at all? The memory of whatever it may have been had escaped from his grandfather, the only one left who could even know. Maybe some old hospital records somewhere? Something in one of these boxes? It wasn't fair. Curt felt he was entitled to know. How serious was it? An accident? Infection? Something genetic? Had his dad suffered? How had he survived? Was there fear that he might not? What did those four words mean?

Curt slipped the photo into the pocket of his flannel shirt and then buttoned it tight.

"Okay, so this pile is trash, Grandpa?"

"Yep. Good riddance. I guess."

Curt slid the photos onto his hand then dropped them in the trash bag. Barely a dent in their big job.

"Your dad's not going to be very pleased with our progress when he gets back, Chris," Joe said, glancing at the boxes they hadn't touched yet. Yet he didn't act rushed. He pulled on his cigar again.

"It's okay, Grandpa. We'll get it done. Or maybe we won't. We'll just deal with it however it is." The room was filled with the scent of his cigar, a smell Curt had forgotten how much he loved and missed since they'd moved away and he didn't see his grandfather so much anymore. "I think we're coming back next weekend to move more stuff."

"Gonna be odd, living in a new place after so many years. Surprised myself by setting down roots here. Didn't think that would ever happen."

"What do you mean?"

"Oh, your grandmother and I flitted about. We didn't want possessions, didn't see any permanence left. The world was going to hell anyway. That was in the Sixties. Maybe you've read about them in history class." Joe chuckled. "But then your father came along and we both knew we had different responsibilities. When you become a parent, you see things differently. Take things more seriously. Take the long view. Maybe the world wasn't such a bad place after all. Not with our little Davey in it now. That was one thing we were certain of. So we settled down here and did our best. Your father was like that too, Chris. When you came along, he really buckled down and worked hard to be a good provider. I was always proud of him, Chris, even if he didn't believe me."

Curt wondered what that meant. And whether it was even true. If his grandfather didn't remember his own baby being sick, how could Curt trust him to remember correctly when that same child supposedly buckled down? From what Curt could tell, his father had mostly just muddled along. If that's what buckling down meant, Curt decided he didn't want to be anything like his father.

"I wish you lived closer. I miss my boy. And your mom. And you." He reached across the table and caressed Curt's cheek. Curt felt a sudden warmth and didn't try to hide his smile. And just as suddenly he wondered how he would feel if his father touched him like that. He didn't do that kind of thing anymore.

"You used to live in this house, Chris. When you were a baby. When your folks were just married and poor as church mice. We were a big, happy family then. Do you remember those days?"

"A little bit. I have some memories."

"I can remember it like it was only yesterday."

"The house seemed much bigger back then."

"I guess to a little boy, it must have. I miss those days, Chris. All of us together. It was a good life. I wish you could all come back and live here again like before. We could add some rooms onto the back of the house. We could make it work, and then I wouldn't have to go away."

Was there plaintiveness in the old man's voice, Curt wondered, or was he just imagining it?

"I wish you could come live with us in St. Louis, Grandpa. We could take care of you. It would be like when we all lived here."

"Oh, no. That would never work. Your house is perfect for the three of you. There's no place for a fussy old man to fit in. I'm set in my ways. Plus, how would you sneak in all of your girlfriends with another pair of eyes living there, eh?"

"Remember, Grandpa," Curt said, eager to change the subject. "At the apartment you have to smoke your cigars on the balcony. You can't smoke inside." Curt had put a note in the cigar box that said, "ONLY SMOKE OUTSIDE." Maybe his grandfather would see the note each time and not forget. Curt thought he probably needed to write a great many notes to put around the apartment. More than he could even imagine then. Forestalling the mistakes, the confusion, the accidents. How did his father possibly think this was going to work?

The comfortable quiet of their afternoon was broken by the sound of a truck door slamming in the driveway. David was back from the apartment, ready to collect another load of boxes to deliver there. Curt cringed a little; his dad wasn't going to like what he found in the front room. Not even one of the boxes fully sorted yet. His dad was back too soon, but there wouldn't have been enough time if he'd taken all day.

David stepped in the front door and stopped to survey the wreckage in the room. "Please tell me all of those boxes are finished."

Neither Joe nor Curt spoke. Joe looked away, but Curt watched his father's face, watched as it fell with disappointment. With frustration. With the weight of it all suddenly fallen on his shoulders. Still on his shoulders.

"They're not, are they?"

"No," Curt said, shaking his head. "It's been kind of slow going."

David looked at his father, who had set his cigar in the ashtray and started pawing through the open box before him, as though he could make up quickly what he hadn't done in the last hour.

"Curt!" his father sighed with frustration, with disappointment. No mistaking it. And while David was doing his recalculation of what was left to be done, Curt, stinging from his dad's tone, thought, *You try to do this! You think it's so easy. You don't understand. You don't get it. Any of it. You never do. You never will!* All balm for his wounded pride, for letting down his father, though he would never admit it and didn't even understand that was what he felt.

"I guess we'll have to haul all of this *stuff*" – he hit the word with an emphasis that Curt recognized was as close as his sniveling old man could ever come to an actual strong word, maybe even a curse word, something he'd never, ever heard his dad utter – "to the apartment. We can't leave it here any longer. Stop what you're doing, Curt, and just start hauling these boxes out to the truck."

There was defeat in his voice too. They were trying to do too much in a weekend. Curt had known it. David was beginning to sense it. David, who knew about moving boxes, hadn't worked out the entanglements, hadn't calculated the weight of the memories in all of those boxes and how impossibly heavy that made them.

Curt rose from the chair and stood before the stacks of boxes. Almost a full truck load themselves. One more trip his dad hadn't counted on when he worked out their moving day. But these boxes weren't just inventory in a warehouse, though his dad didn't seem to get that. Like so much. He grabbed two boxes from the floor.

"Curt!" David barked. "Lift with your legs, not your back!"

The boy adjusted his stance. When it's my turn, he thought, I'm just going to sneak out in the night. Me and my socks and my underwear. Not tell him and be long gone, far away, before he even notices. I wonder how long that will take him.

"And just leave them by the tailgate. I'll pack them the way I want them."

Lifting boxes and loading trucks. Great skill set, Dad! No wonder it took you ten years to get promoted out of that warehouse.

Curt bumped backward out the front door and then duck walked down to the truck. Whatever was in the boxes was heavier than he realized, and he could feel his fingers straining to keep a grip. His dad, he knew, could carry four of these at once. Maybe it would be easier, as his dad had said, if he'd worn the gloves he'd handed him that morning. The kind of gloves with rubber palms that they use in the warehouse his dad had worked in for so long. Curt didn't know where they were now. His arms already ached. How many more boxes were there? He hadn't counted, though he was sure his dad knew. That was his thing. Curt set the boxes on the open tailgate and realized suddenly that he had been banished to the heavy lifting because he had failed at the first job assigned to him. He had failed his father at the one thing he was supposed to do.

It was all stupid. His grandfather didn't need to move. He shouldn't move. His memories were in that house. That little house was his hold on life. How did his dad think moving him to an apartment was a good thing? Was going to be any better? Because he didn't have a lawn to mow? Gutters to clean? Couldn't he see it would push Grandpa over the edge? Couldn't he see what was happening to Grandpa? Didn't he care about his father at all?

"It's all stupid," he mumbled as he walked back to the house. "The move is stupid. The boxes. The truck. The apartment. This wasted weekend is stupid. Father most of all. He's probably in the house right now dumping whole boxes in the trash bag without even checking to see what's in them. Throwing his own father's life in the trash."

Curt hurried inside to save more boxes.

DAVID

"Why does he look so angry?"

"He's not angry. He's just focused."

"It looks like his shorts are going to fall off. Are they really that big on him?"

I can't make it to many of Curt's meets, and I don't go to his practices. And by the time he gets home he's already showered and changed. So I rarely see him in his running kit, at least for the meets. But they should give him a better shirt and pair of shorts. Ones that fit.

Part of the course was laid out around the school, and that's where we hoped to see him race past. Kathy figured out if we stood at one spot we could see him, and then if we hustled across the field, we could be farther along the course when he passed there too. My heel spurs didn't approve, but I think we made it in time. I keep looking up the course to spot him, spot his red hair in the pack of boys. They're thinning out now, so I shouldn't miss him. Still, he's one of the smallest on the team. He's easy to overlook.

"When he comes, you can cheer," Kathy tells me. "But don't call out his name. It will just distract him."

I think he asked her to say this. I never played sports in school, so I don't know the right behavior for parents. At the 5Ks and 10Ks he runs with her, it's not for school or really competitive, so I am allowed to holler his name when I see him. He still stays focused then though. Still looks angry. He doesn't give me a wave or smile then either. Sometimes I think he wouldn't even notice if I wasn't here at all.

Chapter Sixteen

Unmet Expectations

The story he told me went like this: his father was the stupidest man on Earth.

Just drop my laundry and go, Father, he growled to himself. "Father" was his handy, arm's-length term for the man, simultaneously deferential and mocking. David had stomped into his room again with his huge feet in his huge work boots.

But his father didn't go. He never did. He just hung around like a big, goofy dog, muttering his inanities, like he wanted to have an adult conversation, but that, Curt had long before concluded, was way beyond him.

"So," David began, Curt's boxers and running shorts in his paw. "Prom's coming up. You haven't told me who you're taking."

That question again.

"Casey," Curt finally said. "You don't know her."

David looked to the corner of the ceiling. Cleared his throat. Curt's stomach clenched; he knew what was coming. "Curt. We've talked about protection. If you need me to –"

"SHE'S JUST A FRIEND!" As though he were going to bang her after the dance, which, he thought, was what his father must have assumed was his plan. Curt didn't want to hear his protection talk again. He knew far more about human biology, he assured himself, than his father ever would.

His father was silenced for a moment, and Curt hoped he was scared off. But he wasn't. Instead, David put Curt's laundry on the bed and then sat on the corner of it. Great, Curt lamented. Another of his visits. He talks, but it was never *about* anything. Just the usual, mostly monosyllabic words and sentence fragments that drool out of his mouth. Can't he see I need to study? But Curt knew the man was too dense. Thus, he always said as little as possible so his father would leave. Please just leave.

"I'm happy that you have your own room, Curt."

That again? Curt thought he would be more happy if it *were* his own room. If his father didn't keep coming in and just sitting on his bed nearly every night in this endless loop of disappointment.

"Yeah, you've said that." He tried turning back to his biology text and opened it to the illustrations on the female reproductive system to scare his father off, but he went on.

"That old sleeping porch you had at the apartment was . . ." he paused. Looked at his feet. Shook his head. His limited vocabulary failing him as always, Curt noted ruefully. "Well, I'm just glad you have a decent room of your own now."

They'd lived in their house for nearly three years and his father *still* brought that up. How does that make someone happy? Curt wondered. He kept his bedroom door closed, but despite that, his father never seemed to take the hint. At least he knocked first. Curt gave him credit for that. But he always wanted in, like he couldn't abide a closed door. Nearly every night. And just talked. As though he wanted to be Curt's big brother rather than his father. Or, Curt remembered, like when he was little and his father would stop and tuck him in most nights before he went to work at the warehouse. I don't need tucking in any longer, Father.

David didn't realize it, but as far as Curt was concerned, he was just a footnote in his son's life now. Curt was certain he'd outgrown him. Fathers should come with expiration dates Curt told his friends. Why was that so hard for the man to see? Usually turning back to his books and pretending he was studying was enough, but sometimes Curt had to tell him to go when his parrying didn't work. Say the actual words. His father was that dense.

Curt had always pounced when his father asked him where he was thinking of going to college. "Away!" he would blurt just to end the conversation. And to watch his father squirm. He'd eventually stopped asking. Pushing him away was easy to do. Before, when he would go out for his long runs on the weekends – always a reliable way to escape his father – he made sure to ask him where the zinc oxide was. "It's for my *nipples*, Father!" And his father would be embarrassed, his face reddened. Curt even hid the tube sometimes just so he could bring it up. David finally got wise and bought several tubes that he put around the house, including one for Curt's room. But if he ever realized Curt was toying with him, he didn't let on.

Curt doubted he did, thinking of all of the ways he could crush his father. Bring home a B on some test and watch him panic. Quit cross-country and track. Start smoking. Get some girl pregnant. He'd probably die. Brooke and some of the other cross-county guys were talking about getting running tattoos when they turned eighteen. His father actually got angry when Curt mentioned that. "Do you want to be that kind of person?" He'd spat out the words. The closest he'd ever come to actually yelling at him that Curt could recall. He never brought it up again, deciding it was a silly idea anyway.

The fact was, his father was almost never upset with him. Sometimes Curt wished he would be. At least that would give him something to react to. Okay, not like Brooke's dad who still hit him sometimes, but a few strong opinions now and then wouldn't be so bad, would show that his father had some backbone. A few arguments. Even a fight. At least that wouldn't be something *embarrassing* to be resentful about. No, instead he had this passive father who hovered in the background and told him how he was the best son a man could have. That got boring after the first thousand times.

He used to come to meets and embarrass Curt by shouting his name and waving as he ran past. Curt asked his mom to tell him to stop. And then, after his run was over, he went back to work instead of sticking around. Brooke's dad never came to meets to embarrass him.

It wasn't even a challenge. Whatever Curt did he praised. Whatever he did made him proud. Pleased. Delighted. He said he bragged about Curt to his friends at work. His grades. His meets. His awards. He was just making a fool of himself the boy thought. He brags about me because he has nothing to brag about himself. Curt certainly didn't talk about his father at school.

Because, the thing was, David didn't know what kind of person Curt was. Curt didn't want him to know. Curt had his own life to live, not his father's. Not some imagined, scripted life he thought his father had for him. He squirmed, fearing that after prom his father would want to hear all about it. The dinner. The dance. The party at Brooke's house. So he could relive when he and his mom went to their prom, Curt guessed. Try to superimpose their experience on his. Or live vicariously through his son's maybe. But that was not going to happen.

His mom was better at understanding him. In the evenings his father liked to brush her hair for her, but Curt knew she hated it. They would sit on the couch, and she'd pretend to watch TV while he dragged the brush roughly through her hair for ten minutes. After a while she'd take the brush out of his hand and tell him she would just finish up, and Curt knew his father must have felt like some great husband or something. Then he stroked her hair with his big paw like he was proud of what he'd done. But he didn't have a clue. He should keep his hands off her. How had she ever ended up with him?

She made all of his decisions for him. It was so obvious. What he wore. What he did on the weekends. What he thought about this or that. How he spent his money. Who he voted for. She led him around by the nose. Or by the dick sometimes. He was pathetic.

Curt had asked her once why she had married *him*. Said she could have done so much better. It was a stupid thing to say, and he realized it as soon as the words came out of his mouth. She'd made a face. There was hurt in it, but she recovered quickly. "Because I love him, Curt." He thought that was the closest he'd ever come to disappointing her. He tried to respect her feelings after that, even if he didn't understand them. But, he'd decided long before, if he hadn't looked so much like her, he'd be sure he was adopted. How could that man be his father?

He had told Curt many times how Kathy was the best thing that ever happened to the both of them. At least, Curt noted, the clueless man got that much right. But that much wasn't enough. He worked at the same place forever. Curt couldn't see that he'd ever taken a single chance at a better life, done anything with even the slightest bit of risk or challenge. He'd always played it safe. Followed the path of least resistance. Always would. If he thought she was so wonderful, why didn't he get a better job so she didn't have to be a bookkeeper in the basement of that stupid bank? Or drive that broken down car? Or take them on some decent vacations? Sure, his Grandpa's cabin was nice, and Curt liked going there. But Six Flags wasn't Disneyworld. Brooke had been to Europe three times already. They went to the Ozarks.

His father just didn't see it. He didn't understand . . . everything. Sometimes Curt wished he did, that he'd say, "I understand, Curt. I'm on your side." What a relief that would be. But he didn't. And he never would. He was too dense. He was too naive. He didn't have the brainpower to be the slightest bit discerning. He frustrated Curt with his embarrassing, uncritical admiration, never seeing the turmoil inside him. Curt was not the same person with his friends as he was around his father.

Curt had told him that one time, in harsh words. His father was trying to kid him about not having a girlfriend.

"YOU DON'T KNOW ME!"

It just came out. He couldn't stop it. His father's face fell. He'd gone too far. But he was tired of the incessant questions, and he'd just had a big fight with Brooke, and he was worried about an upcoming AP biology test. He'd lost control for a second.

His father ran away with his tail between his legs. Curt could see how much it had stung. He felt bad that he'd said that, surprised he had that kind of power over his father. Not long after he'd heard what sounded like crying coming from his parents' bedroom. But his father wasn't crying, Curt had insisted. Dad doesn't cry!

David rose from the bed. Curt guessed he saw they we're not going to have a chat. Not that time. This was when he always leaned in and tried to kiss Curt's forehead.

"I never realized how difficult and confusing life was compared with what I imagined it would be like," David said. Curt didn't know where these new words came from. "It's hard, and ugly, and unfair. I guess we don't get to live the lives we dream of. Maybe we shouldn't have dreams." He'd turned and stepped toward the door.

His father was not the most worldly-wise person. Curt granted him that. As Curt leaned toward his bed to smooth the mussed quilt, he guessed life *would* be tough for a simple man like him.

David stopped and faced his son. He looked him right in the eye.

"But I still feel like the luckiest man in the world to have a boy like you, Curt."

And then he says something decent like that, Curt mused.

But he hadn't kissed him this time.

Curt leaned from his chair and reached to the bookcase beside his desk, taking down an old wedge of red oak. Running his fingers over its smooth places, he tried to remember.

KATHY

They're fighting again. In their odd, quiet way. Davey, who is too mild-mannered and cautious to raise his voice or ever use words in judgment of anyone, and Curt, too aloof and not as smart as he thinks, withdrawing from his father like he does.

I talk to them separately. Each listens, though Curt pretends he already knows what I have to say, and Davey grudges and agrees, and half the time misses my point.

He doesn't know what to make of his independent son. Davey still clings to his father, still turns to him for advice and even comfort. It will be a bitter day when he finally sees that he can't count on that any longer. A bitter day that's coming soon, I think. But even so, Curt doesn't do the same to him. Curt has always been more my son than his. I know Davey sees it, accepts it. He still finds ways to sneak into Curt's life. Their boys-only trips to the cabin mostly, and Curt falls for it, or falls into it. The warm comfort of their idyllic hours spent there together transcends the barriers they've erected between them.

Curt, for his part, thinks he's too grown up to need a father any longer. He has his friends from school, and his grades, and his running. His interests. I guess that's about normal for a boy his age. But he doesn't understand what is burning inside his father. Sometimes I wonder if he realizes his father has a heart beating inside his chest. And I worry that maybe he won't until he has a son of his own. If that day ever comes.

I think they both know better. They know how good the other is. I just wish there wasn't this stupidity between them.

Chapter Seventeen

Special-blest

David sat, waiting. Waiting for Curt to return from track practice. Or waiting for him to call and say that he was going to be even later and that their trip to the cabin, choreographed for this weekend when their two calendars allowed enough free time to make the long drive to and then from worth the trouble, would have to be postponed. The faucet in the kitchen sink beside him dripped slowly, counting out the seconds. Its repair was on David's list of chores, and it seemed likely he would finally get it done that weekend if Curt didn't walk through the door soon.

Even if they left now, he knew, they would arrive in the dark, and though Curt could easily start a campfire by starlight, would he bother? Was it important enough? Or would they just unload the car and then fall straight into bed and let their weekend start in the morning? And if that, why wouldn't they just head out early on Saturday?

Track practice sometimes ran long. David knew this, and he was pleased that Curt was still dedicated to it in these last weeks of high school when he could be coasting like his friends. His grades flawless. His scholarship secure. His eyes bright, focused on college. Pre-med, he plans to declare. Maybe running there too. Or maybe not. Options. Choices. Opportunities. He had them. He'd made them for himself. Seemed to understand earlier than most young people how life worked, and how you worked life. But that was Curt since he was little. Always ahead of the curve. Always ready with some insight or observation or understanding that David had missed. He was grateful nonetheless that his boy was blessed with such things, always ready for whatever next big step was before him.

And so David sat. The car packed, the tank full. A list of cabin chores in mind. Kathy had assured him she would somehow manage through the weekend without her two men knocking about the house, getting in her way. All that remained was for Curt to walk through the door and then they could go. But he would need to change, of course. And he'd want a shower. And maybe something to eat. More minutes would pass, which David didn't resent, but how can you plan for anything with so much out of your control? Yet Kathy would remind him that such were the hazards of living with others, and wasn't it, on balance, worth the trouble? Hadn't it always been? And he would agree, grateful again to receive an understanding that escaped him.

As he waited, an unbidden memory surfaced. His own tardiness before a cabin weekend with his father. Home late from school on the Friday afternoon Joe had taken off work so they could make a full weekend of it. Davey had slunk in the kitchen door, intending to escape his parents' eyes so he could get into the bathroom and somehow patch himself up, hoping that maybe they wouldn't notice.

But Buddy had started barking and scampering when Davey entered, as he always did for his boy, and Joe was soon in the kitchen. Davey knew then that there would be no hiding the facts from his father. Torn shirt, shiner, swollen lip. Davey, it quickly came out for he could never keep anything from his father, had gotten into a fight on his way home from school, and this surprised Joe since he had thought his seventh grader was surely too mature – and too passive – for fighting.

"With Jon? Davey, he's your best friend!"

"He's a jerk, Dad!" the boy burbled past his swollen lip, keeping his good eye on the floor.

"How did he suddenly become a jerk?" He put his hand under Davey's chin and lifted the boy's face, turning it to examine the damage.

Silence, and then, "He said I was scruffy. Said I have my head in the clouds. He said I don't live in the real world."

Not words to fight over, Joe thought, but little Davey was needing more reassurance lately that he was as good as any other boy his age. His struggle with his schoolwork. Small circle of friends. No good at sports. Intimidated by girls. His body beginning to change. That whole fraught stew of otherwise normal boys on the cusp of their teens. Yet for Davey it seemed more of a struggle than it ought to be.

Joe used a dishcloth to clean Davey's face and then began filling a bag of ice for his spreading black eye. "Well, go put on a clean shirt and then let's get you out of here before Mom gets home. Those fish aren't going to catch themselves!"

Davey's relief was instant. He had expected to be grounded for fighting, to have their weekend cancelled, expected at the very least to suffer the weight of his father's disappointment, yet found the cabin trip still unfolding before him. He didn't understand yet, as his father did, the curative powers of a weekend in the woods.

"Besides, I want to get down to the cabin so I can find out what I've forgotten to pack this time!" said Joe. Davey giggled because it was true. And then Joe joined him. He always forgot something. But mostly it just felt good to laugh with his dad, to know their friendship was unchanged. And now, years later, David could still feel that surge of relief he had felt then.

Outside, a car door slammed, pulling David out of his reverie. Curt's voice, indistinct yet hearty, calling something before the car drove away. He came in the front door, and David heard his track bag fall to the floor. But when Curt turned the corner into the kitchen, David saw, for the briefest moment, surprise and then alarm on the boy's face. He knew then that Curt had forgotten about their weekend. But the boy recovered quickly, darting to the refrigerator to peer inside and hide his face until he could remake it.

"Let me just throw some stuff in a bag and I'll be ready to go. Is the car packed?"

"Yep. Whenever you're ready, we can leave. Don't you want a shower first?"

"No. I'm good. Just give me a second."

So the boy was home and, though he would never willingly show it, contrite for his forgetfulness. Soon enough they would be on the road and then whatever adventures awaited them in the forest would come and they would find a balance, maybe even a return to an earlier, easy warmth that sometimes still slipped past Curt's normal, possibly for one of the last times before he raced off to college and embarked on new changes, changes that David would be, increasingly, only a distant part of. Changes that would make Curt even more unknowable. Inevitable, yes. Natural. Expected. Even hoped for. But no less wrenching.

And so, off. Curt held his father at bay during the drive by studying from his advanced biology textbook for as long as the daylight lasted and then slouching in his seat and closing his eyes. David couldn't tell if the boy was asleep or just pretending, but either way, he didn't venture many words. At least there didn't seem to be any hostility in Curt's guardedness, David thought. There never was. Not yet at least. It was just the protective distance the boy seemed intent on maintaining for some reason David couldn't fathom. Maybe most boys became like this with their fathers, he considered, though he didn't think he'd ever been that way with his own dad. Or if he had, that he could have sustained it for long.

When the car left the paved road and began bumping over the gravel washboard that led to their tiny cabin, Curt roused and blinked into the gathering darkness. "Good to be back," the boy said, and David heard sincerity in his words. "I never realize how much I miss this place until I'm back." He rolled down his window and took in a deep, sharp breath of the oak-scented forest. The cool air swirled inside the car, refreshed now after stagnating during the drive. Curt said, though not especially to David, "Did you know that nostalgia used to be considered a medical condition? A form of melancholy. Now we call melancholy depression, and nostalgia is considered a good thing. Shows we have feelings."

More words all at once, David realized, than Curt had uttered the entire drive down. And not, he thought, words intended to show off his knowledge or to toss some baffling complexity toward his father, as he might have done some other time, but simply an honest, unguarded reaction to being back in their woods, spoken in the boy's own vocabulary.

When the headlights washed over the cabin, Curt tossed his textbook into the back seat and unbuckled his belt. He climbed out of the car and stood in the gathering darkness, letting his eyes adjust.

"I'll get all of this," David said, grabbing the first of their weekend gear from the trunk. "See if you can get a fire going. I'm hungry."

"What's for dinner?"

"Burgers. Chips. The usual."

Curt got to work, even giving himself permission to use several matches to start the fire since the daylight was nearly gone, but then he managed a one-match fire anyway. Soon his flames were pushing back the darkness, and Curt selected larger pieces of seasoned split oak from the rack to turn into glowing embers as soon as he could so they could throw the burgers on the grill long enough to be called cooked and they could eat.

David came from the cabin with a can of beer in one hand and a 7 UP in the other, which he handed to Curt. The boy stopped feeding the fire and took the pop. Then the two of them watched the dancing flames in a comfortable silence. David standing. Curt kneeling in the gravel. In the darkness around them the chirring forest was tuning up.

"We need to add another ring of blocks around this fire pit, Father. The ash is getting deep."

"We can go into Osceola tomorrow and get some at the hardware store, if you want."

"How much of that old fence from the back yard has gone into this fire?"

"Most of it, I think."

When they'd moved to their St. Louis house years before, the picket fence that the previous owners had raised around the back yard to contain their many children and dogs was rotting and falling apart. David had dismantled it and stacked the pieces mostly out of sight as he hauled portions to the cabin each trip to burn in the fire ring. Curt had scoffed at his plan originally, noting that David could have disposed of the fence faster through their weekly trash pickup, but then he realized that all of the nails from the rotten pickets were mixed with the ash of the fire ring, adding their words to the stories that were accumulating there, and something about that had pleased him.

So much ash from countless, countless fires. How many fires over how many years? Curt wondered as he watched the flames. All of his own life, certainly. And all of his dad's life too, as far as he knew. Did it go back before then? He'd have to ask his mom about it when they got home.

"The logs I split have seasoned too long," David said, following his own musings. "A lot are punk now. Make too much ash, not enough heat. Make a mess in the wood stove, too, but I don't think we'll be needing that tonight."

His father's woodcraft, Curt conceded. His own specialized expertise, without broad application, certainly, but well suited to the needs and interests of the simple man who acquired it.

"We should burn as much of that rotted wood as we can and be rid of it."

"Why do I see a session with the sledge and wedge ahead of me this weekend?"

David laughed. "To split new firewood? Maybe not. We don't burn it fast enough anymore. I guess there's still plenty of decent wood on the rack for future fires." And then, "Whenever those happen."

The fire slowly burned down to coals, and when there were enough, David shoveled them under the grill. Once the burgers were sizzling, Curt began stoking his original fire again, careful not to stir ash into the air to fall on their food, renewing the flames and the light while David tended their dinner.

Curt had always found fire building satisfying. It was the one task at the cabin that he could do better than his father. An oddball skill, he knew, but his own. Not that he felt competitive with his father, he assured himself. That wasn't a fair fight. But this one skill felt good anyway.

David left Curt before the fire and went into the cabin to get the rest of their dinner, balancing a tray of buns, paper plates, burger fixings, and a bag of chips. He flipped the burgers on the grill a final time then returned to the cabin again to fetch another beer for himself and a 7 UP for Curt. In the near darkness, a barred owl called nearby.

With dinner now in hand, the two settled in their chairs on opposite sides of the fire, the vagaries of the forest breezes likely to cause one or both to move later to get out of the smoke but good for now as they ate their burgers and fed chips into their mouths.

And this, David thought, sitting across from his pride and joy, was sufficient. One of those infrequent perfect moments that he'd learned to watch for. He no longer got out to the cabin as often as he had in the past, especially as a boy when it seemed like every other weekend meant a visit and what felt like whole summers were spent there. And yet, he came to understand, the infrequency of his visits now made the times when he did come down even more special. Nor could he speak his praise, his love for Curt as much as he did when the boy was younger, knowing how Curt would dismiss it, chafe at its easy overuse. On the verge of manhood, he'd lost the fleshy, open face of a boy and here, in the firelight, had sharper features. A better face for hiding behind. Thus David's words had to be well judged and well timed so the message, always heartfelt, always sincere, got through.

"Want another beer, Dad?"

"Sure."

Curt rose and disappeared into the darkness toward the cabin, returning a few moments later with a cooler that he set down in the gravel beside his chair. He'd also pulled on a flannel shirt, the one that was always at the cabin, left hanging on a nail beside the bed. The thing probably needed to be taken home and washed, David thought. It surely held a lot more smells than just woodsmoke, but if it did, Curt didn't appear to mind at the moment.

"Seemed easier than going back and forth. Here, catch." Across the flames he tossed his dad a beer and then sat in his chair, reaching into the cooler for himself.

David let the can settle before opening it, gazing into the glowing embers, watching the orange light change as the air passed over, as blue flames licked up briefly before dying. Embers soon to be ash. Embers to be mused over. And he did.

"Tie that knot ten times in a row," Joe had told him that long-ago weekend, "and you'll never forget it." Davey was puzzled; his dad hadn't brought up the fight he'd had with Jon – not on the drive down and not at all as they busied themselves about the cabin – and instead taught him how to tie a square knot. "A useful skill for a boy to have." And that seemed true, but when, Davey worried, would his dad want to discuss his fight with Jon? Surely he needed to tell his boy that fighting was wrong. That it was childish. That he was disappointed in him. And then his dad would find out.

Yet it hadn't come up. Instead his dad made a big show of burning a broken wooden ladder in the fire, a true spectacle to Davey more used to tossing scrap lumber into the flames. By Saturday evening, Davey began to worry. How bad was it going to be when it finally happened? Was his dad going to yell at him? Make him cry? Punish him somehow?

Davey fidgeted through dinner and before the campfire as they waited for a whippoorwill to call. He practiced tying the square knot to keep his hands busy, though he had long since mastered it. Finally, when he could stand it no longer, he brought it up.

"Dad, I lied."

"Oh?" Joe didn't look up from the flames.

"About fighting with Jon."

Davey didn't understand that his father's long silence about the subject was intended all along to draw out the boy, to cause him to start, on his own terms and when he was ready, the conversation they needed to have.

"You never need to lie to me, Davey. No matter what."

If his dad said that to make him feel better, Davey thought, it didn't work. It just made it harder for him to tell the truth. Harder to find the right words to say, which was always his problem. How to say what he was thinking, what he was feeling, without sounding stupid because he barely knew himself.

Davey lifted Buddy onto his lap and scratched behind his ears. The dog had been fearful and stuck by him all evening after hearing some coyotes howling on the other ridge earlier. "Jon didn't say those things about me."

"No?" He prodded the coals with a stick. "They why did you fight with him?"

And here his courage failed Davey. He didn't know how to say what he needed to.

Joe waited, knowing the difficulty his son had with words. The campfire crackled before them. The forest was abuzz around them.

"Because he said those things about you, Dad!"

"About me?" It was not a surprise that Jon would say such things; it was his father who obviously had first. Jon was merely parroting them. Joe assumed that man probably thought such things – their few encounters in the past were always uncomfortable – but that he would say them aloud, in front of his son, surprised Joe. More surprising, however, was that if Davey would fight at all, it would be for his dad's honor. Where did that come from? Except that he knew after a moment. Knew the deep-seated impulse triggered in his boy, strong enough to send his fists flying.

"Davey, fighting is always wrong."

"No it isn't, Dad."

Another surprise. Assertiveness in his timid son. A good sign, he thought.

"He said mean things about you, Dad," the boy said to the flames. "He made me mad."

"Davey, we're made of stronger stuff than a few silly words can hurt," Joe said, winging it. "We're like oaks, not like willows. You can't let words get you mad enough to hurt another person."

Davey sat silently, confronted by his father's contradiction.

"So I'm just supposed to let Jon say mean things about you?" "I don't mind being called scruffy. I kind of like it. Means I'm not stuck in some box like most people in the world." Like Jon and his father, though Joe didn't say that. Maybe this was more information than the boy was ready to absorb, he thought. "Anyway Davey, it's always wrong to fight." Yet he wondered what Jon looked like after their scrape. Would there be a call coming from his parents? Was it possible that Peg was at home at that moment fielding the call, unaware of what had happened?

"Maybe when you see Jon at school on Monday, you can tell him you still want to be his friend and put this business behind you both. Sound like a good idea?"

"I guess." If his dad said it, it had to be right. And then, "Thanks, Dad."

Around this very fire ring, decades past. The ashes of that long-ago campfire beneath the many that came after it, reaching from that past to this present between David and his own son now.

Embers dying because their evening was nearly finished. Soon to bed and then to whatever the new day in the woods held for them.

Their spoken words had been sporadic after they finished their burgers and a different kind of conversation ensued.

As Curt had intended, David noticed that instead of pulling another 7 UP from the cooler, Curt had fetched himself a beer instead. He'd set the can on the arm of his chair with the label turned so that David could see it clearly in the orange light.

David was not so naïve as to assume his boy was innocent of the world. There was a time when the boy's whole world stretched no farther than the edge of the blanket they'd spread on the floor for him. But that didn't last, nor should it have. The crunch of his Big Wheel on their gritty sidewalk took him farther. Then his big-boy bike. Soon enough came school and friends and running and his other own interests. And always, the cabin and the hundred acres of forest. His world inevitably expanded, culminating most recently in his spring break trip to Italy with Brooke and his parents. The last time David had seen that boy, he was sporting a pair of earrings. Still, he seemed like a good, levelheaded influence on Curt. A brother he never had.

David had watched as Curt drank the beer without flinching, telling him it was not the first the boy had tasted. Nor would he have expected that either. Curt's flirtation with adulthood was like everything else he attempted: measured but successful, and nearly always private. He would drink a few beers intended to show that he was sensible as well as experienced, both as a way to set his father at ease and to assert himself.

But it was that second part that bugged David. Curt clearly, though subtly, was trying to challenge him. Was it to show he was throwing off the shackles of his childhood and his father's expectations of him? he wondered. Why would he feel that was necessary? They'd never restrained him, always supported him. Was Curt trying to provoke him? Set up a fight? Surely not at the cabin where they valued most of all the peace it gave. One of the last bits of common ground between the two of them. Or was that something Curt was trying to shake off too? Curt's face showed deep shadows in the flickering firelight.

Unsure what he was expected to do, David broke the silence by changing the subject.

"Mom says you might not be running track at Mizzou after all."

And so Curt was stymied. His big statement, his assertion that he was no longer a child, not much longer subject to his parents' rules and expectations, was not missed but *dis*missed by his father's question. For surely it was a question. And maybe not as clueless as Curt might have judged in the past. His father was probing into a different part of his son's personal life. A part Curt hadn't wanted to discuss with him until it was settled, until he knew for himself.

For running was something his gimpy father couldn't do. It was Curt's alone. The solitary sport that was perfect for his ranging thoughts and endless confusion that also distinguished him from his father. Allowed a kind of protective distance that the man could never span.

Curt had long since understood – or believed, he was never sure – that his father lived through him. He knew his father had faced a life circumscribed by the limitations of his intellect and the opportunities that left him and looked to his son for vicarious achievement, for a world he didn't get to live in. The man had never even been outside of Missouri as far as Curt knew. His father was static; he'd reach the point where he wasn't able to change. He had no surprises left. Curt guessed it was natural that he'd want to know about every success his son had. But he wasn't supposed to look too closely.

Which was why, in part, Curt held his father at arm's length. It wasn't just about privacy, he told himself, though there was that; it was also possession. Curt felt entitled to his own life without a requirement to share it, or at least certain parts of it, if he didn't want to. Some things weren't supposed to come out now.

"Don't make too much of this, Father," he began, then pulled on his beer as punctuation. "I just want to make sure I have the academics under control before I commit myself too broadly."

"A smart boy like you? I'm sure you can find the right balance."

Exactly the kind of fawning thing he expected his father to say. Now he just needed to leave it at that. But he didn't.

"I respect your choice, Curt."

Words Curt didn't think he would ever hear. His dad, who never understood anything, who mostly had to have every simple thing explained to him and then only got the rudiments, saying he respected his choice? Did he even understand what he was saying? What the implications were?

Yet he didn't seem to want to pursue the point. A big deal, a huge, huge change in his son's life, and he was just leaving it alone? He had been certain there was going to be a long conversation about it when his father learned of the decision. About missing an important opportunity, an urge to reconsider.

David stared into the embers, quietly winking out to signal the end of their evening. Curt stared at his dad, his face fading into the darkness, quietly perplexed by him. What was this man capable of? When he'd gotten home that afternoon and saw his dad sitting on the chair in their tiny kitchen, Curt's heart had sunk. He'd forgotten about their planned weekend. He'd gone over to Brooke's house after practice and they had talked about Italy, about college, about all of the comfortable subjects they shared. He'd showered in Brooke's bathroom. And then, when he finally got home, he realized what he'd done to his dad. How could he have forgotten?

Should I apologize to Father? Explain my mistake? Open the door a little?

Curt took another long pull of his beer, and then he spoke.

"I wonder why we haven't heard the whippoorwill tonight?"

And David thought that he might come out. There was still time.

CURT

"Are there more like you at home?"

Once again, I'd gone off topic, babbling about my past rather than preparing for my future. I think she's deliberately trying to draw me out. "No," I answer as flatly as I can. Just as well that my father never contributed to the gene pool again. Another offspring might have been more his issue than Mom's. Lightning wasn't likely to strike twice. But talking about high school and my life then and all that was a slip; she must think I'm bragging.

I'd agreed to these study sessions because Shannon is smart and because I have to do really well. All I've done till now, my grades, AP classes, cross-country and track, volunteering with the SPEDs, even my scholarship, seems insignificant, commonplace when I hear myself talk about it. Just your typical high achiever who's now in the deep end of the college pool. Dad taught me to swim in our lake, but he can't help here. All his years at night school, taking whatever classes were offered, piecing together enough passing grades to get a degree finally. Good for him, but it's not the same for me.

Studying is over for now. I'll give it a go later in my room. Sometimes this carrel gets claustrophobic. And Shannon wants to joke around. She's being flirty for some reason.

"I need to get in a couple of miles before it gets dark," I tell her. "Then get a shower." I straighten my notes and gather my books. Grab my backpack from the floor.

"I could run with you."

"Thanks, but I mostly run by myself these days. Get lost inside my head. It's cheap therapy." I hope she hears my joking tone. I don't need a running buddy too.

Chapter Eighteen

Father's Day

The impossible weight of his emptiness would not let David sleep. He wanted to remember what happiness was like, but long days had passed since he'd felt any. He rolled to his side and punched his pillow. He groaned and rubbed his eyes.

They were in the bed that had been Kathy's since the time she had graduated from a crib, in the room that had been hers until the day she moved in with him. The room her mother had preserved unchanged since that day when she had left so abruptly. Preserved at first with the belief that Kathy would soon return and then as a memory to the girl she had lost.

David had never been in Kathy's bed, not even in high school when they were sneaking around for any bed they could find. And now, after twenty years of marriage, he felt guilty being there, as though Kathy's mother were going to crash through the door any moment.

Yet this innocent guilt wasn't what left him restless, what wouldn't let him sleep. His yawning emptiness came from understanding that he felt alone in the world. Married to a woman who loved him unreasonably. Father to a son who didn't. But most urgently, son to a man who no longer knew him.

He had cried in the car after he'd left his father the evening before. Cried without reserve as he hadn't since he'd been a little boy. Cried that way *because* he hadn't since he'd been a little boy. Years of resolve were shoved roughly aside. The strength he thought he had, had collapsed before his anguish. He sat in the parking lot and surrendered to what had been building within him for years. His denial could no longer stand. The desperate hope he'd clung to was lost. He would never again see the man who was his father. The skin that had contained the man who once guided his life now held someone else. Someone less. Someone who did not remember him. And never would.

He had cried until he was empty of tears. He wiped his cheeks with his fingers then put on a stony face and drove back to Kathy's mother's house. He declined dinner, retreating instead to Kathy's foreign bedroom and bed, and to his own shell, the one he had unwittingly been building for himself through the years.

Kathy knew. She understood much of what was happening and did her best to explain it to her mother. Slowly, with carefully chosen words, trying to humanize the man she had married whom her mother had never fully accepted. Kathy had lost her father too, but that had been years before, when Curt was still a baby. His heart had given out, a heart she feared he no longer had after the way he had treated Davey. But that was in the past, and her love now focused on her husband, who was losing his own father. When Kathy climbed the stairs later that evening, she found David already in bed, possibly asleep, with the sheet pulled over his head and gripped in his fist. She'd undressed quietly in the dark then slipped in beside him, kissing his shoulder, which was the only part of him she dared reach.

His fitful stirrings would not cease; sometime in the night, Kathy had said simply, "Tell me."

And then the words flowed. Like the tears, his pent-up words flowed without caution or consideration, spilling into the dark room.

"Dad's gone, Kathy. He doesn't know me anymore. Before I at least saw little glimpses of him. Little things I recognized. He used to know my name. 'Davey' he'd call me. Like when I was a boy. But not anymore. He doesn't know me. He thought I was a doctor. He's gone, Kathy, but he never said good-bye."

David sat up, crossing his legs and resting his arms on them. His head hung before his bare chest. Kathy rose beside him and tentatively rested her hand on his arm. He didn't flinch, so she left it there.

"He was the most important person in my life, Kathy. My first friend. My best friend. Always there when I needed him. Wanted him. He helped me understand things. I remember, he always said that life was messy, but the important thing was how you dealt with it. All my life I've tried to be like him. As good and hard-working and, I don't know, as, as solid as him. I loved Dad every second of my life. I still love him. But he's gone now. I don't understand life anymore. I want my dad."

David's words came in bursts and stutters. He did not cry, not because it would shame him before his wife, but because he had no tears left. Kathy let him speak as the words came to him.

"I miss him so much, Kathy. I sat across from him. I shaved him. I lathered his face and I cut off his stubble. I wanted to find someone I recognized underneath it. Didn't work. His hands kept curling into fists. I'd straighten his fingers, and they'd curl again. He paid our bills with those hands! His strong, gentle hands. Now they're useless." He gave a bitter laugh. "They're supposed to brush his teeth every day at that place, but I don't think they'd done it for a week. I did it for him. He started drooling then. I had to wipe away his spit so it wouldn't drip on his pajamas. I think if they'd known I was coming, they might have cleaned him up a little. Maybe cleared all of the plates of dried food off his table. His glasses are gone. His sheets obviously hadn't been changed in a long time. His pajamas smelled so bad. He's in diapers now. I don't know how long they let him sit in them. It all stinks like piss there. It's a horrible place. That's why you can't go with me. Damn it, Kathy! I can't afford anything better, but where I've left him is awful. I'm ashamed. I'm a terrible son."

No, you're not, thought Kathy, but she held her words so that his words would flow.

"I thought the world ended when Mom died. I thought nothing could be as bad as that. But it's even worse losing Dad like this. I keep losing him every minute. Every time I see him, and he doesn't know who I am, I lose him again." David punched the mattress. "Moving him out of the old house, into that apartment. That was what did it! I should never have made him do that. He lost his grip then. And we moved away. I shouldn't have taken that St. Louis job, Kathy! I ran away from my parents. I'm a horrible son."

Kathy touched her fingers to his lips. For now, maybe, he'd said enough.

"You're not, Davey, I know this is hard in so many ways. I know it hurts. But none of it is your fault. You didn't run away from him, and you're doing all that you possibly can for him. Your dad wouldn't want you to feel guilty. Or ashamed. You know that too, Davey. He'd want you to be the strong man you've always been. You *are* like your father in that way. In so many ways."

David was silent for a moment. He plucked at the bed sheet, and then, without turning to Kathy, he mumbled, "Curt moved away too. As soon as he had the chance. Because he hates me. I might as well admit it."

"He went to college, Davey. That's what boys do after high school. It doesn't mean they hate their fathers."

"He left because he saw how his own dad had cut out. I think abandoning our fathers must be what Clark boys do, Kathy."

"Curt hasn't abandoned you. Why do you say that?"

"Kathy, he made sure I knew he was going away to college when he was a *freshman* in high school. He told me over and over. He worked it out with your mom to pay for it before he even knew where he would go. He wanted out that bad."

"He didn't want out. He wanted to go to college. We wanted him to go. Davey, Curt loves you."

"No, he doesn't. You gave me a beautiful son, Kathy. And I've driven him away. I've lost him. I screwed that up too. It hurts, Kathy. It hurts. And I don't know how to make it stop."

Kathy knew there was a core of boyhood still in her man. She loved this about him. How he could be spontaneous and uninhibited. How he could laugh sometimes without reserve. Love without reserve. But he also often held boyish expectations. She could see that her man, who was still a boy, now felt like an orphan.

"You haven't driven Curt away, Davey. Don't say things like that."

David was shaking his head, not believing her. Not sure of much anymore, but sure of that.

"He hates me because I don't make a lot of money. Because I don't have an important job like the dads of all of his friends. He's embarrassed by me, Kathy. And he's right. Look. We live in a tiny house in, in Richmond Heights! That's the best I can do for us. Richmond Heights!"

"We have friends in Richmond Heights. Our home is in Richmond Heights. We've had good lives there. Happy lives."

"I can't take care of the father I love, and I can't win the love of my son. Maybe it was wrong all those years, Kathy. Not having another child. Maybe we could have had a girl for you. Maybe I could have been a good father for her."

Her words were not comforting him. His torment, his doubt was too much. She could see this. No amount of evidence to the contrary was going to change his mind in his dark place. He needed to ease himself out of it as he always did when he faced his self-doubt. He needed to stop thinking about it. To rest. To heal slowly.

"Try to sleep, Davey. In the morning we can talk about this if you want. Just rest your mind right now." Rest your heart and soul.

David threw himself onto the pillow, obedient to his wife's instructions as he always was. But doubtful, nonetheless. He threw his arm across his face and tried to drift into the solace of oblivion. Kathy sat over him for a little longer, looking at the man she loved who was out of reach across the chasm of his anguish. When she laid herself down beside him again and put her hand on his chest, she felt his even breathing and knew that the sleep he needed had come.

When David woke in the morning, the sun was already in the sky, shining through the bedroom window and filling the space with clean light. They had to drive back to St. Louis, and even though he had taken off that Monday, he hated a late start.

Kathy was already dressed and putting things in her suitcase.

"I'm late," he said, not quite awake. He rested on one elbow and rubbed his hand across his face.

"You needed to sleep, Davey, so I didn't wake you. I went to Mass with Mom while you slept." Kathy deftly folded a blouse and slipped into her suitcase. "She said she prayed for your dad."
Prayed for Dad. Why not? He certainly didn't think his own pitiful efforts were doing any good.

"We'll be late getting home."

"We have all day, Davey. We don't need to rush. Take a long shower. Give yourself some time."

Kathy drove, telling him to sit back and try to sleep. He needed to turn off his brain. He would fret about his dad as long as he was awake, so she wanted him to sleep and get more distance from this worst Father's Day of his life. He needed to get home and back to his routine. He needed to heal.

An hour into their drive, David stirred. He blinked in the sunlight and sat forward with confusion.

"This isn't the way home."

Kathy smiled. "I'm taking a little detour, Davey."

"You're going to the cabin."

"I thought you'd like to see it. When's the last time you were out there?"

He wondered if she remembered the way. He hadn't been there in months, but for her it was years. She had never fully shared his love for the cabin. Never insisted on coming along for any of the many, many "boys only" weekends he'd spent there with his dad and with Curt.

But she knew where she was going, made the proper turns at the proper country crossroads, and easily found the tortuous gravel track that wended through Ozark hill and valley for several miles before finally reaching the little family cabin her father-in-law had built.

She stopped the car on the gravel parking pad, which was giving itself over to weeds. A branch had fallen against the cabin, and Davey had hurried out of the car and headed over to muscle it away.

"No damage," he said, easing the branch from the steel roof it had rested against and dragging it over to the fire ring. "Firewood I don't have to cut."

Kathy stepped from the car. The place looked scruffier than she remembered. Scruffier than the memory that her infrequent visits had led her to expect. Disuse was surrendering the place back to the forest that surrounded it. Everywhere the gravel paths were being overtaken with scrub. A vine was creeping up the side of the cabin. A great spider web hung from the porch ceiling. A phoebe had built her mud nest under the eaves. Nature always wins.

But Davey had come alive. She saw the beginnings of a smile on his face, in the straightening of his back. The vitality that seemed sapped from him was returning.

"This place needs some love," he said, yanking stalks of weeds from the ground as he crossed the gravel beside the cabin. "Maybe Curt and I can come out."

With no picnic cooler or weekend bag to unload, Kathy stood aside and watched her husband as he strode from fire ring to woodpile to porch stairs, pausing before each and summoning memories she could never hope to know. The bright greens of spring were maturing to deeper tones now. The unceasing choir of birds was welcoming him back. David looked toward the lake the longest, sparkling in the June sunlight as dragonflies patrolled its surface. His father had taught him to swim there. He had taught Curt in turn. They had splashed about with childlike abandon, had washed away the grit of uncounted days in that water before sitting at an equal number of campfires. And then fell shamelessly, victoriously into the soft, shared bed of the cabin for a sleep well earned.

David bounded onto the porch and reached into his pocket for the key that had never left his ring despite his infrequent visits. He opened the cabin door and stepped in briefly before emerging with a broom. He took a few swipes overhead at the spider webs then turned his attention to the porch floor, jabbing into the corners to break free the accumulations of leaves and forest droppings.

"What would Dad think if he saw it like this?"

But he paused then, having uttered the wrong words and summoned the wrong memories.

David's eyes were cast to the floor, the broom checked mid swing. With a sudden cry, he threw the broom into the scrub beyond the porch and sank into the old chair, his face in his hands, his shoulders slumped. He had found more tears within him.

"Dad is never coming back to his cabin."

Kathy eased herself onto the arm of the chair and wrapped her own arms around him. Her act of healing was not working as she had hoped.

"The only time I can ever remember really fighting with Dad," David said into the hands that held his face, "was about the cabin. I never told you, Kathy."

He turned and looked into her green eyes, his need to confess in that moment greater than the shame that had held his words in check for twenty years.

"When we first moved to the apartment – remember? – and we could barely pay our bills on what I was making, he had wanted to sell the cabin and the hundred acres and give us the money so you and me and Curt could have better lives."

He looked into her eyes for as long as he could bear it, fearful of her reaction to a decision he'd made for them decades before that he'd never told her about because he never wanted her to know. Then he looked away, toward the lake below them.

"I *yelled* at Dad, Kathy. I still can't believe it. I'm so ashamed. I yelled at him and told him he could *not* sell his cabin. Not because of me and what I had done."

What *we* had done, Kathy corrected, but only in her thoughts. It was clear that David needed this release, needed to let more of his anguish pour forth, and though she'd never had confirmation, she had long ago surmised something of this exchange between David and his father.

"I wasn't thinking of your best interests then, Kathy. Or Curt's. I just couldn't let Dad give up this cabin he had built with his own hands."

"We've had a wonderful life, Davey."

But David couldn't hear her. "Now I have to do to him what I wouldn't let him do for me."

He rose suddenly from the chair and stepped to the porch railing, his hands gripping it both to steady himself and as though to seize the cabin and never to let go.

"I have to sell Dad's cabin to pay for his care that I can't afford on my own."

After his father had moved to the small apartment, they had sold his tiny, outdated house for whatever they could get, eager to have it off their hands. That money had disappeared fast. They'd still had some of his mother's medical bills to pay off. And it never seemed that his father's retirement money, or his Social Security, or even Medicare now, was enough to pay for his care. Or the doctor.

Or all of the medicines. David was strapped each month to pay his father's bills.

Kathy had long understood that their childhoods had ended in that cabin, that their adult lives had begun there much sooner than they should have. Yet even with that intimately shared experience, the very core of their lives together, she also knew that much of Davey's life had happened there that she would never share or know.

Maybe it had been wrong of her all those years to avoid the cabin. The heat. The cold. The bugs. The grit and grime. Curt and Davey would come home from their cabin weekends with a load of laundry, they'd ring the bathtub, their skin that would itch for days, and they would chatter about the adventures they'd had, with an unbounded eagerness to return. She let her two boys have their fun. She *wanted* them to have their fun. But it was a boy's kind of fun, and it was with a feigned eagerness that she took herself along when they had begged her two or three times each year. Maybe, she thought, she should have taken a larger part in this thing that meant so much to her husband.

David had stood silently at the porch rail, staring down at the lake. Kathy stepped over and stood behind him, slipping her hands up under his shirt and gliding them across the skin of his ribs to rest atop his chest. She felt his body shudder.

"How about a swim," she whispered in his ear.

He half turned to her, surprised.

"I didn't bring a swimming suit."

"We don't need them."

"We?"

"It's supposed to be the most natural thing in the world. At least that's what my husband and son have told me."

"Skinny-dipping? You?"

Kathy nodded, hoping her smile looked genuine. The smile in David's eyes told her it did.

She led him into the cabin and began unbuttoning his shirt. He obliged her by pulling her top over her head. But a slow, seductive easing from their clothes wasn't sufficient for Davey, and he quickly stepped back to hop on one foot then the other as he tugged off his shoes and socks. Down came his jeans and as he turned to toss them on the bed, Kathy looked at her man in his cotton briefs as though for the first time. Boy's underpants that he had never outgrown. Underpants she had seen him in thousands of times, that she had washed and dried and put in is drawer. And yet she wanted to touch the soft, personal fabric then, to nurture this moment of unguarded intimacy.

But he had slithered out of them as well and was ready to swim while she was still mostly dressed.

Somehow she managed to get undressed as he waited, the eagerness in his eyes more intent as the seconds passed. But the walk down the stone steps to the lake remained, and her courage faltered.

Someone's cotton flannel shirt hung on a nail nearby, and she pulled it on to wear down to the water. Davey seemed to understand because he didn't object or even take notice. Instead, he took her hand and guided her out the door, across the porch, and carefully down the old stone steps, brushing away the acorns and twigs and bits of gravel with his bare foot before allowing her to descend to each.

At the water's edge he led her past the cattails to the spot when the ground sloped gently into the lake, the easiest access aside from diving off the teetering dock. They stood in water up to their ankles, and Davey slowly slid the flannel shirt from Kathy's shoulders and tossed it onto a small sumac. She smiled, at once nervous and excited, feeling much as she had all those years before when they had visited the cabin together that first time. With his fingertip, Davey traced the freckles on her pale chest, just as he did during their love play.

His torment was far from his mind at that moment. His body ached to float freely in the water, to use his muscles to pull himself forward, to dive beneath, to splash and play and feel alive. He was a child again. They were children again. Without worldly cares for the moment. With only each other and the warm sun and the cool water. And together they played that way for a long time.

Later, up at the cabin, they poked about for towels to dry themselves but found none. Davey proposed air drying in the chairs on the porch, using time that earlier in the day had been urgently needed for the drive home. Kathy, instead, used the flannel shirt to dry herself as much as she could.

He had been collecting his scattered clothes slowly, hoping to let his skin dry for a little longer before he pulled them on, when Kathy rose from the edge of the bed and turned down the quilt.

"Davey."

He dropped his clothes in a heap on the floor and made it over to Kathy in two strides. He lifted her abruptly, and she laughed, they both laughed, then he lay her down gently on the bed, curling in beside her in a moment later.

After Davey had fallen asleep, his head resting on her chest, Kathy stroked his tight blond curls. The scene of the crime, she thought. Only it hadn't seemed like that then. And not a moment since. She wondered if Davey remembered their first time in that bed so long ago. When they were so young. When Davey had become a father himself. She wondered if he could ever forget.

"Let your troubles pass into me," she whispered. "I will always help you bear them."

KATHY

The math doesn't work. It hasn't for a couple of years, but I'd been able to hide it from Davey, protect him from the hard truth. But no more. The cost of Joe's care is bleeding us dry.

Early on we talked about various solutions. Putting Joe in Curt's old bedroom, but then where would Curt go when he came home? And who would care for Joe while we were at work? Hire a nurse to come in? It was obvious that we aren't skilled for the care he needs. It's pretty much constant. Even the littlest things he can't do for himself.

Most of all, though, I didn't want Davey to constantly see his father in this state, to have a daily reminder. In part because it would grind him down but also because I think the more he saw it, the harder he would try to deny it. He'd plunk Joe down in front of the television in the evening and try to joke and chat and pretend things weren't as bad as they are. And then in his private moments, be crushed by unrelenting reality.

So the care home we could never afford, and now we have to face facts. Davey reached the realization on his own, sparing me the need to speak the words. Some part of him always knew what we had to do, but he still sees it as a personal judgment on him, that he's a failure as a son.

There's always been a part of Davey I could never reach. A place where his doubt and insecurities rule. I think only his father ever found a way in there. Only his father could make some difference. And now his father is somewhere else, and this dark kernel of Davey's self is unfettered and taking over.

Chapter Nineteen

Over Under Through

The answers were lost. Answers to questions he hadn't yet thought to ask and answers to questions that burned in him. Burned not because of their importance, so much, but because they could no longer be answered.

His father, sitting across from him, was gone. Mumbling occasionally. Coughing. But mostly resting fitfully, unaware that his son was in the same room, the same city. Unaware, any longer, that David was his son.

Yet after all of the decades there was still one more thing they had to discuss. One thing beyond the usual stuff all sons and their fathers fought about or laughed about. None of it really important in the end, except that all of it was important because all of it added up. It accumulated. The doubts and disappointments. The certainties and uncertainties. The shared secrets. The dirty jokes. The harsh words, sometimes necessary, sometimes not. All of it answers to questions unasked, unthought. And the more answers, the better, the more complete, a life story could be told. Until there could be no more answers and all that was left, was all that would ever be.

On his phone, David opened an email from Curt to read while he sat with his dad in the care home. This was as close as Curt came to actual letters – he rarely even sent birthday cards but merely called him, usually near the end of the day – but still not as though written to him with pause and reflection. Curt had sent an uncommonly long email this time that, David suspected, he wrote at the urging of his mother. Longer than his usual weekly note certainly – seemingly always prefaced with his need to dash to class or rounds, so much so that for a long time David was in honest awe of the rigor in Curt's schedule that could only allow him time to write between urgencies – but still no more informative, no more revealing. Pleasantries. Anecdotes. The usual challenges of his classes. The struggle to eat right, to get enough exercise. But never anything truly personal. David sometimes thought that he must not be trying hard enough and that there might be some messages hidden for him in Curt's emails. Why else would the boy keep sending him more or less the same thing every week? Yet if David had felt capable of reading between the lines, if he had dared himself to try, he wondered if he would be able to find whatever it might be, or if he did, that he would want to know it. He'd long known Curt wasn't telling him everything he could. There had to be a good reason if this was so. His son's emails were at once a casual conversation and an impenetrable wall. Something said, but across a protective distance of space and shielded emotion.

"Am I pathetic, Dad, to feel grateful for even that little bit?"

His father did not respond.

David read:

> It's going to be harder to find much free time to visit now. We started biochemistry this semester. They say it's supposed to be worse even than gross anatomy. But over, under, or through, I'll come out eventually, Father.

Curt's words led David to a memory, maybe even a real memory. He believed he could still recall when his son had sought a particular, important answer from him. Back when his son still did that. Decades before. At the cabin. A boys-only weekend when he and little Curt could cavort and fish and skinny-dip and cook hot dogs over the campfire and unknowingly craft important moments of their lives in the honest disguise of spontaneity and innocence. Curt was young, not long out of diapers at the time. Too much soda pop and a sudden need to go. He'd hurried Curt to the other side of their little road. But when they got there, David believed he remembered, Curt was stumped.

"Dad, should I go over, under, or through my underpants?"

He no longer remembered the answer – he couldn't truly be sure that Curt had even asked the question, or if it was just a sweet story he'd made up in his head – but he was certain nonetheless that that moment had established his boy's manner for the rest of his life.

Despite their many trips to the cabin in the years following, Curt had soon stopped asking him these kinds of questions. Little Curt began working out most things for himself. David had come to see that his aloof, independent son almost didn't need a father. Or maybe what he needed was a different father. A better father. His clever mother seemed to be all he wanted growing up. And even she appeared barely necessary any longer.

"Dad," David said into the silence between them. "Dad. Do you remember all of the good days at the cabin? Do you remember the cabin? I love that place." The older man's dry, curled fingers opened slightly and touched a button of his flannel shirt. Nothing more. "Do you remember me? Do you know your boy Davey? Dad?"

Joe coughed dryly.

Unfair questions; David knew it. Nothing could come of asking but his own disappointment. More in a lifetime of disappointments so it hardly mattered. Yet the questions remained. The questions burned.

Mom told me about the trouble your friend Jon is having with his boy. I was sorry to hear it. When I was thirteen, I was still afraid to go into public restrooms on my own. (I guess I never told you about that little fear of mine.) I can't imagine running away from home at that age.

And yet, David knew on well-worn reflection, Curt had begun his own flight even before that age. More than just a once-unguarded child growing into his own private life. Something deliberate. What seemed like an *intentional* separation from David. Why? Had he failed Curt in some essential way? Where had he failed? How?

"What did I do wrong, Dad?"

First Curt's precocious wall of sarcasm, and then later the increasing distance his bright mind allowed him to span. David watched helplessly as his boy drifted farther from him. Not drifted, navigated. He ran his race in ways that seemed *intended* to leave his father farther and farther behind. Not seeking any particular replacement that David could see but just putting miles between himself and dear old Dad, whose advice and influence and guidance and discipline, Curt had made obliquely clear, no longer seemed necessary, no longer even seemed valid. David saw that he had become a triviality in his son's life. Irrelevant. An embarrassment.

How much of this was necessary for the boy to become his own person? David pondered. How much was not? The good-natured digs that came too often. The big words Curt peppered into his comments. The casual regard he gave to his father's feelings, if he thought his father even *had* feelings. The slight, chuckled, but unhesitating corrections to much of what David said, until David found himself often saying nothing at all. The revelations Kathy would casually share with him about their boy that the boy hadn't chosen to tell him. The good news. The bad news. The big news. The private news. The milestones passed that David only learned of later. And undoubtedly intimacies about his boy that he would never learn. And just that smug look in Curt's eyes that suggested he knew more than he was telling. Why was this happening? Why was he being left behind? He didn't think he'd been that kind of son himself. He thought he'd been a decent father.

"I guess if you'd warned me, Dad, I wouldn't have understood. This is the hardest job I've ever faced as a parent. Not the thousands of diapers. Not the sleepless nights. Or the crying. None of that. It's letting Curt go. Letting him make his own choices, and sometimes they aren't the choices I would make. Or even understand. He's going places I haven't been, Dad. Places I can't follow. I can't give him advice anymore. I don't have any experience for him. I don't have any answers. I no longer have anything he needs."

And when it came time for Curt to leave for med school, to start that chapter of his life, the break was more or less complete. A civil son, but a son more in name, it seemed, than in his heart. Curt hadn't even wanted David's help moving his few things into the apartment Kathy's mother had rented for him, along with paying his tuition, which widened the chasm between them. But David had insisted this one time – what felt to him as possibly a last time – to be involved, somehow, in his boy's life. For in some dim way David realized that, contrary to his son's evident wish, he was going to be a parent for the rest of his life. Despite how grown and capable Curt certainly was and would be, no matter how far he might try to distance himself, David was always going to worry about his boy, fear for him, wish for him. And though such feelings might go dormant, when they were called back in clear moments, like his move from home, David felt them with unremitting intensity.

Weeks later, when David stopped by Curt's apartment unannounced, he was greeted at the door by a stranger named Pat. Curt had a roommate that David had known nothing about. And yet if Curt had not chosen to tell him, David never felt he should ask about it. Curt, Pat had told him, was at a study group and wasn't expected back for several hours. Pat was wearing the flannel shirt that David had given Curt as a parting gift.

> You should investigate wearing orthotics – inserts – in your shoes, Dad. Ones designed specifically for arch support. They may help with your *plantar fasciitis* that is resulting in your supination. I'll show you some stretches you can do next time I'm home. If you're diligent about doing them, they may help.

It had been no surprise to him or Kathy that their son was bright enough to go to medical school. They saw early on that his trajectory, as Kathy called it, would be high, and David realized just as early that in this there was little he could contribute aside from heartfelt encouragement and mostly just not getting in the boy's way. Which is how it happened.

And why not? David had his own life, which had been as demanding as anyone's, as unremarkable as most, stretching him thin to be a provider for his little family and to care for his own father, who had been growing more frail and forgetful as each year passed. David wondered sometimes – they were bitter sometimes – where his life might have gone if he hadn't had his father's care eat every spare dollar in his wallet and every spare feeling in his heart. But he knew where. He knew what his own, unimpeded trajectory would have been. Never so lofty as his son's. He would have gladly given every one of those dollars to Curt's schooling rather than let his mother-in-law so eagerly do it. David knew that his life had no great destiny. He was not made for such things. It was a realization he'd had when he was young. His life would not have been an accumulation of fine possessions or achievements, great travels, or honor or praise or respect. His work was ever hard and uncertain. His insights were never deep or profound. His dreams were always kept humble.

And none of it enough. Never ahead of the race. His father drifting away. His son hurrying away. And his own inability to hold on to either, whether by the limitations of his capacity or some inner, self-destructive conviction that it was himself, him, David, that wasn't enough. He didn't have the answer and guessed that he didn't want to know the answer. He was afraid to ask the question.

And so the struggle continued day to day. Keep food on the table and the car running. Give long-suffering Kathy as much as he could of a life that was not nearly all that she deserved. Give Curt as much attention and love as the boy – now the man – would allow. And give his stubble-jowled, forever lost father the care that he needed.

"I don't know how to do it, Dad! Tell me how to do it."

The bills were mounting. They were behind in their payments to the care home, and David was surprised that his father hadn't been evicted. Yet, as Kathy had pointed out, the conditions there sounded bad enough that the facility was probably grateful David hadn't reported them. David's visits were usually unannounced, which meant he found his father in an appalling state most of the time. The small window of his room, looking on a boarded-up warehouse, was always filthy with fly specks and dirt. How small his life had become, yet it was the best David could afford.

He thought that maybe if he told them when he was coming, they might clean up and care for their charge so David could pretend, at least for the moments of his infrequent visits, that his father lived with some dignity. Yet that might lead to them to pointing out more insistently that their fees were in arrears. And so David was saddled with the irony that the way to ensure his father had any care at all was to ensure he had terrible care.

Thus the best he could do for his father. The man who gave him life. Who gave him a good life. Who taught him how to build a fire and catch a fish and pee in the forest. Who helped him struggle through math and science and English. Through friendships. And fears. Who kindly never told his son how limited he truly was. Who gave him all that he could, which David saw he could never repay, especially now when it was needed most.

"I'm sorry, Dad." And even his words, he knew, were insufficient.

His father didn't respond. No, his silence, David knew, wasn't because Joe was disappointed by the mess his boy believed he had made of his life. David had managed to keep most of that stuffed inside, hidden from his father. Nor that his father no longer loved his son. That had *never* been in question. Even when you can't always see something, you can know that it is there. Be certain it is there. It was simply and painfully because his father was gone. Leaving only this shell behind. A shell that felt less like his father with each of David's visits.

More was left of David's father in the cabin. Memories formed there, found there. All of the bits and pieces of their lives accumulated there, waiting to be picked up and used, and savored, with each visit. Visits so infrequent these days that David sometimes wondered if the place existed at all, or if it was only some make-believe he had contrived for himself to escape the rude reality of what passed for his life. He hadn't built a fire or wetted a line in months.

> I read the other day, Father, that whippoorwills are in decline throughout their range, and no one is exactly sure why. I always loved when we were at the cabin for an overnight and I could hear the sound of those three notes, in their many, many, many iterations. It would be a shame if I never got to hear them again.

"I wonder how the cabin is doing, Dad. Do you ever wonder that?"

Would his father be stirred at all by seeing the cabin again? Would he remember his own hundreds of perfect moments there? The joining of each board by his own hands? The sandstone steps down to the lake they had laid together? The fish caught? The smoky fires? The meals cooked and eaten? The cigars he loved so much?

Or, as David half hoped, was that mercifully lost to his father too? For David had come this visit to deliver bad news to the man who most needed to know yet was least able to hear. News that was the greatest confirmation to David of his own inadequacy, the final ripping of his father from his heart. Words David least wanted yet most needed to speak. The faraway cabin, the lake, the hundred acres of Ozark forest around it demanded attention. Worries about taxes and insurance, unexpected costs for maintenance, worries about the locals vandalizing, about fire, forced him and Kathy to finally decide – no more second guessing – that the place would have to be sold.

Sure, the rationalizations made sense. His father no longer knew the place. David no longer visited the place. Curt no longer cared about the place. It was a liability, an underperforming asset, as Kathy called it. Another drain on his thin wallet. A memory from his past that could no longer be part of his future. And the money from the sale, such a lot of money in David's circumscribed life, could be directed to pressing needs. His father's care foremost. Their mortgage. Maybe a better car. Maybe something added to their paltry savings. Even a bit of frivolous pocket money if there was anything left.

The word he'd rehearsed with Kathy also made sense. The way he would tell his father the painful news. Words to be spoken to a man who could not hear them, but words that had to be spoken aloud lest they devour David like all his other repressed regrets. Hard, bitter-tasting words that a son had to say to his father, that one adult should be able to say to another. To the only adult who could forgive him for his need to say them. Words weighed and considered. Words practiced. Words it had come time to say.

David rose from his chair and bent over his father, kissing him on the forehead. Then he fell to his knees, dropped his head in the man's lap.

But he could not say the words.

DAVID

"Many were chosen," Curt would say, "but few were called." He told me he was talking about when he was in cross-country. Because nobody was cut, just about everyone who tried out made the team, but it was smaller number who were really called to the sport. I'm not sure where he thought he fell.

I'm pretty sure I am not called to the sport. Once I'd gotten my heel spurs under control, I must have said something foolish about maybe trotting around the neighborhood, because on my birthday Kathy surprised me with a really nice pair of running shoes. Some brand I'd never heard of, Hoka, with thick soles. I admit they feel like the second-best thing in the world when I put them on, but that's about it. Not much else about my running has been so nice. Still, I try.

Kathy often goes with me, step for step. She waits when I have to stop and rest, and other times she encourages me to walk for a while instead. But then sometimes when we're running side by side – usually it's not very far – I really feel like I'm doing something. She talks to me when we run, even though I can barely breathe, like it's no trouble at all. I think she misses when she and Curt used to run together.

I see now why he took to running so much. Especially going out on my own. It takes my mind off of everything. It's an escape. Just me, trying to throw one foot in front of the other for a while. No worries for the time except that. The world gets small, in a good way, more manageable, and I can just focus on this one thing for a while.

Chapter Twenty

Men at Rest

"My poor father," said Curt to the trees and the water and the air. "In love with a man who cannot love him back."

Curt had wandered down to the tilting dock, filled with jumbled thoughts but mostly startled by the overall collapse he'd found when they'd arrived at the cabin that morning. Too long away. Not just the dock falling into the lake, but all of it. The road overgrown. Weeds lush in the fire ring. Piles of leaves on the porch. Branches down and someone else's beer cans everywhere. Scrub thick, massing, closing in on the cabin. The cabin. Even the cabin seems weary of the fight, he thinks. It looks sad, lonely. Needs fresh stain. The cabin looks confused, unsure if it is loved any longer, abandoned, as though it has somehow failed us. Silly thoughts, he told himself, but some people, he knew – some people he *knew* – thought more readily with their hearts.

He had wandered to the lake, picking his way down the polished stone steps, crunching on sticks and desiccated acorns and bits of loose gravel, wrestling a large, fallen branch aside, before reaching the bottom and considering the teetering dock. The wall of cattails had conquered nearly every inch of the shoreline on this side of the lake, so going onto the dock was the only way he could get close to the water. He had learned to swim in this lake. Had splashed and played with his dad and his friends and himself here. Had burned his pale, freckled skin. Had wasted countless hours here, though it didn't seem like that at the time, he reflected, and maybe they weren't so much wasted as just used differently. Devoted to different priorities. So long ago. Before they moved. Before college and med school. When he was young and life was full of infinite futures. Before the demands of his life and his own conflicted self had erected barriers so that nearly everyone he knew could only see glimpses of him. He'd made sure of that. And then, he found, he had to live with that.

The staff at the care home were surprisingly nonchalant about his father's plan for an excursion. His grandfather was no longer coherent, no longer present, and needed constant overseeing. But when they arrived – David first told Curt to stay in the car and then reconsidered and asked him to come inside – and explained what their plans were, the staff had no problem with them hauling the old man away for a day trip to the family cabin. David made sure to note that Curt was in medical school and that Joe would be in good hands, but they didn't seem to give that any more regard than they did to whatever David's plans were for the day. They asked no questions and gave no instructions. Suggested no cautions. Didn't even ask when he would be back. Nor did they offer to help take Joe out to their car. They weren't being supportive or even cooperative, Curt quickly realized. They really didn't care.

He understood then why his father had always deterred him from visiting his grandfather, and with him so busy in school, Curt never had. It was a disgrace the way his grandfather lived, the care he received. The lack of care. "He won't know you anyway," David had told him, more times than seemed necessary. "He's gone, Curt. He's not there." But Curt had learned this day what his father hadn't wanted him to know, the ugly real reason: that the deplorable care was all that he could afford, the *best* that he could afford for the father he loved. This was his dad's deepest personal shame. What toll it must have taken for him to let Curt see that secret!

But then a day at the cabin. David had gotten the idea that his father would somehow benefit from a visit. He had come all the way from St. Louis for the weekend, picking a time when Curt was home from school. Planning and preparing and considering and second guessing. It seemed pointless to Curt. If his grandfather really was no longer there, what would a trip to the cabin achieve? Why upset his routine, as pathetic as it was, for something he couldn't appreciate? Why, Father? And at the end of their day, when his father would finally realize this, in his plodding way that never thought things through, Curt knew his dad would be more than disappointed; he would be destroyed. What did he expect? That Grandpa would perk up? Recognize the old place and resurface with his old mind again? Chat and laugh with his son and his son's son for an afternoon? Curt knew that wouldn't happen even as he saw that his dad was going to try nonetheless. The helpless old man still had that kind of power over his dutiful son. David wanted his son with him when he tried. Poor man. No wonder you have so much self-doubt. You should just let things go, Dad.

David and Curt had managed to get Joe onto the cabin porch and settled into one of the chairs there, well back so he was in the shade. Curt had remembered his grandfather as a tall man, nearly as tall as his father, not the shriveled, ashen-skinned stick figure they had helped onto the porch. A ramble in the woods was out of the question. Wetting a line as well. There had been talk of a fire and cooking hotdogs, having a couple of beers. Curt had looked forward to building a one-match fire again. But just getting Joe up on the porch seemed a superhuman effort, and as he watched from below Curt imagined his father thinking "Now what? Now that I have him here, what happens next? What do I do next?"

Despite Curt's misgivings, David *did* have an idea of what he wanted to do, though the possibility that he might be doing it solely for himself was not yet clear to him. He had disappeared inside the cabin briefly then emerged with a small table that he set before his father. He adjusted it, sliding it up so that Joe could rest his arms, his curled hands, on it if he wished.

"Pretty good, huh, Dad? Are you comfortable? Not hot? Can you see the lake down there? See Curt on the dock?" David waved to his son hoping he would wave back, which Curt did, but Joe took no notice for he wasn't in the chair on the cabin porch. He was inside his head, deep in some lost and found past that was all the life he had any longer.

David slipped into the cabin again while Joe sat unmoving in the chair. But Joe was, rather, sitting in his old truck. The brown one. Beat up, but still running, so why replace it? Maybe when

Davey started driving they'd get something better, safer. And Davey was sitting beside him. Joe was going to be late for his union meeting, but Davey had breathlessly begged to be dropped off at McDonald's first so he could see his friends.

"How will you get home?"

"I can get a ride from Jon's mom. Or I can walk home. It's not that far."

And so they drove, and then, as though from nowhere, Davey asked what color his mother's hair had been, before it had gone gray, which was all he had ever known.

"Blond, Davey. Just like yours. Curly like yours too."
Joe pulled into the parking lot and reached for his wallet. "Do you need some money, Son? Five dollars enough?"

"Ten would be better," Davey said, and Joe was so tickled with his clever son that he didn't hesitate to hand over the money. He was a different boy since starting high school. Full of a newfound confidence and even a bit of swagger.

"Thanks. You're the best dad in the world," the boy said, giving his father a quick peck on the forehead then bolting from the truck.

Joe watched him hurry into the McDonald's. Watched as he and his buddy, Jon, traded punches. And watched as his beautiful, beautiful boy then blushed and fidgeted when a girl with long red hair had walked up to him and smiled. And Joe smiled.

David came out of the cabin with more things. An ashtray and a cigar.

"I got you an Upmann, Dad. The kind you always liked. When's the last time you had a cigar, Dad? Do you want me to light it for you?" And because Joe didn't respond, David went ahead. He cut the tip and struck the match and coughed only a little as he pulled on the cigar to get the cherry going. Then he held the cigar before his father, ready to help him if he wanted to take a puff. But Joe didn't react and after a few moments, David rested the cigar on the ashtray. Smoke curled slowly from the tip, its aroma gathering on the porch, the perfume of his boyhood cabin days and surely of countless hours of his father's life that he had never known. The scent that infused so many of their memories.

"One more thing, Dad." And David disappeared into the cabin again, returning this time with a notebook and the mechanical pencil. "Your Visit Journal, Dad. We're making a trip to the cabin. We need to record it in your Visit Journal like you used to."

He placed the journal on the small table and flipped it open to Joe's last entry, from years before. Then David wrote the current date on the next blank page and turned the notebook toward his father. He even worked the mechanical pencil into the man's crabbed right hand so he could make his notes when he felt ready.

Part of David knew how foolish he was being, how foolish his hope was that any of this, any of his effort to put the stimuli before his dad, would spark some moment of recognition, the briefest reunion. But it was a part of him he was working very hard to ignore as he tried to retrieve even a few desperate seconds with his father. Just a glance of recognition. Some confirmation that he was still Joe's little Davey, somewhere in his mind. Or maybe in his heart.

Early on, Joe's doctor had told David that everything his father had learned in his life would eventually be lost. Every skill he had mastered. Every name that he knew. Every memory. Every moment. The brain cells were dying. There was no going back. It might begin slowly, but they couldn't win this race.

A few years after they had moved his father to the sensible apartment, once David had finally been able to admit that the tiny, warm house where he had grown up was too much for his dad to take care of, David had received a call from the Highway Patrol. His father had been pulled over on the interstate, driving only twenty miles an hour. A hazard to himself and other drivers. The State Trooper told David his father was distracted and mostly incoherent, saying again and again that he needed to "get there."

Get where, the Trooper couldn't learn. David wanted to believe that he was trying to get down to his cabin. Obviously impossible, but it took this shock for David to accept that the giant who was his father could no longer live on his own, not even in the sensible apartment.

But that wasn't the memory David had hoped to conjure by bringing his father for this last visit to the cabin. He leaned on the porch rail, gripping it, doing his best to ignore the defeat all around him. "Nature always wins," his dad had often told him when the two had spent so many long-ago yesterdays cutting down the cedars that were ceaselessly marching toward the cabin. And so it was. The cabin far away. His father far away. His son far away. David was losing it all.

Curt was still standing alone on the dock. The day was warm enough for a swim, and he had been debating the idea for a while. His father didn't seem to need his help up at the cabin. There was really nothing else for him to do. Hike in the woods on his own? Build the fire for the hotdogs he knew they weren't going to cook? Make a futile effort at cleaning up around the cabin? Speak empty words to the man who wasn't there? Or to the man who wouldn't listen?

From his vantage on the porch, David could see his son begin shedding his clothes on the dock. You can't really raise a child, David thought. Another late lesson. The best you can do is try to nudge them in the right direction. What you think is the right direction. Hope is the right direction because you don't know yourself and it wouldn't matter if you did. Curt had mostly figured it all out on his own.

Curt undressed slowly, folding his clothes carefully. When he was finished, he turned to wave to his father, to make sure the man knew what he was doing. The sunlight flashed in the orange blaze of his pubic hair, and David waved back to his faraway son before Curt turned and dove and disappeared into the murky water.

There were no mysteries for him here. Fish, yes. Turtles. Plants under the water. Algae. Microbes, even. But all of it known or at least knowable. His muscles remembered how to pull him forward, and he wished he could stay under the water in the silence, away from the books and the labs and the lectures and the study groups. His fellow students. His friends. His entanglements. All of it. Better to be alone. To cultivate isolation, to embrace it. The deeper he went, though, the colder the water was, and with every kick more of it swirled up and around him.

When Curt surfaced near the middle of the lake his momentum slowed and he rolled onto his back, letting the water suspend him, the sun kiss him. He filled his lungs with air and closed his eyes. If today were my last day on earth, came a spontaneous thought, this is exactly where I would choose to spend it. This much is good enough. Good enough for now. His life, with all of its intrigues and demands, would be waiting for him when he returned. But for now, at the cabin, he could rest, relax, release. And this, he then realized with surprise, was exactly what his desperate father was trying to do. For all three of them.

"You are not dumb," Joe was telling his son in an urgent, long-ago moment. "My boy is not dumb." Davey's head hung before his father, convinced that his dad was wrong this time and that he really didn't know anything, certainly not the kinds of things the other kids already knew. Sure only of his inadequacy. Embarrassed at school. Tearful and stammering before his father at home.

"You are not dumb at all, Davey. You're a good boy. The best boy in the whole world." Joe crouched before his five-year-old and put his hands on the boy's bony shoulders. Davey's wet eyes stayed on the floor between them. He sniffled.

"It's my fault. The thing is, Davey, that I've tried really hard to teach you right from wrong, and I forgot to teach you right from left." He slid his hands down Davey's arms. "This is your right hand, Davey," he continued, grasping the boy's hand, pulling his fingers free from the balled fist, "and this is your left. They're useful for all kinds of things. Like drying silly tears for one." He brought Davey's left hand up to his face and stroked the little fingers across his wet cheek. Then Joe put his boy's hands around his neck. "Or for giving your old Dad a big hug when he needs it," which Davey did instantly, burying his face in his father's shoulder because more tears were coming. Different tears this time.

They drove to the hardware store then, and Joe bought him a pair of white cotton gloves, much too big for Davey but the smallest size he could find. At home Joe wrote on them with a marker in sure, bold letters LEFT and RIGHT and worked with Davey to learn the words. Little Davey was so pleased with these treasures, pleased more deeply than he had the words to express, that he wore them constantly, even to bed. Decades later Curt had found them in a box and learned the story.

The cigar had stopped giving its trail of smoke, and David put it to his lips to bring it to life again. Joe had shown no interest in it. No sign at all that he knew where he was or who he was with. He wasn't fussing. He had no objection to being in the comfy chair on the shady porch of the cabin. Or to the warmth of the day. Or to the forest filled with a choir of birds around him. But he was hardly present in any of that.

To David this was a bittersweet reality. If his dad knew of the cabin any longer, it was in his memories, whatever they might be, where it could remain and be lived in. Be enjoyed and savored and held onto forever. David hoped that was the case.

Because David's other purpose for bringing his father to the cabin that day, the purpose he hadn't shared with Curt, was to do, finally, what he could not do the many, many times he had tried before. He had to stand before the man who had given him life and love and example and adventure and one hundred acres with a cabin and a lake, to stand before that man on the porch of the cabin he had built with his own hands and tell him – even if he couldn't hear – that his son had to sell this property because in the end he wasn't a good enough provider to pay the bills.

And if his father could give him the slightest acknowledgment, even a glimpse of recognition – of his cabin, of his son – that would make the words immensely harder to say and yet more real and right. "I love this place, Dad. I love you, Dad. I know I've let you down a lot over the years. I have to do it again now. I have to tell you something, Dad."

But Joe wasn't listening. Not to his son in the present moment. He was, instead, at the cabin in a different moment. Passing on an important skill to his boy who was to enter kindergarten in the fall. "The secret to a one-match fire, Davey, is not how good you are with the match but with the *preparation* you put into building the fire. Lots and lots of tinder. A fair amount of kindling. Once that's going, you can add the bigger logs, the fuel. But the trick is to have the right amount of tinder and kindling. It's all in the preparation, see?"

Little Davey listened, because his dad was speaking to him. And he watched as his dad crumbled scraps of paper, balled wads of dried grass and leaves, and piled them carefully on the cold ash of a previous fire. "If you prepare properly, your fire will burn long and hot, my boy Davey."

Curt had finished his swim. The lake was warm at the surface, but the cold water touched him if his foot or hand dangled too far below. Every stroke brought up more chill. And so he was done. He pulled himself onto the tilting dock and wiped the water from his face, shook it out of his close-cropped red hair, blinked it out of his eyes. He could already feel his skin starting to redden from the sun. It was all too much. The falling dock. The cattails. The encroaching forest. The weary cabin. Who had time anymore to keep it up? They lived too far away. Their lives were too full. Their priorities were different now.

Curt's eyes wandered across the still, glinting lake and the sweep of trees beyond, and he turned to look up toward the cabin. There were his father and his grandfather. Strong men with broad backs and powerful arms. Big hearts. Half of who I am comes from them.

As he watched from below, though, Curt saw his father give a sudden cry, fall to his knees, and throw his arms around his own father. Curt bolted toward the cabin, running barefoot and naked up the littered stone steps and across the weedy gravel, leaping onto the porch in a single bound.

His father was crying, sobbing, his body quaking as he rested his head on his own father's shoulder. His grandfather appeared to be crying too.

And then Curt saw it. Saw the impossible thing that had made the impossible true, that had brought these two men to tears in each other's arms.

There on the page of the notebook, in a shaky, barely legible hand, were five letters. Five letters that spelled the word DAVEY.

Curt fell onto his father's back and wrapped his wet arms around the two men, his own tears joining theirs, dripping onto their flannel shirts.

As the world paused for them, the three men held that embrace for a long, long time.

JIMMY

Was after that summer old Joe Clark died. Hadn't seen him or his boy, Davey, much in years. Heard from him that Joe had drifted away, and then he died. Difficult business for a family, dying.

Talk of selling the place now. Checking around the cabin like I always did for Joe. Seen the newest bunch up from Osceola to party a few times. Figured I needed to pick up their beer cans or whatever else they left.

And there was a crow. Standing on one of the stones around Joe's old fire ring. Just perched there, staring at the ash and weeds. Looked up when I approached, but didn't fly off. Looked at me for a while like maybe it was trying to remember where it knew me from, cocked its glossy black head, then looked back at the ash.

Up in the old white oak betwixt Joe's cabin and his pond another crow called. One at the fire ring looked up then, looked toward the second crow. It called again. First crow took a last look at me then lifted itself into the air and lighted on the branch beside the other one. Some cackling. Bobbing heads. Stretching wings.

Then the two of them took off. Flew across the pond. Lost them in the forest beyond.

About this time I heard a truck, big one, coming down the road to the cabin. Kids from Osceola likely, or someone taken a wrong turn and lost. But it was from the hardware store in town.

"Think you've found yourself at the far end of the wrong road."

"Old Clark place, right? Got a load of lumber. They're going to add a room."

Across the pond I heard those two crows calling.

Chapter Twenty-one

Spring Fever

On the first day of spring, Kelly Shepherd made a decision. He laced up in the battered sneakers he'd had since high school and went for a run.

It wasn't a success. By the first block, his feet hurt. By the second block, his lungs hurt. And by the time he got through several stoplights and crosswalks and reached the park, he was spent. The evening light was already fading, so he abandoned a run around the lake and walked back to his apartment, not defeated, he insisted, but maybe chastened.

The next evening he tried again, walking to the park to warm up and then forcing a half-mile trot around the lake, dodging goose droppings and cyclists and little children with big dogs on long leashes. He mostly did it, coming up a bit short but telling himself that what counted was that he had tried. Back at his apartment he peeled off his sweatpants and hoodie and sprawled in a chair for twenty minutes before he got in the shower.

It was on a weekend run at the park that he first noticed a spur from the lake loop; a paved path led into the trees. Though it might hold poison ivy and snakes and untold wild beasts, he thought that, at the very least, it ought to have fewer goose droppings. So Kelly steered his reluctant feet onto this path into the trees, uncertain how far to go because he had no idea then where the path would take him.

This part of the trail, he soon found, was where the more dedicated runners were. They darted past him with concentration (or was it anguish?) painted on their faces. Barely dressed in skimpy shorts and bright shirts. (Weren't they cold?) Guys with no shirts at all. (Weren't they *really* cold?) Couples running together, somehow having conversations as they whizzed past his wheezing self. Plenty of solo runners, too, self-contained and committed. Whether pushing or punishing themselves, Kelly couldn't decide, though he wondered if maybe that amounted to the same thing.

As his visits increased, he began noticing regulars. Dressed the same or running in the same exaggerated way that was hard to miss: short strides or arms flailing or more motion sideways, it seemed, than forward. The same groups, the same colorful shoes. And as they grew familiar to him, he did to them. A returned nod or wave. A word or two spilled his way. And he started to feel like he was among friends.

Except for one guy. A pale, red-headed man who seemed focused solely on his run. Pounding out miles for what? Fitness? Escape? Relief? If so, it didn't look like he was finding any. He looked angry.

So Kelly imagined stories for the man. Spurned in a relationship. Fired from his job. Struck with some hidden affliction. Rejected by his family. He ran to get away from whatever it was. To find some kind of solace, or if not, then at least some kind of solitude.

Kelly imagined this compact man – not bad looking really: kind of exotic even with his close-cut red hair and freckles, and later, Kelly learned, green eyes – running alone for miles and shaking off every attempt at casual greeting. He pictured a woman running alongside him, getting no more than a curt "Hey" before he quickened his pace and left her behind. After a couple of tries, she found a different part of the trail to run. But the man kept to his regular route, his regular times.

Though he wasn't sure why he did it, if Kelly timed it right, they would often pass along the same woody stretch of the trail, Kelly always on the lookout so he would be "running" when they met.

And one day, there *was* a nod from the man. Next, a wave. A smile. And then, a word. "Hey," the red-headed man grunted once, raising a solitary finger in greeting. "Hi," the next time. Escalation! Kelly began to look forward to his runs, not because he was recommitted to his earlier rash decision but because he thought maybe he had, somehow, cracked this solitary man's shell and earned his notice.

Spring grew warmer, and though Kelly was getting better with distance and possibly endurance, he still sweated heavily, and his pants and hoodie were always sodden by the time he got home. He considered this funk to be his runner's credentials, though he feared maybe he was trying to graft a sport onto his body that wasn't going to take. Yet he kept at it, in part because he didn't know what else to try and in part because he felt fellowship, even *acceptance*, from the other runners on the trail.

One Saturday afternoon as he was trotting he heard, above his gasping breaths and slapping feet, footsteps coming from behind. So he hugged the edge of the path to let the person pass, but the footfalls slowed, and then the red-headed man fell in alongside him.

"Hey," the man said. "Thought I'd missed you."
Astonished by so many words coming from him all at once, Kelly wasn't sure what to say or if he had enough air in his lungs to speak at all. But he tried.

"Don't you usually . . . go the other way?" Lame. What do runners talk about?

"Out and back. I was hoping I'd find you. Run with you a while."

"Really?" And then, "Not sure you can call . . . what I do . . . running." He *was* sure that was the stupidest thing he could say. The man let it go.

"My name's Curt."

"Hi. Kelly." Better.

"I see you on the trail a lot."
Kelly still wasn't sure what to say. Had this Curt been watching for him? He let a few strides pass and tried not to show how much he needed to suck air. Curt spoke again.

"I hope you don't mind me running with you. Is it okay?"

"Sure. Don't know how much . . . I have left in me."

Curt slowed his pace then, not by much, but Kelly noticed. And because of that, Kelly thought he could be honest. "Really new to running . . . don't know what I'm doing."

Curt had already worked this out. How Kelly was dressed, his shoes. The barely hidden alarm in his eyes, like it's not supposed to be this horrible, is it? Endearing in a way.

"We can stop whenever you want. I've already got my miles today."

Kelly pushed out some words. "How far . . . do you . . . go?"

"Depends. As far as I can." A few more strides. "I don't like to head out if I can't get at least five miles, but my schedule dictates my distance more than anything."

"What do you do?" Maybe this guy wasn't as private as he thought. Nor as angry as he seemed.

"I'm finishing my clinical rotations."

"At the hospital?" That made sense. The trail they were on passed below the giant university medical center.

"Yeah."

"You're a doctor?"

"Almost. What do you do?"

Kelly thought for a few strides, considering how to phrase it so it didn't sound pathetic in comparison. Realizing he had no chance of that, he plunged in. "Wage slave in a cube farm. Insurance analyst. Not what little boys dream of being . . . when they grow up." Not like being a doctor, he thought. "Pays the bills."

"So, you live around here?"

"Other side of the park." He cranked a thumb behind them and tried to make his words sound as effortless as Curt's.

"With the geese. I know it."

Easy to talk with him. Easy to fall in with him and match his stride. *Try* to match his stride. Funny how running with someone even *felt* easier, like he had more endurance. Was that the word? Maybe more reason to keep pushing? Kelly let himself consider this. What it might mean. Where it might lead.

"Listen, I have to go now," Curt said, as though reading Kelly's thoughts. He slowed and then stopped where the path forked. But then, "Let's do this again."

"Doctor's orders?"

Curt smiled. "But first I have to get you out of those pants."

"Sorry?"

Curt realized the moment he said those words the innuendo Kelly heard. Instead of correcting himself, though, apologizing, rephrasing, he let it hang between them. After a beat he said, "Those sweatpants. Nobody runs in cotton sweatpants. You need tech shorts."

"Tech shorts?"

"Like mine." He pinched the wispy fabric of his black shorts.

"Where do I find those?"

Kelly could feel Curt's green eyes on his body then. Assessing him. Caressing him

"I can lend you a pair." Back in high school Curt and his best buddy often exchanged running clothes as a secret joke between them. Even at cross-country meets. Every stitch but their shoes. "I'll bring some next time."

"Okay," Kelly said, having no idea what he could politely say to the offer of another man's scanty shorts. "Doctor's orders?"

"Something like that. When is good for you?"

They both found time in the week ahead to meet again on the path, and then Curt disappeared up the trail toward the hospital, leaving Kelly to wonder if it had all been a fever dream, some delirium born of dehydration or exhaustion. Did he have a date with a doctor?

The passing days relaxed their pace, and each evening, if storm clouds didn't hide the sun, the light stayed a little longer. Kelly wondered whether he should go for his regular runs or save himself for Curt. And then, where on the trail, exactly, were they to meet? And what if Curt couldn't make it? His rounds at the hospital running long. Or a difficult patient. Some unexpected meeting he couldn't tell Kelly about because they hadn't exchanged numbers? Or he simply forgot. Or changed his mind. No longer interested in running beside a wage slave from a cube farm who dressed wrong and couldn't run anyway. Was that his plan, then? Kelly wondered. Keep it vague so he could skip out?

But Kelly mastered his doubts, just as he mostly had his running, and walked to the park and past the lake, only stepping into a trot when he got to the woodsy stretch where he'd first seen Curt. The pavement was wet; an afternoon storm earlier had threatened their plans. The trees were still dripping as Kelly peered ahead to spot Curt before Curt spotted him. Even so he was surprised when Curt came up behind him again and fell in stride.

"Your pace or mine?" Curt said.

Kelly's initial worries fell away, leaving him with only all of his other worries about how best to get sweaty with this man on their first date. If it was a date. If he wasn't getting it all wrong. Which seemed right.

"I brought you a present."

Curt slowed and they stopped, Kelly careful to hide the panic in his lungs and act as though he could breathe normally. When was it going to get better?

Curt reached into the front of his shorts and pulled out something: a second pair of shorts he'd had tucked in there. "These ought to fit you."

Kelly took the black shorts – silky, weightless – but was baffled. How was he supposed to put them on? There was no restroom nearby. No parked car he could duck behind. Not even enough leaves on the poison ivy yet to hide him.

"Um."

Curt looked up and down the path. "Right now," he said. "If you're quick." And then, "Don't worry, I'm almost a doctor."

The suddenness of the chance, that it could vanish in a moment, sparked Kelly. Trusting Curt, he tugged down his sweatpants and wrestled them over his shoes.

"Next time I'll need to get you out of that jockstrap."

Kelly yanked up the shorts; the light fabric felt funny against his skin. But not as funny as realizing that Curt had just peeked at his bits, if funny was the right word. Embarrassing, maybe.

"Wear whatever you're comfortable in, but most guys wear compression shorts."

"Compression shorts?"

Curt pulled up his own shorts to display a second, skin-tight pair beneath. "Good for muscle performance, too. I'll bring you some next time."

Kelly saw a birthmark on Curt's freckled right thigh. It had been hidden by his running shorts. He felt he was seeing something private, a glimpse at a personal detail Curt kept hidden. How many people had ever seen his birthmark? Kelly wondered. Maybe very many? Or very few? And was Curt holding up his shorts longer than necessary? After a moment Kelly shook himself out of his reverie.

"I thought all I needed was shoes."

"Yeah, and we need to get you some decent running shoes, too."

Kelly didn't miss the plural in Curt's words.

"Anything else?"

"I guess that will depend on how long you want to keep it up."

"Well, thanks for the loan of the shorts." Kelly held out his hand, and Curt took it. Maybe Kelly held on too long, because Curt shook loose and took off. "C'mon," he shouted over his shoulder.

Kelly followed the instant after, a little confused, a little excited, leaving his shed sweatpants puddled and forgotten on the ground.

Curt had noticed a twig in Kelly's brown hair when they'd held hands for that endless moment. He'd wanted to brush it off, to pluck it, to remove what was marring the man, but someone had trotted by then, and Curt had lost his nerve. Instead, on impulse, he bolted ahead, turning back to grab a low-hanging branch and tug it, showering Kelly with the drops still clinging to it. They both laughed.

Back at his apartment, a good and interesting run with Curtis David Clark behind him – they had shared names and numbers and had talked about everything and nothing – Kelly fell onto his kitchen chair to recover. He'd slithered out of the running shorts Curt had given him. "Keep them," the almost-doctor had said. "I have plenty." Kelly examined the shorts more closely, the way he couldn't when he'd stood briefly in his jock on the public running path before Curt. The waistband maybe just starting to soften. The zippered pocket on the side, good, Curt told him, for holding his phone and ID and maybe a credit card for "rehydrating" after a run. The mesh liner that Curt had said was sufficient support for some guys, and Kelly was too shy to ask what he meant by "some guys," though he thought he knew, thought maybe he was one of those guys. He studied every inch of the wispy fabric, of these shorts Curtis David Clark had pulled onto his body for his runs. Sweated in. Slipped out of afterward and threw into his laundry basket. Or on the floor of his bedroom.

He thought he hadn't thanked Curt sufficiently. Lending him – giving him – his own clothes. Lucky they fit so well. They wouldn't get together again until the weekend when Curt said they could go to the running store and find Kelly some legit shoes. Maybe grab a bite and a beer. Kelly decided he'd text Curt. Simple but clear thanks for the shorts. For the running advice. Maybe not mention the companionship. Not yet.

Curt surprised him, however, by showing up at Kelly's apartment the next evening. Kelly met him at the door with a finger in the pages of a paperback, marking where his reading had been interrupted by the doorbell.

"I hope it's okay. Coming by unannounced."

Kelly felt breathless then, like when he was running.

"It's fine. Come in."

"A meeting was cancelled. Thought if you were free, we could find you some running shoes now."

"Sure."

"So you're a reader." He pointed to the book in Kelly's hand. "What book?"

Kelly looked at it, as though to see for himself and wondered what Curt would think of his choice. "*Frankenstein*. About a father who won't acknowledge his son. Among other things."

"I thought it was about a monster."

"It is. But who is the monster?"

"Too deep for me. Hey, I brought you something." Curt tugged at the back pocket of his jeans. "Compression shorts. Don't worry. They're washed."

"Do I have to put them on right now?"

Curt laughed.

"As I thought about it, I realized you wouldn't be able to slip into them on the trail, so I wanted you to have them before we ran again. Now you won't need to buy any. I've got loads of this stuff. By the way, how did those tech shorts fit? Not too snug?"

Kelly considered as he examined Curt's, well, underwear. Curt seemed generous, and interested. Much more open than he'd first appeared. Was that just his nature, guarded at first? Careful? Or was there something more? And what could he possibly give Curt in return?

The running shorts had not been snug. Not in the waist or anywhere else. And since he wasn't sure how to respond, he took the question at face value.

"They fit fine. Thanks again, by the way." He held up the compression shorts. "I guess these *are* supposed to be snug."

"Where it counts. Hey, mind if I use your bathroom?"

"Oh, sure. It's off the bedroom. Please don't look at the mess."

As he passed through the bedroom Curt *did* look at the mess. A mattress on the floor, but with only one pillow among the twisted sheets. A heap of laundry near the closet. Scattered shoes. Several tilting stacks of books. He was a reader. Bare walls. No photos. Not of his parents. Not of a girlfriend or anyone else. Under cover of the flushing toilet, Curt peeked into Kelly's medicine chest. No surprises. Some floss. Good. A single toothbrush in the cup. Better.

When Curt returned to the front room, Kelly was standing before him wearing the immodestly snug compression shorts. He held his shirt above his waist to show the skintight shorts and maybe a bit of his stomach. Perfectly legit. Two runners. Talking gear. Talking shop.

"How do they fit?"

"Like a glove. You look great, Kelly!"

"I guess I'll get used to this." He tugged at the crotch.

They didn't make it to the running store that evening. They never left the apartment.

"It was ugly," Kelly said in the darkness. "I think it was what happens when an irresistible force meets an unmovable object."

Curt stroked Kelly's hair softly, listening.

"I mean, I knew it was going to be a huge shock for him. I'd practiced in the mirror a thousand times. But I couldn't have dropped enough hints or found enough right words to make a difference. His expectations, his prejudices, and I failed him in every way. Why do our fathers mean so much to us?"

This was a question Curt had struggled with most of his life too. He'd never found an answer and had none for Kelly. The room was quiet for the moment, only the swish of cars on the wet street outside intruded.

"He said all the usual things. I was disgusting. An abomination. He said I was a woebegotten miscreant." Kelly was pushing out his thoughts. "Didn't think he knew those words. I have three older sisters, so he'd finally gotten the boy he wanted . . . but no more . . . said I was no longer his son."

Curt pulled the sheet over them. Meager protection, but it was something.

"I expected his reaction. He used to hit me as a boy. When he was angry. But this time, he threw . . . he threw his coffee at me. Mom by the sink. Crying. Whole dramatic scene."

Curt listened. He felt Kelly's shudders as he stammered these difficult words. Rejection so certain, so final. Each man faced rejection in his own way.

"Said he never wanted to see . . . my ugly face. Haven't been back home. Six months. Not a word."

Kelly was breaking down, perhaps crying. Curt wondered if this was the first time he had spoken about it to anyone. Had he no one to talk to? Had he held in this poison for that long? Except that long was nothing. Each in his own way.

He let the solace of quiet suffuse the room. His fingers coursed through Kelly's hair. The room in twilight. The traffic sounds diminished. The world shrank, at least for the moment, to this mattress on the floor among the murmurs and shadows, with these two men huddled upon it. Kelly's stuttered breathing softened. If tears had fallen, Curt left them unremarked, left them private to Kelly. They held each other.

"What about you?" Kelly finally dared.

What could he say after Kelly's confession? How would his own story compare, both better and worse as it was? He wanted to let Kelly's words persist, remain their most important exchange for a while. Not be diluted or diminished by other words so they could keep their full weight.

Or, Curt considered, was this just a rationalization, just another way to keep his secrets, keep himself protected? A skill he'd refined from years of practice. Yet, in Kelly's arms, in the quiet and dark of his room, almost a confessional where he could expect no judgment and seek no forgiveness but meet only acceptance and even understanding, maybe he *could* breach his barrier a little. Maybe this was the person he could, he should, try to be open to. Wasn't that his real point in coming over anyway?

A few deep breaths. Not enough to prepare but what he could manage. "I'm not out to my parents," Curt said.

There was more to say. Certainly, his scant words did not balance with Kelly's painful release. And so he tried.

"I'm sure my mom has guessed. She can see right through me. But my father, well, he doesn't get it. Maybe he doesn't want to or maybe he's just never let his thoughts stray there. He's not very imaginative. I don't know if that's his nature or if that's what he retreated to after life dealt him such a crappy hand."

His fingers found Kelly's ear and traced it. This wasn't so difficult. Not in the darkness. Finally spoken. Not with Kelly for some reason. No need for the bluster of the trail. No need to be abstracted and clinical. Kelly's silence, he felt, wasn't indifference or even mere patience, but generosity. A kindness he could give him. Curt found, now that he'd finally started, that he didn't want to stop his words.

"My father is a good man. But he's elemental. He used to load trucks for a living. He can cut down a tree, split the logs with a sledge and wedge, catch a dozen fish, and then have breakfast. He can build a fire in the wood stove that will burn hot all night. Knows the names of every tree in the forest. All that manly stuff. This is how he meets the world. This is what he understands. I could tell you stories about my father."

Kelly heard exasperation in Curt's words, but also, maybe, admiration. He hoped someday to hear Curt's stories about his father.

"Did you grow up in the country?"

"No, we have a little cabin down in the Ozarks. My grandfather built it. It seems I come from a long line of manly men." He paused, caught his breath. "Half of who I am, genetically, comes from my father, but aside from my curly hair, I can't see what I have inherited from him!"

Is this, perhaps, why he wore his hair so short? Kelly wondered. It wasn't the first time Curt had considered this, had followed this thread of his thoughts. But it was the first time he'd shared it, and hearing his thoughts out loud showed him how insufficient, how incomplete they were.

"The way things are now, Dad loves me. I think I fit, barely, into his idea of what a son should be. The one thing I can do better than he can, in the forest, I mean, is light a one-match fire. Every time. He respects that, and I guess it's enough. College. Med school. Even running. All foreign lands to him. Stuff he doesn't comprehend. He's proud of me, sure, but that's normal."

Normal for you, Kelly thought.

"What happens when he finds out I'm gay? When he finds out I'm not manly in that most conventional way? By his simple understanding of things, I mean. That I don't measure up. What if his love is conditional on that? Is he going to throw a coffee mug at me? He's never been violent. He's never even used harsh words with me that I can recall. But maybe he's saving up. Maybe his trigger will be those three small words: 'Dad, I'm gay.'"

"Perhaps you're not giving him enough credit." He rested his hand on Curt's freckled chest.

"I've thought that too. That all his years of acting like a decent man means that's truly what he is. But what if he's not? What if his mind can't expand to fit this? He used to tease me about not having girlfriends in high school. Now he talks about grandchildren and taking them to our cabin. What if *I'm* no longer the boy he always wanted?"

So many pained words pouring from this man, Kelly thought. They left him unsure what to say. Or rather, how to say it. The problem wasn't with Curt's father, Kelly guessed. The problem was with the edifice of protection Curt built around himself. Kelly understood that bit. But with a few words, not even clever words or the best words, maybe his emotional fortress, this house of cards he'd trapped himself in, could come tumbling down. They both knew about repression in its forms and guises. How is it that this almost-doctor didn't see the very affliction in himself? Because the human heart is always going to be mysterious? Because the familiar paths are easier? Because striking out is frightening?

Curt would stay the night. They would sleep in each other's arms. In the morning they would shower, find some breakfast, and maybe, if they were both lucky, Kelly thought, continue their conversation, both of them needing to do so. Both of them needing to heal.

He traced his finger along Curt's chin, crossing his lips and lingering there. Silence for now, he said without words. Silence and rest.

KATHY

A mother knows. We all have our secrets. Because we're afraid or ashamed or protective of our hearts. Or because we know that no matter what, there will be judgments or dismissals or grudges or questions, and we don't have the answers, haven't prepared responses, haven't prepared ourselves for standing naked and unguarded.

I know Curt holds his father at a distance. I know that Davey is dismayed and hurt but doesn't see how to reach him. I tell Curt he must talk with his father. I tell Davey to be patient and open. They're two good men with bleak voids inside them. Strong men. Stubborn men. Incomplete men.

Peg once told me about Joe, about how his father ran off when he was a boy and how she understood, better than he did, his deep longing for that kind of relationship. How he masked it with his drifting. She said it was in Davey that he had the chance to make it real, though as a giver rather than a receiver. But he never wanted Davey to know his secret. All that he wanted his own son to know was solid and deep and eternal love from a father. And for better or worse, that's what my Davey got.

But maybe he should have known of this thing that plagued his father. Maybe I shouldn't have kept this secret. It might have better prepared Davey for some of the unpleasantness of life and love. It might have even deepened his love for his father. And perhaps this is what Curt needs as well. A shock to his carefully balanced, sterile system. A jolt that will show him that his father is a person with a heart and soul and a depth of feelings that he keeps hidden too.

Chapter Twenty-two

Little Gray Birds

As long as there have been campfires, there have been storytellers. On that early summer Saturday, as twilight had given way to inky night and the stars in the deep, cloudless sky wheeled in the blackness above them, as the sounds of the dark forest enfolded them, Curt seemed to have an endless supply of stories. But this was not so. He was nearly finished telling his stories. They were stories of real people with real lives, lives a part of and also apart from his own. Stories he had lived. Stories he'd been told. And others he had to conjure from scraps and rumors and desperate inference.

Curt thought that Kelly, who sat close beside him and sometimes held his hand as he spoke, had been feigning interest and fighting sleep for a while.

"You're probably sick of hearing all of these stories about my family."

"I like your family stories. They're much better than mine."

"You should write them down then, though maybe you only like them because you idealize my family." It wouldn't be hard to do, given what Curt had heard about Kelly's family life.

Curt drew a cigar from the pocket of his shirt and examined it in the firelight.

"Why do you smoke those things?"

"I don't," he said after a long pause, carefully cutting the tip then lifting a burning stick from the fire to light the cigar. An Upmann. "A few times a year. Hardly constitutes being a smoker." He puffed on the cigar to get it going, coughed a little to make Kelly chuckle, then threw the stick back in the embers. Curt let the redolent white smoke curl from his mouth. "They remind me of my grandfather. It's a way of understanding someone. Living in his skin for a moment."

"I'm not sure I want to be kissed by a mouth that has smoked a cigar."

Curt knew better.

"I'll be sure to brush my teeth," he offered. "I'll even floss."

Their day in the woods had gone well enough, Curt thought. Kelly, bookish and thoroughly city-bred, had expressed skepticism about an overnight at a cabin in a forest – off the grid, no less – but they both knew they needed something, some spark to rekindle what seemed to be sputtering between them because the demands of his life had been pulling them apart, pulling Curt back toward his cultivated, lonely, but familiar solitude.

Kelly had tried to remain open, even seemed enthusiastic sometimes, as Curt led the two of them on a ramble through the dappled sunlight touching their Ozark hills, watching for what in all of it might be of interest. They'd each carried loppers and together had set about liberating cedars – a job Curt always enjoyed not only to continue the tradition his grandfather had begun but for the perfume the trees gave when cut – until Kelly complained of getting itchy from the needles. Then off came their shirts as Curt tenderly brushed Kelly's shoulders and back and chest, surrendering himself for the same.

"About Tuesday, when you're cursing my name because the chigger bites all over your body are driving you insane, I prescribe an over-the-counter antihistamine orally and cortisone cream topically. And try to refrain from cursing too much as well."

"Doctor's orders?"

Prevention is better than treatment. You really should have tucked your jeans into your socks as I suggested this morning."

After that chore, they took a more passive approach to appreciating the forest by looking for birds.

Curt had pointed out the easy ones, those few he knew. Bright red cardinals. Commonplace robins. Raucous blue jays. Maniacal laughter from woodpeckers. The pair of crows that were nearly always there and that Curt sometimes let himself believe were the souls of his grandparents. And the more obscure birds that he'd learned over the years. The chickadees, the nuthatches, the tufted titmice, a name that made Kelly snicker. "I saw a bald eagle here once. One winter visit when I was a boy."

"But what," asked Kelly as they paused on their hike, betraying what Curt thought might be an actual, budding interest, "are all of these other birds flitting about in the branches?"

Too small, too quick to identify. No distinctive markings that they could see. So Curt fell back on the honored taxonomy he'd learned from his father without even realizing he had.

"They're called little gray birds. Not obvious or flamboyant, but they're all around the forest. Happy to go unnoticed except by their own kind. Happy just to go about their lives. Adds a little mystery, I think. Always more to be learned. More ways of knowing the world."

That evasion had sufficed, Curt thought, for Kelly then seemed content merely to watch these little gray birds, to listen to their songs, and not impose a category on them.

"I didn't realize you were such a naturalist."

"I'm not really. That's Dad's thing. He can name every bird in the forest," Curt said. "Every tree. At least, I grew up thinking he could."

Their warm afternoon was capped by a dip in the lake. "To wash off the ticks." Curt had deliberately failed to mention the possibility of a swim so that Kelly wouldn't pack a suit and they would be forced to swim the natural way. A challenge Kelly was surprisingly willing to meet.

"I've never swam in a pond before," Kelly said as the two paddled in the cool water.

"And you still haven't because this is a lake."

And later, burgers and chips around Curt's one-match fire. A bottle of wine that passed between their lips. And long musings in comfy chairs before dying embers. It had been a good day after all. Maybe what the two of them needed. And Curt felt free and open once again, garrulous. To tell his stories. To be listened to. To speak his mind. He still had more to say, though it would be mostly for himself since Kelly, he feared, was fading, though his next words suggested otherwise.

"We tell stories to make sense of our messy lives, don't we?" Kelly said. "Our stories make us who we are, and if our stories were different, we would be different. We tell stories to understand people, too. To humanize them. To convince ourselves, once we're finally ready, that they exist as separate, individual persons and not just as walk-on characters in our own life's story."

Curt held the cigar before his face. How can people like these nasty things? he thought.

"And when we don't have all the facts, we fill in with what we can figure out. Or what we imagine is true. But some of it we have to make up, either in the spirit of what we already know is true or, sometimes, in the spirit of what we *want* to be true. There is a deeper, deeper truth than actual truth."

Kelly's words seemed right because in recent months Curt had been unearthing stories like fossils, frantically trying to puzzle out what they could tell him about his past, trying to assemble bones that didn't always want to fit. But the farther back he went, the more he had to rely on imagination. He'd come late to the job, had realized his need for the stories late.

The forest around them was filled with the love songs of the tree frogs and the occasional hoots of the resident barred owls, the heralds of their night. They would never see that bird in their ramblings, but its presence was certain nonetheless.

"My grandfather built that cabin. With his own hands."

"Yes, you may have mentioned that once or twice today."

"After he died, the bills for his nursing care finally ended. I never fully realized how hard paying those was for my father. Anyway, after a while we were finally able to make all the repairs the cabin sorely needed and add that second bedroom on the back. Dad and I took it apart and put it all back together."

He pulled on the cigar and let the smoke slowly drift from his mouth. Curt was drifting now as well, rehearsing a story mostly for himself this time.

"When Dad and I were tearing out a wall, we found a surprise waiting behind it. My grandparents had written a message onto the boards with a black marker. From 1970, if you can believe such an ancient time ever existed. It said they had built the little cabin at the end of the road as their fortress of solitude. For the three of them. Joe. Peg. And, it read, 'for the Best Little Boy in the Whole World: Our Davey.' They had traced their hands onto the wall. A hand inside a hand inside a hand. They fit each other like gloves. My dad blushed when he saw that; he ran his fingers across the words, and then he started to cry. Right in front of me!"

Kelly was silent. Whether out of respect or sleepiness, Curt wasn't sure.

"It takes a strong man to cry. There was strength in his tears. A manliness I don't know that I can ever achieve. We stopped the remodeling work then until Dad could get Mom out to the cabin so we could write our own messages behind the wall. Leave our own handprints there. And we did!"

Curt took another puff from the cigar. The orange embers in the fire ring before them snapped and glowed. The frogs called in the trees. "Who cooks for you?" asked the barred owl. "Who cooks for you all?" The stars above them dazzled. The two sat in silence for a while before Kelly spoke.

"You look lost in that big shirt."

Curt had found it hanging on a nail in the cabin and pulled it on when the evening cooled. The elbows were threadbare and the cuffs frayed. "It's Dad's, I'm pretty sure."

"Have you told your dad yet? About us?"

"Not yet. I haven't come up with the right way to do it. The right words to say."

In his subtle way, Kelly was trying to force the issue, to convince Curt to share this one essential thing with his father, for good or bad, though from what he could tell about the man, it would be good.

And Curt almost seemed complicit in his understanding of this.

"It's funny," Curt said. "My mom was the one who helped me with my homework. She'd answer all of my existential questions about life and the universe. But Dad, well, he taught me how to whistle. How to ride a bike. How to swim, right there in that lake. How to pee in the forest. That man made sure I knew right from wrong." Then he added with a chuckle, "as well as right from left."

Curt examined the cigar as he let more thoughts surface. "He taught me other silly things too. Like how sometimes you have to work all your life at a job you hate because people are depending on you. How to give up what you want so the ones you love can have what they want. How to wear a brave face every single day of your life even when you doubt yourself." Curt paused to let his voice settle. "Especially then. And I know he does. I realize now that the only person Dad has ever judged, ever *will* judge, is himself. And he's been severe about that. But he shouldn't be. Sometimes I think that if I try very hard I can maybe, someday, become half the man Dad is. Half the son he was."

Curt wiped his eyes. "Now you're making me sentimental."

"I like making you sentimental."

"This isn't how I wanted our day in the woods to end."

"Then let's end it differently. You did promise me a *thorough* tick check, remember?" Kelly rose from the camp chair and bent over Curt, kissing him gently on the lips. "Be sure you brush those teeth before you come to bed, Dr. Clark."

"Go on. I'll be there in a little while."

Curt had one more item on his agenda for the day. The coals needed to burn down before he left them anyway, and there was still half a cigar to be smoked; it would be a shame to waste it. Most importantly, though, he had one more bird to find.

It was only recently, after a stray comment by his grandmother, that Curt had started down the perilous road to understanding his father, to begin drawing out the guarded secrets so common, he'd found, among stoic men. And thus, unprepared, he had unearthed the one huge truth, the most dangerous story of them all. One he should have pieced together long before yet hadn't because he thought his father had no life of his own, no past, no secrets worth knowing. How wrong he was!

He had taken the stray comment to his mother. Innocently. Openly.

"I was talking to Grandma the other day and she said something odd. I didn't think about it at the time, but then it came back to me." He was standing in the kitchen doorway, leaning against it and munching on an apple.

"What did she say?"

"She said something about your *real* wedding. What did she mean by that?"

"She said that?" Kathy looked up from the dishes in the sink and stared, unseeing, out the window for a few moments, steeling herself. Then she grabbed the dish towel and began drying her hands.

"Yeah. What did she mean?"

So the conversation had finally come. She was glad he had brought this question to her, as glad as she could be about such a thing, rather than to David, for from him Curt would not be given all of the story. Kathy almost blindly seated herself in one of the kitchen chairs. She had always thought she was prepared for this moment, but she could feel now that she wasn't and never really could have been. Kathy allowed several seconds to pass before she spoke.

"We had two wedding ceremonies, Curt. The church wedding, the one you see in all the photos, where I'm always holding that big bouquet in front of me, was our *second* ceremony. Our first was at the courthouse in Kansas City, several months before."

"Grandma didn't think that a civil ceremony was as valid as a church wedding?" He slid out a chair and seated himself, already sensing in her voice, in her manner, something of the import in the story she was about to tell him. The apple rolled from his hand and came to a stop between them.

"Partly." Kathy paused and looked at her son. She drew her hand softly across his freckled cheek. "You never did the math, Curt?"

"Did the math?"

A smile formed on her face. A smile of resignation, but also of relief. "You were born one month after the church wedding."

"One *year* and one month."

"No, Curt. Just one month."

The sands were suddenly shifting beneath him and for a moment Curt lost his practiced reserve. "You never told me this!"

"We always thought you would figure it out on your own and come to us."

Except that to Curt, the story had begun with him. Anything that came before was just preparation for his life on his earth. Nothing really that important came before him. This new fact didn't fit his view.

"So, you and Dad had a shotgun wedding?" He realized after he spoke that he hadn't phrased his words very tactfully, and he winced, but his mother didn't seem to notice. This *did* explain why she had ended up with a man like his father, a matter that always puzzled him. "Well, um, I guess these things happened. It was a different time." He felt his face redden; he wasn't doing a very good job of recovering. Some stray bit of Catholic guilt was still lodged in his soul.

"No, Curt." Her eyes took on a faraway look, a frightened look. Her words became little more than whispers. "No," she said, drawing out the word as she shook her head. "No."

The little kitchen fell silent around them. His mother rarely betrayed her pain. Curt understood that something big was approaching him. Racing toward him. A story he didn't know and perhaps didn't want to know. He searched her face for a clue but found none. He had no idea how to prepare himself.

"This is hard for me to say, Curt. And it's going to be harder for you to hear."

Curt held his breath, a child again before his mother. Powerless before her words.

"We were teenagers, Curt. Your father and I. We were *children*." She tried to look into her son's green eyes but had to look away. "We'd snuck out to your grandfather's cabin one beautiful December day. And that's when . . . when you entered our lives, Curt."

Curt reached his hand across the table and rested it on his mother's hand, the one that was clutching and crushing the dish towel.

"You were loved from the first moment we knew about you, Curt," she said urgently. "You were loved. You must always remember that, Curt. *Always* remember that, because . . . " She turned away again. He could see the pain in her face. A pain, he suddenly understood, she had been silently carrying for a lifetime. His lifetime.

"You have to understand what my life was like then, Curt. Good Catholic girls didn't get pregnant at seventeen. What I had done to my parents was more than just the sin that the Church taught them. It was a rejection of all their values. Of all that they had raised me to be. I had shamed them."

"But," Curt said, and then found he had no further words.

"You don't know this, Curt. I *never* wanted you to know this." She looked at him again. "Oh, I love you, my baby boy. Your father loves you. You are the most precious thing in our lives, Curt. You. Our son. Curtis David Clark." She said those three words clearly. "Our beautiful son. Almost taken from us."

"Taken?" He thought then of the photo he still had of his father as a baby. "Healthy again," it had said on the back.

Tears were welling in Kathy's eyes. Several fell onto the tabletop, her hand with the towel heedless of them.

"Almost taken from us. Yes. I was a child, Curt. A daughter. A good daughter until I had done what my parents thought was so very wrong. And so, when my father did what he did, what he tried to do, I guess, I couldn't resist him. My father had decided. And so, it would be done."

"What, Momma? What had he decided? What would be done?"

"I couldn't have fought him, Curt. Not then. And I don't know if you can ever forgive me for that." She freed her hand from his and wiped her eyes, without much effect.

"Mom." He reached for her face but stopped halfway.

"You were to be . . ." She swallowed and tried again. "You were to be taken from me, Curt. Given up for adoption. Given to a different mother. A different father. Raised by strangers. My boy, *forever* unknown to me. I would never know you, and you would never know me. Or your dad."

All that Curt thought he knew was falling apart before this revelation. All his life he had been Curt, but who was that? Who might he have been instead? Had he almost been – what? – discarded? Every single fiber of himself would have been gone. Curtis Clark would never have existed. He would have had someone else's name. Someone else's life. Someone else's parents. Someone else's everything. Someone else would be living in his skin. And he, he would be annihilated. There would be no Curtis Clark. Curtis David Clark.

His world, his universe shrank into that kitchen, into nothing more than two people in those eternal seconds, sitting at the little table where he had eaten so many meals with the two who *were*

Mom and Dad. The only family he ever knew. The only family, he realized then, he *ever* wanted.

And might not have had. He was reeling as he sat there. He could feel his heart pounding, hear it in his ears. He grabbed the edge of the table because his head was spinning. His mother was right. He should never have learned this story.

"But." His words came slowly. Unconsidered. "But . . . I wasn't . . . I wasn't adopted, Mom." He knew this in his head to be true, but he needed to hear it with his heart to be certain.

"No. You weren't."

"What happened?"

Kathy took several breaths as she gathered her few words.

"Your father happened."

"Dad?"

"Davey wasn't going to give you up. Not ever! *He* was the one who realized that if we were married, no one could take you from us. No church. No parents. No law. No one. We could keep you. Keep our boy. It was your father, Curt, who understood this and then *insisted* on this. He arranged the courthouse wedding. Because he loved you before you were even born, Curt. He loves you that much!"

"Dad?" Curt could feel his eyes filling with tears of his own. Who was this man he didn't know?

"He showed me that I could defy the most powerful man in my life and join him in a new life. A new life that included you, my baby boy." Kathy was sobbing then, but Curt was deep inside himself.

"Dad did this!" he whispered. "Dad did this to save me!" The greatest, most important, most essential fact of his life, reaching to the very core of his soul, and he had not known it. Each moment of his life, each word his father had ever spoken to him meant *vastly* more than he had ever known. He would never be the same. Nothing would.

And all of his life had flowed from that one moment, from a brave defiance by a frightened boy, the boy who was his father. Coming down to this moment, in this place, to this person he was. All because a father had held his son tight and would not let go! Strong and brave and self-sacrificing. More than he had ever known. More than he thought *he* could ever be. All that a boy needed.

A giant. A hero. His father. Say it out loud! "DAVID JOSEPH CLARK IS MY DAD," Curt shouted to the dark forest around him. The forest fell silent for a moment.

Curt threw the cigar onto the embers then lifted his hands to his face and didn't try to hold back the tears. Why should he? These were good tears. Cleansing tears. Tears of love. Of bottomless respect. And tears of regret for all the years he had wasted. He would beg for forgiveness.

He let the tears flow, felt his body shudder with his sobs, with the immense, wild love he felt for his father. A love that had been long smoldering yet unknown to him. So clear to him now in this place. He let it take him for as long as it needed, and then he let it subside.

Curt sat in his solitude and listened. He would stay and listen all night if he needed to. But it soon came. Three notes. Three notes, like three syllables. The call of a whippoorwill.

"There it is," Curt said to the universe. "Now I must tell Dad. I must tell Dad everything."

CURT

Nobody would talk about it. I mean, I'm sure Mom said something to Dad privately, probably several times and in different ways, but he was in his deep, industrial strength denial then. Sure, it had to be tough, half-knowing that the person you loved so hard all your life was slipping away. But he let it go on too long. He ignored all the signs, or maybe outright denied them, not because of the hard choices that would have to be made by admitting it but, I think, because just admitting it was going to be hard enough.

Maybe I should have spoken up then. Mom has always been so careful about everyone's feelings. I could have been more blunt, even as the scrawny kid that I was then. Though that would have been out of character at the time. I remember I tried to go for days without talking to Dad – yes, because I was a jerk. But I still wanted to grab him by the shoulders, look him in the eyes, and tell him that his father was falling into dementia.

Instead, we all let it fester like the sad secret it was. Everyone dancing around it, afraid to bring it up. Afraid of what it might mean, how things would change, what would be lost as a result. It wasn't healthy.

But it wouldn't have changed the love he felt for his father. It might have even deepened it. Given it a new dimension, a new means of expression. He could have loved the man his father had become and still loved the man he had been before.

But now it's time for me to say other difficult words to Dad.

Chapter Twenty-three

Deadfall

How could it have been worse? Not only the three-hour drive, mostly into the setting sun, and their wooden conversation, mostly about nothing, but in the last half mile of forest, just before they finally got to the cabin, a tree lay fallen across their road.

David had watched the tree for a few years, a hackberry. He watched it die limb by limb and drop branches slowly, watched it shed bark in sheets, watched new pileated woodpecker holes appear in the bare white trunk, watched the tree and wondered if it might do exactly what it had finally done.

Had watched and done nothing because this was the natural course. A snag like this served its own purposes in the forest. After it had dropped its leaves for the last time, it became a home to furred and feathered cavity nesters taking their turn. It allowed sunlight to return to the forest floor. And then finally, when it came down, it began to merge with the ground again, returning its decades of enrichment to the soil. To David, a fallen tree wasn't bad. It was just, well, next.

Curt saw none of this, however. To his green eyes the fallen tree was a roadblock, a new chore to hijack their weekend, a bad start to a difficult visit that needed to be a good one or else everything would be wrong for all time.

David shut off the truck's engine, and both of them stepped out. The tree was a blowdown, its withered roots heaved from the ground and coated with the rocky Ozark soil the trunk had risen from. The hole it left behind still held water from the storm that had toppled it. His father had once said – had he said it, Curt wondered, or was it just a story he liked to believe? – that it would be among the roots of such a fallen tree that he could ever hope to find an arrowhead, and Curt scrutinized the rocks there, looking for a worked stone lost by a hunter centuries before and then entwined in the roots of a sapling begun as an acorn or nut that had fallen beside it. He wasn't sure what kind of tree it had been, but his father would know.

"A snag like this could have stood for another twenty years or fallen in a day," David said. "Our tough luck that it came down now, across the road."

"Must have made a lot of noise when it fell." Curt paused, waiting for a response that didn't come. "I guess we need to walk the rest of the way to the cabin and bring back the chainsaw."

"Maybe not." David broke off a branch as thick as Curt's arm and tossed it aside. "C'mon." He returned to the truck, and Curt followed. David shifted into four-wheel drive and steered into the trees, picking his way, pushing down and pushing aside the scrub and saplings, bumping over rocks hidden in the damp leaf litter, finding a path through all of it that would fit his truck and get the two of them past the problem and back on the gravel road that led to the family cabin. Branches scraped the side of the truck, stuttered across the roof of the cab, slapped the windshield, and plucked the antenna. But David did not relent, and as they crept, Curt watched in silence as his father found a way that was invisible to him. When they bumped onto the road once again, David didn't pause to relish his success but stepped on the gas and continued to the cabin.

The cabin waited, waited to welcome them, waited as it had for decades past and would, they all hoped, for decades more, its roots sunk deep in the Ozark hardpan. For David the cabin was the most evocative memory he had of his father; for Curt the feeling was more diffuse. It was family and memory and stories and a sanctuary that would always be ready, both safe and sacred. As it needed to be most of all for him this weekend. All that was wrong could seem right, seem fixable, when he was at the cabin.

The fallen snag, they both knew, would wait for the next day. They would return rested, with the tools they needed, and when the day was fresh. An hour or two of harsh noise and heavy lifting, then the road would be clear again, showing remnants of the fall and their clean up, but that would soon be absorbed by the living forest that would keep to its eternal cycles. Before them now, though, was the work of getting settled in the cabin and a fire built before the summer sun had fully set. Chores practiced through the years, both together and alone, that were simple to Curt. Simple and clear compared to his real, his dreaded task for their weekend. This complicated and conflicted son of a good but possibly not good enough father. He would soon know.

"Talk to your father," Kathy had told him. She had watched her boy in the days and weeks following his graduation from medical school, saw how the completion of this one great thing had now meant that another, greater thing took its turn and lay before him, no longer to be shunted and put off. "Say what you need to say to him," she urged as the two of them sat at the kitchen table and picked at the threads of Curt's next life. Kathy knowing, without having been told, what her son needed to tell his father, and also knowing, better than her son could, what his father would say in response.

"Do you think maybe you underestimate him?" Kelly had said, his turn to press counsel on Curt, unasked but not, he knew, unwelcome. "Has he ever given you any sign that he is not broad-minded? Or at least incapable of being so?" Kelly knew, guessed, with an objectivity Curt did not have, that the picture Curt had painted of his father was incomplete, even unfair, and further, suspected that this most important conversation of their two lives would finally breach that false barrier, and Curt could begin to see the depth in his father that he hadn't allowed himself to across most of his life.

And so here he was, in the place that was refuge for them both. Where, Curt knew, he had always felt most clearly the love of his father, a man who was not so good with words but who had an eloquence of both action and stillness that better expressed his heart. But if his love was unspoken it was also, Curt believed, unguarded. As natural and boundless as the sky above them. All that remained was for Curt to say three small words. But his life would not be the same after he spoke them. Nor would his father's. And he cared deeply about both. So, Curt asked himself as he built the fire he would certainly light with a single match, should he upend their entire weekend at the cabin, or wait for the last possible moment so he, they, could relish most of this time they had together just as they had countless weekends of their past?

Yet if Kelly was right, then so many of those uncounted visits – most of Curt's life as a son really – had been incomplete, not as fully or as deeply lived as they should have been. If Kelly was right, then Curt had cheated his father and had cheated himself. And if his mother was right – there was no question of this to Curt – then he shouldn't wait a moment longer.

Still, nothing would be the same afterward. Who would think that it could? Each moment of each day for the rest of their lives would be filtered through this new knowledge. And it was this aftermath that Curt feared the most. Even the best outcome would mean a subtle but permanent difference in how they saw one another.

Curt's fire burned brightly, pushing back the falling darkness, and he readied the larger pieces of wood to add so they would have flickering flames and coals for conversation and quiet musing. He wondered how many of these fires he had built in his life and wished he had kept some record of it, some record beyond the buildup of mute ash in the ring. David came from the cabin with two beers in hand, giving one to Curt, and they both popped them open. The night sounds of the forest were beginning. A barred owl had been calling across the lake below them, and they hoped, as they always did, to hear a whippoorwill, their totem sound. David commented that he'd seemed to hear the bird less frequently than he had in his boyhood. Even with the regular cycles of the forest, some things changed. This delight of theirs might disappear someday, and David was glad Curt had experienced it.

"Doctor Clark! It's easy to be proud of you, Curt."

Stop, Curt thought. You're making this harder. He dropped a chunk of split oak onto his fire. Orange sparks spiraled into the air and winked out.

"Maybe so," Curt said. "But maybe med school was the easy part. Being a doctor, a resident in the real world, might not be so easy."

David pulled a chair closer to the fire. He sat. In a moment, Curt did the same, sitting across the fire from his father. Once on an evening much like this, a screech owl had pierced the forest with its call. Sudden silence had followed; every other creature had ceased its noise in awe or terror. Curt remembered that.

On this night they were instead gifted with the three notes of a whippoorwill, somewhere in a tree beyond the firelight. Both men sat in silence, savoring the sound.

The whippoorwill had spoken. Curt would as well.

"Dad," Curt said, not lifting his eyes from the orange glow of the consuming flames between them, and David knew from Curt's use of that word, this less formal name for him he rarely used, that important words were about to come, words he thought he could guess.

He tried again. "Dad, I'm gay."

And now the aftermath.

Curt did not know how long his father had been waiting to hear these three small and so hugely complex words from his son. Curt had always been a clever boy. And the depth of his compassion had led him down the path to becoming a doctor. But for all of the range in his heart and mind, Curt had never seemed able, or perhaps willing, to grant sufficient humanity to his own father. Early on he had formed a concept of who the man was, what his essential nature was, and he had been so busy hiding his own essential nature, that he missed all of the evidence that David Joseph Clark was the one person on the whole planet who loved him most of all. It was an understanding he'd reached only recently and so viscerally that he still had no words for it.

David hadn't understood, at first, why his son had cultivated an uncrossable distance between them. They could joke and laugh and discuss most things and even skinny-dip in the lake together without hesitation, but he knew there was always something in the way. As his realization of what this must be slowly came to him, and he stopped joking about girlfriends and stopped speaking about grandchildren, he understood that if it ever were to be broached, it would have to be on Curt's terms. His boy grew, never giving him a single moment of rebellion or cause for grief that he could remember. He finished high school well. He went to college and came back a man of insight and achievement. Then he went to medical school and came back a doctor. And yet during all of this,

Curt had not found the opportunity – or was it maybe the desire? – to be fully open with him.

David never knew why, just as he didn't know why this time, this visit to their cabin, was when it had finally happened. What about the universe had changed?

And then it struck him. He pulled on his beer then cleared his throat, wanting to say the right thing and not realizing how even the short time he took for this reflection was rending Curt's heart, filling him with a certain fear of an outcome that he had been equally certain wouldn't come.

"So, is there someone special?" David asked, not yet ready to meet his son's eyes. He would follow Curt's lead in the moments ahead.

Curt slumped into the most immense relief he had felt in his life. David's question told him that his father, whose opinion counted most of all, had jumped past objection or rejection or confusion or whatever wrong might have been, had even jumped past immediate acceptance, and had effortlessly moved on to opening his heart to Curt's fuller life. Someone special! Someone his father would greet and hug and welcome as a second son and bring to the cabin and their forest because this was his way of expressing love.

The part of Curt that had known this all along pushed aside his unfounded fears and joined his father on the other side.

"Yes, actually. His name is Kelly." Then a moment later, "I met him on the running trail."

"A runner like you! That's great."

"Yeah," he said, barely able to suppress a chuckle of giddiness.

David was about to ask when he would get to meet this Kelly person, this person who loved his son, but another thought pressed itself ahead.

"I don't suppose you even need to tell Mom."

"She can see right through me, Dad!"

"I know. Me too." And he'd heard that word "Dad" again. "Still, you should tell her anyway. Just to get it in the open."

Maybe they were exhausted by their achievement because they let a comfortable silence fall between them, filled, mercifully, by the chirring forest. Each man had been unprepared for the other's words, but each man had been relieved and released by them. David finally attempted.

"Curt." He scuffed the toe of his boot in the gravel. "I'm not very good with these things. With speaking my mind. I don't know the right things to say, the right ways to say them. All I can say is that I love you. I always have. I always will. You're my perfect boy and I've always been proud of you." He paused and set his beer on the gravel then clasped his hands. "I don't know what else to say, Son." In a husky voice Curt said, "You don't have to say anything else. What you said is perfect." And then, "Thanks, Dad."

And so, for a while neither of them said anything. The fire between them snapped and sizzled. The insects and frogs sang in the trees. Faraway owls hooted. A breeze came from the other side of the cabin and blew smoke into Curt's face. He closed his eyes for a moment, but when he opened them again, the smoke was still coming at him.

"Well, if that's the way it's going to be," he said, rising from his chair and dragging it through the gravel to the other side of the fire beside his father. His dad. Dad.

In the orange of the firelight David reached across and rested his hand on Curt's bare forearm.

"You know what I don't see a lot of out here?"

Curt, not expecting such an odd question and unable to imagine where it might lead, said simply, "What's that?"

"Mosquitos. I guess the dragonflies and the bats take care of that for us."

What could he say in response to that? Curt wondered. Was any response necessary? His father had eased right back into common cabin conversation, into the mundane they shared as though Curt's monumental words were now well behind them and maybe even not so monumental at all. More importantly though, when, beyond a perfunctory handshake or a clap on the shoulder, was the last time his father had touched him, touched his skin? When had he let him? His arm tingled.

They both knew, each at his own level, that what had passed between them at this campfire would need more thought, more slow absorption into their lives. That their few words to each other would eventually be followed by other words, mostly good words surely, but words that would pick and poke at their changed relationship, furthering it, deepening it, and discovering what it would mean going forward.

David was already beginning to sense this. Now that he had his son back – and he was back, wasn't he? After more than a decade of holding himself at his distance Curt had finally spoken his truth and together they had gotten around what had been between them, right? – David realized that he was also losing him. Soon he would no longer have Curt to himself. Because Curt was going to give himself to another. To Kelly. David would have to learn to share him, to accept – once again, ironically – whatever bits of Curt were allowed to him. He held this bittersweet tension in his heart, feeling it but not understanding it.

Curt, in turn, tried to find his own new equilibrium. It wasn't so much that his father's automatic acceptance of his son's life had been unexpected; he realized how he should have seen this, should have seen it years before. No, it was that so much time had been lost, so much love had been tempered, so much chill had been cultivated and then endured. So much needless waste! Why had he allowed himself to create such a mess? To let it last for so long? His diagnosis: he hadn't been a very good son to a very good father. Never mind that the cure had come easily or that they could both now be healthy again. That the affliction had existed at all was his real shame.

The whippoorwill had ceased its call. David thought he had heard one across the lake, up on the far ridge, but it was too distant to hear clearly. The air had stilled. A thread of smoke rose unmolested from the few coals still glowing in the ring. Time to spread them so they could burn out. Maybe quench them with whatever liquids the two men had at hand. And then to the cabin for the night. The usual routines before going to sleep.

David screwed his half empty beer can into the gravel and pushed up from his chair. He prodded the coals with a stick and considered whether they needed further attention or would burn themselves out overnight. The recent rain meant the forest was wet, so he wasn't too worried, but he also knew he would rise in the night, more than once likely, and he could check on the coals then. Curt had watched in silence, thinking much of the same thoughts as his father, the result of having shared countless campfires with him in this place.

David said, "I'm turning in."

"Be right there," Curt said, rising from his chair and stepping closer to the coals. "One thing first." As David walked the familiar path to the cabin he heard Curt quenching the coals.

When Curt reached the cabin, David had already turned on the lantern that hung from a hook in the ceiling. The light was dazzling to his dark-adapted eyes and he looked to the floor at first as David opened the windows to ensure that whatever breeze passed before the cabin would also pass through it and keep them cool as they slept.

And it was in this moment that Curt was overcome with the horrible realization of how fully his three words had changed his life.

Before him David was undressing, getting ready for falling into bed. He would strip to his briefs, unabashedly before his son and move about the room nearly naked. Curt would do them same, peeling down to his boxers with nothing left but to say a few words and then get into bed himself.

Together, the summer before, they had added a second bedroom to the cabin, which, Curt came to see, was his dad's big indulgence. Curt understood that putting on that second bedroom was important to David, a way of leaving his mark, and, Curt considered, perhaps a way of grieving for his lost father. More than anything, David wanted the little cabin and their hundred acres to be a part of the family forever. He was preparing it for further life that he wanted to be lived there, for further perfect moments.

Yet Curt feared that the second bedroom would soon be witness to a different kind of moment. One that would forever evoke its own memories. This realization tainted his whole weekend. On the face of it, an inevitable consequence of his three words, yet harrowing because nothing could speak more clearly of a new and irreparable break with his father. It was this: that no longer could they share the old bed in the old cabin. No longer could these two men, in nothing more than their underwear, curl beneath the single quilt as they had hundreds of times and fall asleep side by side. For despite the love he knew his father felt for him, Curt was certain that the man could never again sleep beside his son, his son who was now an openly gay man.

Curt stood beside the bed, hesitating. He was waiting. Waiting for a word from his father or the will in himself. Waiting for direction.

"It will be good to get some sleep before we tackle that fallen tree tomorrow," Curt offered as innocuously as he could, trying to fill the lacerating silence and maybe prod the right words – or even the wrong ones – from his father.

"I'd completely forgotten about that!" David chuckled at his own forgetfulness. "Yeah, that will be quick work for the two of us."

Left with nothing, and close to tears, Curt paused for a hopeless moment, then grabbed the second pillow from the bed and began to walk to the other bedroom.

"Hey, where are you going?"

Curt stopped but didn't turn.

"Aren't you going to sleep here with me?"

Curt spun around and didn't try to hide his smile as he threw the pillow at David. He shed his clothes and hurried under the quilt with his dad.

David in his briefs and Curt in his boxers. Two grown men, nearly naked, happily in bed together. And they would slip into the lake fully naked the next day, to wash off the grit and grime of their work on the deadfall, just as they had so many times before.

CURT

"We'll go at your pace, Dad. The Trolley Run is downhill all the way."

I'm taking sly glances at Dad, trying to read him. He's betraying neither the excitement nor the dread of new runners. His face has hardened in his years, taking on the edge of a scowl. I'd only noticed this recently. So unlike the many photos of him I've seen in Grandpa's albums. That boy had a softer face, a face that was more open and bright. But this man beside me has a practiced face, a mask, giving nothing away.

"Mom and Kelly will be waiting for us at the finish. How are you feeling? How are your feet?"

"Good. Those inserts really help. All those years with that heel pain. Gone."

"You'll do great, Dad."

"Never gone four miles all at once. I'll probably collapse."

Lifetimes ago, back in the days of our apartment, we would go to Sunnyside Park so Mom and I could run the figure eight path. Dad's heel spurs were already crippling him, so he would sit on a bench and wait for us to come around each time, waving and cheering. But three or four laps were too much for me then, and I would come staggering toward the bench at the end, red curls pasted to my neck with sweat, my gait sloppy. Dad would hold out his arms and I would fall into them, exhausted.

Which is the story I let him believe because I knew, even then as a little boy, how much Dad loved to catch me and hold me for a moment. And how I wanted to be held. How I always have.

"If you collapse, Dad, I'll catch you." And I won't let go either.

Acknowledgments

No one achieves anything of worth without the help and support of a great many others. From what began as a single story about a little cabin in the woods grew a novel about the love three men have for each other. I could never have realized this without the support of those around me who listened to my ideas, read part or all of this work, and offered their insights. Foremost is my wife, Libby, who was with me at that little cabin from the start. Thanks as well to Peter Anderson who read the manuscript in its early form and helped shape its maturity. His fingerprints are all over this novel. Also to Rachel Johnson, who offered her words for individual chapters. And a thousand perfect moments to the poet Ellen Goldstein, who suggested the title.